Praise

"[Sorokin's] disorienting prose forces the mind to react—to focus, to sharpen—and urges us to be on guard against revered forms and the literary conventions of authority."—*Harper's*

"Sorokin is widely regarded as one of Russia's most inventive writers."
—*The New York Times*

"His books are like entering a crazy nightmare, and I mean that as a compliment."—Gary Shteyngart

". . . an extraordinary writer—a brash, Swiftian ventriloquist whose best work spars ably with the Russian greats of the last century and a half."—*The Nation*

"Sorokin, global literature's postmodern provocateur, is both a savage satirist and a consummate showman."
—Dustin Illingworth, *The New York Times Book Review*

"Sorokin is both an incinerator and archaeologist of the forms that precede him: a literary radical who's a dutiful student of tradition, and a devout Christian whose works mercilessly mock the Orthodox Church. It's this constant oscillation between certainty and precarity, stability and chaos, beauty and devastation, homage and pastiche, plenitude and rupture that makes Sorokin's fiction unique."
—Aaron Timms, *The New Republic*

"Translated with equal parts delirium and precision by Max Lawton, *The Sugar Kremlin* collapses reality and satire, present and past with a heedlessness that only Vladimir Sorokin can muster. A brilliant, hilarious, terrifying triumph."—Mark Krotov, coeditor, *n+1*

Other Work by Vladimir Sorokin Available in English

Dispatches from the District Committee
Their Four Hearts
Ice Trilogy
The Blizzard
The Queue
Day of the Oprichnik
Blue Lard
Telluria
Red Pyramid: Selected Stories

THE SUGAR KREMLIN

**BY
VLADIMIR
SOROKIN**

TRANSLATED FROM
THE RUSSIAN BY
MAX LAWTON

FRONTISPIECES BY
YAROSLAV SCHWARZSTEIN

DALKEY ARCHIVE PRESS
Dallas, TX / Rochester, NY

Deep Vellum | Dalkey Archive Press
3000 Commerce Street
Dallas, Texas 75226
www.dalkeyarchive.com

Deep Vellum is a 501c3 nonprofit literary arts organization founded in 2013 with the mission to bring the world into conversation through literature.

Text copyright © 2008 by Vladimir Sorokin
Translation copyright © 2025 by Max Lawton
Originally published in Russian as *Сахарный Кремль*
by AST, Moscow, Russian Federation, 2008

Introduction © 2025 by Joshua Cohen
Illustrations © 2009 by Yaroslav Schwarzstein
First English edition, 2025
All rights reserved.

Support for this publication has been provided in part by grants from the National Endowment for the Arts, the Texas Commission on the Arts, the City of Dallas Office of Arts and Culture, the Communities Foundation of Texas, and the Addy Foundation.

Library of Congress Cataloging-in-Publication Data
Names: Sorokin, Vladimir, 1955- author. | Lawton, Max, translator. | Schwarzstein, Yaroslav, illustrator. Title: The sugar kremlin / by Vladimir Sorokin ; translated from the Russian by Max Lawton ; frontispieces by Yaroslav Schwarzstein. Other titles: Sakharnyĭ Kremlʹ. English Description: First English edition. | Dallas, TX : Dalkey Archive Press, 2025. | Originally published in Russian as *Сахарный Кремль*. Identifiers: LCCN 2025009265 (print) | LCCN 2025009266 (ebook) | ISBN 9781628975789 (trade paperback) | ISBN 9781628976168 (ebook) Subjects: LCGFT: Dystopian fiction. | Novels. Classification: LCC PG3488.O66 S2513 2025 (print) | LCC PG3488.O66 (ebook) | DDC 891.73/5--dc23/eng/20250404 LC record available at https://lccn.loc.gov/2025009265 LC ebook record available at https://lccn.loc.gov/2025009266

Cover art by Yaroslav Schwarzstein
Wrap design by Zoe Guttenplan
Interior design and typeset by Douglas Suttle
Printed in Canada

THE SUGAR KREMLIN

TABLE OF CONTENTS

Introduction	11
Marfusha's Joy	23
Minstrels	49
The Poker	63
A Dream	87
Chow Time	97
Petrushka	119
A Tavern	135
The Queue	151
A Letter	167
At the Factory	181
Cinema	191
Underground	205
A House of Tolerance	221
Khlyupino	235
Disfavor	249
Translator's Note	263

"Rus', you are but a kiss in the frost!
The midnight roads are going blue."
    Velimir Khlebnikov

"But how much despotism lurks in this silence,
which attracts and fascinates me so much!
how much violence! how deceptive is this peace!"
Astolphe de Custine, *Russia in 1839*

THE GUTS OF THE RUSSIAN BRONTOSAURUS-COW:

*A Conversation with
Vladimir Sorokin*
by Joshua Cohen

MY PROBLEMS STARTED MUCH earlier than the night before deadline—they started in my childhood, when I completely failed to learn Russian, and though an inability to function in a writer's original has never stopped me and shouldn't stop anyone from pronouncing upon a translation, I admit that in my maturing years I ran into compounding difficulties, including the facts that I've never lived and written in a country that proscribes me, that I've never had to leave the country of my language and gone to settle abroad, that I've never had to live up to or live against a new identity projected onto me in exile as something of an artist-spokesman for political opposition, and—believe it or not—that I've never been mistaken for a one-man repository or symbol-embodiment of my literary culture, which happens to be one of the foremost literary cultures in the history of the world. It's so much easier, I'm realizing now, to introduce a book by a writer who stayed at mediocre home, surrounded by his more-or-less admiring publishers who publish him, and his more-or-less admiring readers who read him; it's so much easier, in other words, to introduce a book by a writer who is dead, which is admittedly how I feel sometimes, in my shut-into-my-apartment-and-English existence.

Vladimir Sorokin, however, is alive; he is quite alive, and when I asked him how and why (along with a clutch of other questions even more sincere), he obliged me with answers that contained all the intelligence and humor I expected, but also with a startling and I'd even say troubling tenderness and grace. Perhaps I'd missed this in what I'd read of his two-dozen-or-so-books, or perhaps this is new—a new element that in complete contradistinction to the extraterrestrial Ice that falls to the Siberian earth in his *Ice* trilogy is loving, positive, constructive (I should also say, speaking in these optimistic terms is novel *for me*).

The interview that follows transpired via email, and via the author's prodigious translator Max Lawton in winter 2024-25. I hope its contents convey the high respect I have for Sorokin, who is one of the great prose-writers of his remarkable Russian generation born around the death of Stalin, a generation that includes at least one other estimable Vladimir, the late Vladimir Sharov, and whose best still-living prose-writers and poets now dwell in Berlin, Paris, London, Tbilisi, Yerevan, Zurich, Athens, Rome, Tel Aviv . . .

Joshua Cohen

Reading you over the years at the inevitable delay of translation, I've always thought to myself: this is brilliant, but beware! If I have to distill this thought—this feeling—into questions, I'd ask the following: Is parody dangerous? Does satire of a regime ultimately serve the regime? I guess I should ask a politician instead: can you make fun of something without making it stronger?

Joshua, you're asking a very important ontological question. I could easily fall into conceptual speculations on this theme so as to justify myself and, I think, would be able to find justificatory arguments regarding my use of satire and humor, referring to Rabelais, Swift, and Hašek, I have done so in many interviews and have also grown a fairly thick skin, off of which such questions quickly bounce. But, in conversing with you, another writer, I don't wish to do this. When I was writing *Day of the Oprichnik*, then *The Sugar Kremlin*, what I was thinking of least of all was the benefit or harm of such texts vis-à-vis the state's evil or a potential victory over it (and, for me, Russia's pyramid of power has always been evil). When I start writing any book, I want one thing: for the book to turn out well, which is to say for it to be a self-sufficient work of literature, one unconnected with current issues of people or the state, even if the very subject of the book is the vileness of power.

I asked this because you come from a culture in which writers were once extraordinarily important. What does it mean to be a Russian writer today, though? A Russian in exile—does it feel like exile?—in Germany? (We'll agree for present purposes that Berlin is Germany.)

I'm going to be frank here: I don't know what a Russian writer is today. The simplest answer would be someone who writes in Russian. On Nabokov's grave in Montreux is simply written "écrivain." I feel very close to this sentiment. In the West, alas, there are still a great many clichés regarding Russian writers: spirituality, the metaphysics of Russian spaces and Russian nature, suffering, deadly love for a femme fatale, the horrors of the Gulag, totalitarianism, etc. I'm not against all of those themes, but I am against the cliché. Circumstances conspired such that I ended up in Berlin. But the last thing I want is to consider myself an emigrant, as Nabokov did. Unlike him, I can return to Moscow at any time, there's no Iron Curtain. I just don't wish to go to Putin's Moscow right now. Nabokov's situation was a great deal tougher. He was fleeing from death. Whereas I simply moved to Berlin. Even before this, my wife and I lived between Moscow and Berlin. And I hope to return to Moscow if the situation changes and the war in Ukraine ends.

The Sugar Kremlin, *like certain strains of your work, partakes of multiple genres, multiple forms: folktales, theater or film scripts, letters, dreams, and songs—but there's a sense that this variousness isn't yet another postmodern reinvention of the novel so much as a waking-up-from-a-long-nightmare declaration that the novel never existed. Do you recognize this reading? What does the novel mean to you?*

It seems to me that the best novels are produced when authors creatively disrupt the form of the novel. We need simply recall *Gargantua and Pantagruel*, *Ulysses*, or *War and Peace*. These are referred to as great novels, even though, formally speaking, it's almost as if they weren't novels at all. They're simply novels that are well suited to their time, which is why they turn out to be *great* novels. The contemporary world is so complex and protean that it is no longer possible to describe it with linear prose and squeeze it into a traditional novel's structure. In order to conceive of the contemporary world, I make use of complex optics, which can be referred to as faceted vision, like what insects have. Keeping in mind that, today, in post-Soviet Russia, the imperial past, which was not buried in time, presses in on the present like a glacier, the question of the future is suspended. As young Russians admit to me: "we do not feel the future as a vector of life and development." This is an absolutely pathological situation and a writer needs a special sort of vision in order to adequately recreate this on the page (you'll notice I say "recreate" and not "describe"). For this, I make use of a system of mirrors set up on two platforms—one is the past and one is the future. You can call this postmodernism or grotesque metarealism, I don't mind either way. But the grotesqueness of Russian life didn't begin with post-Soviet Russia, we need only recollect the worlds of Gogol.

Why do you prefer the verb "recreate" to "describe"? What's the difference? And why, when it comes to the contemporary, does recreation-on-the-page seem to be possible or at least more possible than description? Has something happened to realism or reality?

I don't like the term "description of the world," it contains a clear reference to *secondariness*—to illustrativeness. No, instead, a writer must conceive of his own worlds—not describe the world that's already been created. Tolstoy, Kafka, and Joyce were able to create their own worlds, which is why their prose stuns with its intellectual authenticity.

And what does style—the music of your sentences—mean to you, especially given that fools like me must read you in translation? What am I missing?

Joshua, I am simply a fool of literature who trusts his intuition alone—it's all that I have. To put it generally, a book's intonation is very important to me. That is the locomotive able to pull a novel toward new expanses, new horizons, but also able to knock it down into the abyss of routine. The intonation of a first page is like a melody you catch—a melody that begins a symphony. Which is why there are many books I don't even finish ten pages of, sensing that they "don't sound right." But, alas, I'm also a bad reader . . . In my life, a great deal has been and continues to be devoted to the visual arts.

In what way? I mean, you just scoffed at "illustrativeness."

Until I was twenty, I thought I was going to be an artist and devoted a great deal of my time to both painting and drawing, which I don't even remotely regret. In the eighties, I made my living by illustrating books, which allowed me to support my family and write prose in the evenings. You might well say that, ever since, I've been standing with only one leg in literature and the other in the *art-ocean*. This gives me the unique opportunity to look at literature as an *art-object*. Which is why I really do understand Nabokov, who wished to turn the reader into a viewer, as he once put it. Art helps me to create literary spaces, this way of seeing is always with me, but to explain the principles of such a way of seeing is difficult.

What do you see as the relationship between the chapter here called "The Queue" and my favorite of your early novels, translated as The Queue? *Is the line the great unit of our time—and is there anything besides the word itself, or an impatience for meaning, that unites the lines we wait in and the lines we read?*

The queue is an eternal theme of the Russian world—but not only of the Russian world. During the pandemic in Berlin, my wife and I stood out in the November cold and rain for four hours to make our way onto the bus where they were administering the Moderna vaccine. All of this was organized with a disgusting lack of humanity. I saw a queue of people trembling in the cold, as if this weren't the twenty-first century, but the forties of the European twentieth century! Which is why, for me, a queue is an archaic monster that lives inside of us and can easily emerge at any moment, paying no mind to time or century.

So you were vaccinated! Which brings me to questions of paranoia and conspiracy. I feel that novelists, especially in the so-called West, when faced with suspicions or dread, used to ask themselves: "is this true?" Now, in a time when anything, when everything, "can be true," the new thing to ask is: "can we live with it?" How has fiction changed as the culture has become more and more explicitly self-fictionalizing?

"Is that really true?" is an eternal question in our world, where *fakes* multiply with each passing minute. But I rely on my intuition, as I did before. My life experience and my inner feeling are all I have when assessing a phenomenon, person, or event. It seems to me that we have nothing else. To take something on faith is a dangerous act in our time.

The politics of this book are quite direct: the Sovereign, who reigns supreme, who builds the wall, is also "a sewer rat," whose dominion is some amalgam of the Soviet revolutionary era and the near-future New Russia. What connects that historical age to this coming age—or is there no difference, save a few technological breakthroughs and better Chinese food outside of China?

In Russia, all epochs are tied together by one thing: the pyramid of power. It was built by Ivan the Terrible in the sixteenth century and hasn't fundamentally changed since then. The language spoken by Russians in the sixteenth century changed, but the system of power did not! This pyramid is archaic, opaque, unpredictable, inhumane, and absolutely vicious to the populace around it. At the summit of the pyramid sits a single person who has all of the power for himself—the laws that exist for ordinary citizens do not apply to him. All of the ills of Russia are a function of this pyramid. It was an apposite structure in the eighteenth and even the nineteenth centuries, then, in the twentieth, it gave birth to a beastly totalitarian regime, but, in the twenty-first, it's a total anachronism, putting the brakes on the development of the country and frightening its neighbors. The consequences of this have now become visible to the whole world. The pyramid of power is a kind of reactor of imperial energy that produces hard radiation. The one sitting on top of it mutates, losing all human qualities and turning into a slave of the imperial idea. Like in *The Lord of the Rings*.

Is the Russian pyramid primarily a tomb, like its Egyptian predecessor, or some sort of gods-appointed abattoir, like the pyramids of Meso-America? And how does the Russian pyramid—at least your use of it—jibe with Marx's class pyramid? Or with Freytag's literary pyramid? Why so many pyramids—and what kind of pyramid is your book's Kremlin?

The Russian pyramid of power is a mystical object. It was created over the centuries, starting in the sixteenth. In it were united the authoritative principles of the Golden Horde and Byzantium, as well as Russians' pagan beliefs. In Russia, power took the place of God, this having been especially clear during the Soviet Union when Stalin became a living god and Lenin—a dead one, a mummy who was placed into a pyramid resembling an ancient ziggurat on Red Square. And the Soviet people worshipped this mummy.

Here is my favorite passage of this book:

> Sixteen months ago, six members of the mystical, anti-Russian sect "Yarosvet" were arrested. Having drawn a map of Russia onto a white cow, they performed a certain magic ritual, dismembered the cow, and began to take pieces of the cow's body to remote regions of the Russian state and feed it to foreigners. The cow's hindquarters were taken to the Far East, boiled, and fed to Japanese settlers, the flank and underbelly were taken to Barnaul, where they were folded into pelmeni and fed to Chinese people, they

made borsch from the brisket in Belgorod and fed it to eighteen dumb fuckin' Ukrainian overseas traders, they made a meatballs out of the cow's front legs for Belarusian farm laborers in Roslavl, then made kholodets from its head, which, not far from Pskov, they fed to three old Estonian women. All six of the sectarians were arrested, interrogated, then admitted to everything, named their accomplices and abettors, but, nevertheless, a dark place still remained in the case: the cow's offal.

Here we have what you call the "magic ritual of the 'dismemberment' of Russia"—but of the Russian state, or of Russian culture—both? And what is the offal in this metaphor? The "intestines, stomach, heart, liver and lungs"—by reading you are we reading them? Or, to put it another way, to what degree are you consciously performing literary haruspicy on the Russian corpse and corpus?

If we speak of Russia as a "sacred cow," this is indeed an image in the heads of many of our officials and patriots. But, when looking at a map of Russia and its size, you understand that it's not a cow, but a brontosaurus. The fear that the neighbors of this brontosaurus will bite it in the ass haunts our patriots. Which is why Russia periodically attacks its neighbors. An act that usually ends sadly for Russia. Imperial Russia collapsed after the war it lost against tiny Japan, just as the USSR collapsed after the war it lost against Afghanistan. About what will happen now, one can only fantasize . . . If you wish to speak of the guts of the Russian brontosaurus-cow, then this is pure Russian metaphysics.

MARFUSHA'S JOY

A RAY OF WINTER sunlight beat through the frosty window and fell upon Marfushenka's nose. Marfusha opened her eyes, sneezed. The little ray had woken her up at the most interesting spot: Once again, Marfusha had been dreaming of the enchanted blue forest and the shaggy ne'er-do-wells therein. The shaggy ne'er-do-wells were winking out from behind blue trees, sticking tongues of fire out of their hot mouths, and writing luminous hieroglyphs onto the bark of the trees with yon tongues, oh yes, the most ancient of all ancient and most complex of all complex hieroglyphs, hieroglyphs unknown even to the Chinese, the sorts of hieroglyphs that reveal great and terrible *secrets*. Such dreams petrify the soul, but somehow they're also a very pleasant thing to behold.

Marfusha kicked off her blanket with her foot, stretched out, saw the living picture of Ilya Muromets galloping about atop the long-maned Sivka-Burka on the wall, then remembered: Today was the last Sunday . . . the last Sunday of Christmas week. How nice that was! Holy Christmas still wasn't over! She wouldn't have to go to school until tomorrow. Marfushenka had been resting for a week now. For seven days, her *soft* alarm clock hadn't gurgled at seven o'clock, her grandma hadn't tugged at her legs, her dad hadn't grumbled, her mom hadn't rushed about, and her satchel with her smart machine hadn't pulled at her back.

Marfusha got up out of bed, yawned, and knocked on the wooden partition:

"Mom-m!"

There's no reply.

"Mo-om-m!"

Mom began to toss and turn behind the partition:

"What d'you want?"

"Nothing."

"If y'don't want nothing, then keep sleeping, y'little fidget . . ."

But Marfushenka doesn't want to sleep anymore. She looked out the frosty window lit up by the sun and immediately remembered *which* Sunday it was, jumped in place, and clapped her hands:

"The gift!"

The sun and the frosty patterns on the glass reminded her of the *main thing*:

"The gift!"

Marfusha squealed with joy. Then grew frightened:

"What time is it?!"

She jumped out from behind the partition in her nightgown, her braid disheveled and beginning to come undone, then glanced at the clock: only half past nine! She crossed herself in sight of the icons:

"Glory be to you, oh Lord!"

The gift would only be ready at six in the evening. At six in the evening on the last Sunday of Christmas!

"Why on earth aren't ya sleepin'?" Mom raised herself up unhappily on her bed.

Lying next to Mom, her father tossed, turned, and sniffed, but didn't wake up: he'd come back from Miusskaya Square late last night, he'd been selling his wooden cigar cases there, and all night he'd been pounding his chisel, crafting a cradle for Marfusha's future brother. But her grandma over by the stove woke up right away and set to coughing, wheezing, spitting, and muttering:

"Blessed Virgin Mary, bless us and have mercy . . . "

She saw Marfusha and hissed:

"Why won't you let your father sleep, you little snake?"

Grandpa coughed in his corner too, behind another partition. Marfusha sequestered herself in the lavatory—as far from Grandma as possible. But Grandma could get annoyed with her there too. Mean ole lady! Grandpa was nice and talkative. Mommy was serious but kind. Daddy was always silent and gloomy. And that was Marfusha's whole family.

Marfusha did her *business* and washed her face, looking at herself in the mirror. She liked the way she looked: a little white face with no freckles, even, smooth, fair hair, gray eyes like Mom's, a little nose that wasn't snubbed, just like Dad's, big ears like Grandpa's, and black brows like Grandma's. Marfusha knows a lot for her eleven years: she gets "good" grades, is on amicable terms with her smart machine, can type on the keys without looking, knows a lot of Chinese words, helps Mom, can embroider crosses and beads, sings in church, memorizes prayers with great ease, folds pelmeni handily, cleans the floors, and does laundry.

She pulled her toothbrush—shaped like a little yellowish-red dragon—out from its glass, animated it, watered it with dental elixir, then put it into her mouth. The dragon sprinkled her tongue with *minty pleasantness*, pounced on her teeth, and began to purr. Meanwhile, Marfushenka launched a comb into her hair. The *layered* comb set about its usual work, crawling and buzzing through Marfusha's fair locks. How nice Marfusha's hair was! Smooth, long, and silky. It was a pure delight for a comb to crawl through such hair. It did its combing, returned to the crown of Marfusha's head, and began to plait a braid. Marfushenka spat the little dragon-brush out of her mouth and into her hand, washed it, then put it back into its glass. The dragon tooth-cleaner winked at her with its eye of flame and froze until the morrow.

And, already, from the kitchen her restless grandma calls out fussily:

"Put on the samovar, Marfa!"

"In a sec, Gram!" Marfusha shouted back, then hurried the Chinese comb along:

"Kuaiii—i-dyar!!!"[1]

The comb began to purr more loudly, and its *soft* teeth flashed more quickly through Marfusha's fair hair. Marfusha picked out an orange bow and a pair of hair clips and waited for the comb to complete its work, then—through the partitions and into the kitchen.

Marfusha managed to fill up the one-and-a-half-bucket samovar: she poured the water, set fire to the birch bark, threw its blackening matter into the center through the vent, then put pine cones in on top of them—pine cones they'd go to collect in Silver Grove as a class. Marfusha managed to collect three bags of them every week. This was a great boon to her parents. And to Mother Moscow.

The birchbark crackled, Marfusha put a handful of birchwood chips above the cones, inserted the ventilation tube, then put its other end into a hole in the wall. There, behind the wall, was the stove pipe shared by the entire sixteen-story building. The samovar hummed merrily and the cones crackled.

And Grandma was already right there with her: barely had she finished reciting her morning prayer when she immediately set to stoking the stove. These days, everyone stokes their flames in the morning and cooks their supper in a Russian stove, just as the Sovereign ordained. This is a great boon to Russia and a wonderful economization of precious gas. Marfusha loves to

---

1. [Chinese] faster.

watch the firewood burning in the stove. But there's no time for that today. Today is a special day.

Marfusha went into her corner, got dressed, prayed quickly, and bowed down to a living portrait of the Sovereign on the wall:

"Health be to thee, Sovereign Vasily Nikolaevich!"

The Sovereign smiles down at her, looking at her affably with his blue eyes:

"Hello, Marfa Borisovna."

With a touch of her right hand, Marfusha animated her smart machine.

"Hello, Smartypants!"

The blue bubble lights up in response and winks.

"Hello, Marfusha!"

Marfusha knocks on the keys, goes onto the InterYes, and tears forth broadsheets of school news from the Tree of Learning.

CHRISTMAS SUPPLICATIONS PERFORMED BY STUDENTS OF THE PARISH SCHOOLS

AN ALL-RUSSIAN ICE-SCULPTURE COMPETITION (*WHO CAN SCULPT THE SOVEREIGN'S HORSE BUDIMIR???*)

A SKI RACE WITH CHINESE ROBOTS

SLEDDING DOWN THE SPARROW HILLS
AN INITIATIVE BY THE STUDENTS OF SCHOOL 62

Marfusha went to the final broadsheet: *On the Bright Day of the Birth of Christ, students of Parish School No. 62 (PS62) elected to continue their patriotic assistance to a Bolshevik brick factory working on the state program "Great Wall of Russia."*

She didn't manage to *leap* into her personal news before her grandfather started to breathe tobacco fumes down her neck.

"Mornin', grasshopper! What's new in the world?"

"Schoolchildren molding bricks on Christmas!" Marfusha replies.

"Oh boy!" Grandpa shakes his head and looks at the shining bubble. "Good kids! That's how the Wall'll get done by Easter!"

And he jabs his finger into Marfusha's side. Marfusha laughs and Grandpa chuckles through his gray mustache. Marfusha's got a nice grandpa. He's kind and talkative. How much, oh, how much he's seen and how much he's told his granddaughter about Russia: about the Red Troubles and the White Troubles and the Gray Troubles. About how the Sovereign's father Nikolai Platonovich ordered that the Kremlin be whitewashed and that the Mausoleum with its troublesome red be demolished overnight, and about how the Russian people burned their overseas passports on Red Square, and about the Renaissance of Rus', and about the heroic oprichniks, the enemies of internal destruction, and about the Sovereign and the Sovereigness's wonderful children, about their magical dolls and about the white horse Budimir . . .

Grandpa's beard tickles Marfusha:

"Well then, y'little fidget, ask your Smartypants how many bricks are missing from the Wall."

Marfusha asks. The Smartypants answers in an obedient tone.

"In order for the Great Wall of Russia to be completed, 62,876,543 more bricks must be laid."

Grandpa winks moralizingly:

"There y'go, Granddaughter, if every schoolchild molded a single brick out of our native clay, then the Sovereign would finish the wall immediately and a happy life would begin in Russia."

Marfusha knows this. She knows the Great Wall isn't going to be finished any time soon, that internal and external enemies will prevent it. That many more bricks need to be molded in order for universal happiness to come into being. The Great Wall grows and grows, fencing Russia off from external enemies. And internal enemies are torn into little bits by the oprichniks. Indeed, beyond the Great Wall, there are accursèd cyberpunks illegally sucking up gas, hypocritical Catholics, unabashed Protestants, batty Buddhists, rancorous Muslims, entirely corrupt atheists, satanists shaking their stuff to *damnèd* music on town squares, thuggish druggies, insatiable sodomites who bore into the darkness of each other's asses, sinister werewolves able to change their God-given image, and greedy plutocrats, and malicious virtuals, and merciless technotrons, and sadists, and fascists, and megaonanists . . . Marfusha's girlfriends had told her about these megaonanists, that they were shameless European people who locked themselves in basements, taking tablets of fire and trifling with their pussies with special trifling machines. Marfusha had already dreamed of the megaonanists twice: they'd caught her in dark basements and slid electric, iron hooks into her pussy. How frightening . . .

"Go get some bread, Marfa!"

Well, then, time to go out onto the street. Of course, she wasn't eager to do so this early in the morning, but what could she do? Marfusha pulled on a cardigan, threw the old fur coat she'd already grown out of over it, put her feet into gray felt boots, pulled a downy kerchief off of the stove, and threw it round her head.

And Grandma slips her a silver ruble:

"Get a round loaf of white and a quarter-loaf of black. And don't forget the change."

"And buy me cigarettes, Granddaughter." Grandpa twists at his mustache.

"He's already smoked through the whole household . . . " Grandma grumbles, tying Marfusha's kerchief.

And cheerful Grandpa gives Grandma a finger in the side:

"OK, then, Mother Hen!"

Grandma shudders and sputters.

"Why don't you just . . . y'old devil."

Cheerful Grandpa hugs her from behind, his arms round her skinny shoulders.

"Stop hissin', Timofeyevna, you snaky lady! Later on, I'll siphon you off some from my pension."

"Oh, you'll siphon off from it alright, ye old vacuum cleaner, you just wait!" Grandma shoves him away, but Grandpa kisses her on the lips handily.

"Ach, you ragged wolf!" Grandma laughs, hugging and kissing him back.

Marfusha goes out the door.

Their elevator doesn't work on holidays—'tisn't allowed for by the city council. Marfusha goes down from the ninth floor on foot, slapping her red mittens against the graffitied wall. The staircase was filthy, trash everywhere, dried-up piles of shit, but there was no mystery as to why: this was a zemsky building, and the Sovereign had been upset with the zemskys for the last six years. Thank God Malaya Bronnaya paid off the oprichniks, otherwise it would be in the same situation as Ostozhenka and Nikitskaya. Marfusha remembers how they set flame to seditious Nikitskaya. The smoke spread all across Moscow . . .

Marfusha walked out the door. The courtyard was covered with snow, and sunlight was shining down onto it. And the kids from the building were already playing their hearts out: Seryozhka Burakov, Sveta Rogozina, Vitka the Elephant, Tomilo, a guy from House No. 13, and some *shaggy* ragamuffins from the Garden Ring. For all of Christmas, they've been playing the same game: Oprichniks vs. Nobles. The nobles build their estate from snow and move into it. Then the oprichniks surround them: "Word and Deed!" The nobles bribe their way out of it each time with icicles. But, as soon as they run out of icicles, the oprichniks are on the attack, reclaiming the noble estate.

Like now—snowballs were whizzing into the estate and the oprichniks were whistling and cheering:
"Hail! Hail!"
Marfusha skirts round the battle. A snowball hits her on the back.
"Come on and peel 'em with us, Marfa!"
Marfusha stops. Svetka and Tomilo, both flushed, run over to her:
"Where you headed?"
"Must needs buy some bread for breakfast."
The narrow-eyed Tomilo sniffs:
"I heard some boys cursing on Vspolnoy. The f-word and the c-word."
"Wow!" Marfusha shakes her head. "Who reported them?"
"Sashka the Dovecote. He called Seryoga and Seryoga told his dad. His dad went to the precinct right away."
"Nice goin'."
"Play just one round with us! You'll be Princess Bobrinskaya!"
"I can't. My parents're waitin'."
Marfusha set off once again.
Coming out of the courtyard, she headed for Khoprov's shop. The shop was beautifully decorated—two dressed-up fir trees were standing by the entrance, the windows were shimmering with *living* snowflakes, and Santa Claus and the Snow Maiden were riding on an icy sleigh in the corner of the window. Marfusha walks into the shop and a copper bell tinkles. People are already waiting in line inside, but the line's not too big—just thirty people. Marfusha got in line behind some old guy in a Chinese vatnik and stared at the display case. And there, beneath the glass, lies everything that one could ever trade: meat with bones and without, ducks and hens, sausages boiled and smoked, milk whole and sour, plum and apple jams, "Clubfooted Bear" and "Bear in the North" candies. Plus rye and wheat vodka, "Homeland" and "Russia" cigarettes, plum and apple jam,

gingerbread with peppermint and without, rusks with raisins and without, granulated and lump sugar, millet and buckwheat, white and black bread. Yep, she was gonna have to wait through the whole line for the bread and her grandpa's cigarettes. Suddenly, Marfusha hears a familiar little voice in line:

"A half-pound of lump sugar, a round loaf of black, a quarter-loaf of rye, and a dime's worth of apple jam."

Zinka Shmerlina from Marfusha's building's third stairwell. Marfusha immediately went over to her:

"Get some bread and cigarettes for me, Zin."

The black-eyed, black-haired Zinka reluctantly takes the ruble from Marfusha.

And the line immediately comes to life.

"She's in such a hurry, the little fidget can't wait in line like everyone else, huh?"

"Where's she goin' without standin' in line! Don't let her through!"

"We also need no more'n bread!"

"What a cunning little thing!"

But now, Khoprov himself is standing behind the counter, and he loves lil' girls:

"That's enough yappin'! Aggrieve not the maiden. What's the rush? All of you'll be off to work tomorrow."

The owner of the shop was wide in torso, tall, had a thick, red beard, was dressed in a red kosovorotka, and in a sheepskin coat too. Khoprov gives Marfusha her bread and cigarettes with his big hands, gives her the change, and winks at them with his little eye, droopy and lost in the fat of his face:

"Set forth, dragonfly!"

Marfusha and Zina leave the shop. Zina's family is poor and unfortunate: even though her father is a craftsman of *warm robots*, he still drinks like a fish. And her mom has no desire to work at all. That's why Zina's dressed so poorly—thin felt boots, a patchwork quilted jacket, a hat that, though it's made of fox fur, is old and worn and appears to have been handed down from her older sister Tamara.

"Are you gonna go to Red Square with Tamara?" Marfusha asks, taking more comfortable hold of the bag of bread.

"Nope." Zina shakes her head. "Stupid Tamarka's in Kolomna right now—she's coming back anon on the night train. Vaska and I'll go."

Vasya is Zina's little brother. Good for them—they'll get two presents. Marfushenka must needs wait for her mom to give birth to a little brother.

They'd only passed by two buildings on Malaya Bronnaya when—look!—Amonya of Kiev City himself comes out onto the lane, stalking along with his faithful electric dog, and behind them, a whole crowd of rubberneckers. Marfusha has solely seen blessèd Amonya once before, when they hung him up over Trubnaya Square by ropes so's he might see the *trouble* at hand. And he saw that the Sovereigness would have a second miscarriage because of the Streltsy widow's evil-eyeing. The people treated the widow pretty harshly after that—they dragged her down Vasilyevsky Descent to the Moscow River and shoved her under the ice with pike poles.

The girls stopped in their tracks and looked at the blessèd one. He's walking, stooped, thin, ragged, somehow reminiscent of a frog, dragging along his electric dog named Cadet on a leash. There's a heavy iron cross on Amonya's chest, chains across his shoulders, and oaken corks protrude from his ears so's he might protect himself from the noise of the people. Marfusha's grandma always said that Amonya took yon corks out of his ears only once a year, at the Feast of the Transfiguration, so's he might "hear the whispers of the Tabor Light." Because of yon oaken corks, Amonya never converses, but only screams and shouts. Like now.

"I can't see the way! Dark is the path!"

Even though it was a sunny morning, Amonya couldn't see the way. He stops, and the crowd stops too.

"Shine! Shine forth!" the blessèd one cries.

Cadet lights up his blue eyes and shines them in front of Amonya's feet. Amonya leans onto a staff, tilting his big head toward the ground, sniffing at the snow and shouting:

"Something sips of blood!"

The crowd shuffles around Amonya:

"Whose blood is to be spilled, Amonechka?"

"Who must take care?"

"Wither are they to creep?"

"Where are the candles to be placed?"

"To whom shall the gifts be given?"

Amonya sniffs at the snow. Everyone freezes.

"A lesser trouble!" he shouts out.

The crowd approaches, worried now:

"Show us the trouble! Show us the trouble!"

Amonya straightens up and casts furious looks off to the sides from beneath his protruding brow:

"A lesser trouble! A lesser trouble!"

"Show us the trouble! Show us the trouble!" The crowd approaches.

Merchants and members of the petty bourgeoisie, tramps and beggars, drinkers and cokeheads, Chinese peddlers and Tatar sbiten sellers, adolescents and children, all of them beg:

"Show us the trouble! Show us the trouble!"

Amonya straightens up and throws his hand into the air:

"Lift me up!"

The crowd began to fuss about and rushed to knock at the doors and windows of nearby houses. Faces flashed into the windows and the four silent companions of the blessèd one took skeins of strong rope out from their shoulder bags. In just a moment, the ropes are hung from the balconies and snaked down from the windows. Immediately, a sentry appeared and shut down Malaya Bronnaya: *Amonya's gettin' raised up!* The law is simple: in whatever part of the capital Amonya is showing trouble, everything has to freeze immediately.

They tie ropes around Amonya's waist, his trusty dog stands up on its hind legs, and the crowd parts. They pull the ropes, raise up Amonya, and he lifts up off of the ground.

The crowd froze. Everyone's watching. They raised the blessèd Amonya up over Moscow. Higher and higher. Third floor, fourth floor, fifth floor. Sixth floor.

"I see the lesser trouble!" his voice rings out above the crowd.

They stopped pulling at the ropes. Amonya of Kiev City was hanging between heaven and earth. The crowd was standing down below, not stirring at all. Marfusha's mouth fell open. She stares with total attention at Amonya hanging there.

"Archers' blood is to be spilled in ZaMoskvorechye!" Amonya broadcasts from the air. "The oprichniks are to crush two colonels on Monday. But this disfavor shall not be meted out to their subordinates."

The crowd sighed with relief: that really was a lesser trouble, Amonya was right. There were no archers in the crowd either. Solely one woman wearing an Astrakhan fur crossed herself and ran away.

"Lower me down!" Amonya hollers, shuddering on the ropes.

They lower him down and release him from his fetters.

And he starts up again:

"Remedials!"

Hands shoot out from the crowd holding gifts for him. Some give money and some give food. His companions and his electric dog help him to gather up the gifts.

"I'm ill! I'm i-l-l-l-l-l-l!" Amonya cries mournfully.

They cross themselves in the crowd and bow down to him. Marfushenka crosses herself and bows down to the blessèd one as well. Cadet's blue eyes come to rest on her bag of bread and cigarettes. A broad-shouldered companion approaches her with a sack, then silently opens it in front of Marfusha and Zina. The girls submissively put everything in their hands into the sack.

"I'm i-l-l-l-l-l-l! I'm i-l-l-l-l-l-l!!" Amonya hollers so much that many people in the crowd begin to sob.

The blessèd one walks away down Malaya Bronnaya. The crowd rushes after him. And Zina and Marfushenka see them off numbly with their eyes.

The sentry whistled, letting the cars building up at the entrance to the street pass. The girls came to their senses: they must needs go to the shop once more. Marfusha had eighty whole kopecks left over from the ruble, but Zina only had three.

"I must needs tell my parents," Zina thinks aloud. "Lend me a lil' call?"

The payment on Zina's talker is always overdue.

"Go ahead." Marfusha takes her talker out of her ear and gives it to Zinka.

Zinka attaches the reddish-brown talker to her earlobe.

"Alkonost, two, two, nine, forty-six, half-a-hundred, eight."

Zinka's family's distance-talking service is the cheapest one—Alkonost. Marfusha's family uses Sirin. But not because the Zavarzins are that much richer than the Shmerlinas. It was just that, six months ago, Marfusha's father carved an icon case with the Savior and his Apostles for the table-minister of the Chamber of Communication's manor. And yon icon case pleased the table-minister so much that he gifted the Zavarzins nine free months of Sirin.

"Ma . . . I gave all our grub to blessèd Amonya," Zina says.

"Foolish girl," Marfusha hears the reply. "Your father won't let you through the door without vodka."

"I only have three kopecks left."

"That'd better be enough."

Zinka gives the talker back to Marfusha with a sigh.

"Nothing to be done—I'll go to Pushkin Square and tear up my throat singin' 'Separation.' 'Haps they'll give me enough for a quarter bottle."

"Go with God." Marfusha nods and heads back to the shop herself.

This isn't the first time Zinka's had to beg. And Marfusha doesn't have the right to lend her money.

The line had gotten even longer while Marfusha was gone—plus everyone was running out of food on the last day of the holiday. And, as luck would have it, she didn't know anyone in line. Nothing to be done—Marfusha waited through the line and made it back to the broad-bodied Khoprov:

"A round loaf of white, a quarter of black, and a pack of cigarettes."

The shopkeeper squints his swollen eyes:

"Huh? Gettin' what you just got, dragonfly? Wasn't enough for everyone? They ate up the bread and smoked all the cigarettes?"

"I gave it all away to blessèd Amonya, Paramon Kuzmich."

Khoprov scratches at his red beard:

"Well, well! Nicely done! Yon was a charitable act."

Then, after only a slight pause, he launches his hand into a box of hard candy and gives some to Marfusha:

"Here y'go."

"Thankee."

Marfushenka takes the candies, bread, and cigarettes—then straight off home she is. She puts the candies into her mouth, sucks, hurries, turns off of Malaya Bronnaya, then, in the building on the corner, on the first floor, through an open ventilation window, she hears:

"Ai, I won't do it again! Ai! Ai, I won't!"

And the rod whistles and spanks. Marfusha slowed her pace, stopped.

"Ai, I won't! Oy, I won't!"

A boy is being whipped. The rod whistles, slaps against his naked buttocks. It seems like it's his father doing the whipping. Daddy never whips Marfusha, 'tis Mommy alone does that. Yeah and rarely too, thanks be to God. The last time had been before Christmas when, due to Marfusha's oversight, two lines of precious coke had blown away. On that evening, Mom and Dad sat down in the kitchen after a difficult day and chopped out three lines of *white* just as Marfusha was taking out the trash, leaving the door wide open as she did. And, as luck would have it, the ventilation window was open in the kitchen. Wind blew in from the broken window in the stairwell, so much so that all of the coke was blown into the four corners of the room like dust. Dad and Grandpa cry out. Grandma pinches her. And Mom silently laid Marfusha out on the double bed and whipped her bare booty with a jump rope. Marfusha was crying and Dad and Grandpa were crawling around in the kitchen, licking their fingers and collecting the white dust . . .

Marfusha entered her building and saw three beggars drinking by the radiator. They'd spread out a copy of the newspaper *Revival*, laid out everything they'd managed to collect that morning, and were eating chasers after taking swigs from a bottle of moonshine. But these beggars were newcomers, not locals, and you could see from their appearance that they weren't Muscovites at all: one was old and as gray as a harrier, the other was swarthy, strong, but missing both of his legs, and the third was an adolescent. And it seemed they'd bought their moonshine from the Chinamen on Pushkin Square, as the liquid was contained in a *soft* bottle.

"Health to ye, girlie." The old man smiles at her.

"Don't you fall ill either," Marfusha mutters as she passes by.

She started to head up the stairs, then she had a thought: She had to go report to the super. There were all sorts of beggars. They'd let a group of mummers into Building No. 15 during

Svyatki and the mummers had passed through three apartments with gas revolvers and stolen away with three bags of stuff, singing Christmas carols all the while. In the best case, beggars in from out of town will shit on the staircase, but, in the worst, they'll steal something.

Marfusha rings at the super's apartment on the third floor. The super's wife opens the door with curlers in and a cigarette between her lips:

"What d'ya want?"

"Beggars are drinking moonshine downstairs!"

She said it, then ran right up the stairs. Made it to her floor and leaned out of the broken window: What's gonna happen? A little bit of time passed, then she heard a sound down below and a door slammed:

"Oh beloved mother of mine!"

The old man tumbles through the door, holding onto his behind, the adolescent runs out behind him, then the invalid sways out on his crutches. And behind all of them comes Andreich the super with an electric cudgel. He aimed, then cast a blue bolt into the seat of the invalid's pants. The invalid screeched and swore:

"Fuck your prolapsed mother!"

The super threatens him:

"Watch out or I'll cast a red one! Then take you to the precinct, you mischief maker!"

The old man and adolescent pick up the invalid and drag themselves away. The boys in the courtyard see them off with hoots and snowballs. The red-nosed Andreich spits into the snow, puts away his cudgel, then disappears back into the building.

A useful, stately thing had been done. Now content, Marfusha rings at her own door. Grandma opens it, trembling with rage:

"Where'd you get off to, you little snake?!"

Coming out of the lavatory, Grandpa chuckles over Grandma's shoulder:

"Bet she got wrapped up talkin' to a girlfriend!"
And her gloomy father chimes in from the kitchen:
"Marfa's slower than molasses."

"I saw blessèd Amonya," Marfusha explains herself. "He got raised up right there on the street, then asked for remedials. I gave him the bread and tobacco. I had to get everything all over again."

Grandma quiets down, but continues to grumble:
"I s'pose he had great need of it . . ."
"What'd he see?" Grandpa wonders.
"They're gonna crush the archers."
"Well, God be with them." Grandma waves her hand, taking the bread from Marfusha.
"They can afford to shed a few," her father mutters.
"They've got a few to spare, that's for sure!" Grandpa lights up.
"They've gotten fat with no war to keep 'em busy." Her bare-headed mother yawns, peering out from the bathroom. "That monkey Voronin has three Merstallions. So, are we gonna sit down to eat or what?"

The entire family prayed to Saint Nicholas, had their breakfast of millet porridge with milk, drank Chinese tea, and finished the meal with white bread and apple jam. Her father fiddled around with his cigarette cases, then set off for Miusskaya Square to trade. Mom and Grandma went to church. Grandpa went to get firewood in Arbat on a sleigh. And Marfusha stayed at home—to wash the dishes. She washed the plates and pots, then washed and ironed her school collars. Then sat down to play "Guojie"[2] on her Smartypants. She played until lunch, but couldn't find a *baojian*.[3] It turned out she must needs have been looking for it not in the castle, but in the dungeon, where clay warriors stood stock-still before coming to life and rushing at her, coming

---

2. "Godza"—Chinese for "state border," a 4D computer game that became popular in New Russia after the infamous events of August, 2027.

3. [Chinese] sword.

out from underneath the earth and crawling toward our border. While you're fighting with them, the *baojian* glows blue, and, as soon as you overpower them, it disappears right away. Then you just *try* and find it! On the other hand, Kolka Bashkirtsev had told her how, as soon as you find the *baojian*, all of your enemies immediately topple over dead and the young Sovereign marries Princess Sun Yun, then there's a *side quest* for girls: the wedding. It's very beautiful there, he said, the bride wears six outfits over the course of the feast, then there's another *side quest*, a forbidden one: what the young people do at night in the bedchamber. Playing this level is *strictly* prohibited! And Marfusha was never going to play it. But the little boys who find the *baojian* always do . . .

Another couple of hours passed before the cuckoo on the wall cuckooed. Mom and Grandma came back from church, Grandpa slid back with his sled full of logs, and her dad came back from Miusskaya Square filled with joy: he'd sold three cigarette cases. What luck! First of all, he went to the pharmacy and bought a vial of coke. He and Mom snorted it up and washed it down with braga, plus Grandma and Grandpa had a little bit of it too. It was only under the influence of coke that her father lost his habitual gloominess. It was as if he became a different person—loquacious, restless, and full of life. And when her father was full of life, he immediately set to singing songs: "Fall," "I Just Slept a Little, Little Bit," "A Pure Falcon in the Snow," "Little Sadness," and "Khazbulat the Sporty." He, Mom, and Grandpa sat down in the kitchen to sing. They sang and sang, sang until they wept, as they always did. At the same time, Marfusha fixed up some warm porridge, went to the School Tree, and looked to see what she had at school tomorrow.

1. God's Law
2. Russian History
3. Mathematics

4. Chinese Language
5. Labor
6. Choir

Six classes—that was too much.

Marfusha's always gotten along well with God's Law, reveres the history of the Russian state, diligently studies Chinese, is always expeditious in Labor, sings well in Choir, but Mathematics... it's far from a simple discipline for Marfusha. Nor is her teacher, one Yuri Vitalievich, a simple fellow. Oh, how unsimple! He's tall and thin, slender as a *baojian*, but terribly strict. Back in first grade, when they were studying arithmetic, Yuri Vitalievich walked round the class, repeating in his squeaky voice: "Arithmetic is an enormous discipline, children." And that's without even mentioning mathematics... It gives itself to Marfusha with great difficulty: Yuri Vitalievich has already put her into the corner eighteen times, onto her knees seven times, and onto dry peas four.

Marfusha leafed through her despisèd mathematics textbook, closed it, then put it back onto the shelf. Some of her teachers were frightening. But there were also good and kindhearted ones. Like, for example, her PE teacher Pavel Nikitich. You just look at him and he tosses you a dime. His favorite thing to do with the girls is running races. The 500-sazhen jog and 50-sazhen sprint. He's in Chinese sneakers in the summer and on skis in the winter. The girls run and he cheers:

"Burn, baby, burn!"

Marfusha turns out to be best at sprinting—she's super fast, quick and crafty. She's gone to the district competition twice. She got fourth and sixth place.

Marfusha was surfing the InterYes and, again, decided to play "Godza." It was her favorite. And that's how the time passed until evening: four o'clock, five o'clock, half past five... Right then, Marfusha's heart jumped: It was time! Mom got her ready, dressed her up, tied a new kerchief white as down around her, and blessed her journey:

"Go forth, Daughter."

Marfusha went out into the courtyard, her heart pounding. And dressed-up children are milling about in the courtyard, coming out of all six of the building's stairwells. There's Zina Bolshova and Stasik Ivanov, there's Sasha Gulyaeva and Mashka Morkovich, there's Kolyakh Kozlov. Marfusha went out onto Bolshaya Bronnaya with them. And other children are already walking down the street—dozens, no, hundreds of children! At Pushkin Square, Marfusha turned onto Tverskaya Street—and all of Tverskaya was filled with children. The children were walking down Tverskaya to the Kremlin in an enormous throng. There were absolutely no adults among them—it wasn't allowed. The adults had already gotten their gifts. At the edges of the juvenile crowd, keepers of public order rode along on horseback. Marfusha walks along with the crowd. Her heart is pounding and she's frozen with delight. The juvenile river moves more and more slowly, more and more children are pouring into it from streets and little lanes too. And here's Manezhnaya Square, Marfusha passes by it with the crowd. Another step, another and another—and now Marfusha's boot steps out onto the cobblestones of Red Square. The crowd moves at a slow pace, crawling along like an enormous caterpillar. Red Square is beneath Marfusha's feet. Red Square always takes her breath away. Here is where the heroes of Russia are recognized and here is where its enemies are punished. A moment later—and the chimes of Spasskaya Tower ring out: six o'clock! The juvenile river came to a halt—froze. Their chatter went quiet. The lights around them were extinguished. And, up above, 'pon the winter clouds, the Sovereign's enormous visage shone forth.

"HELLO, CHILDREN OF RUSSIA!" thundered out over the square.

The children cried out in response, leaping up and down and waving their arms. Marfusha leapt up and down too, admiring the Sovereign's image. He smiles down from the clouds, his blue eyes watching them warmly. How wondrous is the Sovereign of All of Rus'! How beautiful and kind! How wise and affectionate! How mighty and invincible!

"MERRY CHRISTMAS, CHILDREN OF RUSSIA!"

And suddenly, as if by magic, out through the clouds, out through the Sovereign's face, thousands of red balloons begin to drift down. To each balloon is attached a little box. The children catch the falling boxes, jump up, and pull down the balloons. Marfusha grabs a balloon as it comes down from the sky, then pulls the little box over. The children standing next to her grab other boxes.

"BE HAPPY, CHILDREN OF RUSSIA!" thunders down from the sky.

The Sovereign smiles. Then vanishes.

Tears of joy splash out of Marfusha's eyes. Sobbing and pressing the box to her beaver-lamb fur, she moves along with the crowd toward the Vasilyevsky Descent and past St. Basil's Cathedral. And, as soon as it becomes easier to move through the crowd, she impatiently opens up her shining box. And in this little box is a Sugar Kremlin! An exact replica of the white-stoned Kremlin! With its towers, cathedrals, and bells of Ivan the Great! Marfusha puts the Sugar Kremlin to her lips, kissing and licking it as she walks . . .

Late that night, Marfusha is lying in her bed, squeezing a Sugar Spasskaya Tower in her sticky fist. Marfusha is cozy 'neath the quilted blanket with the sugared tower in her maiden's fist. 'Tis the peak of the tower with its two-headed eagle alone that peeks out of Marfusha's hand. The moon shines through the frosty window, glittering on the two sugared heads of the great bird.

Marfusha looks at the eagle, glittering with sugar, and fatigue pulls at her eyelids. 'Twas a big day. A good day. A joyful day.

It was a festive evening for the Zavarzin family: They put the Sugar Kremlin onto the table, lit candles, looked round at one another, and conversed. Then Dad pulled out a hammer and split the Kremlin up—breaking off each tower separately. And Marfushenka gave the towers of the Kremlin to the members of her family: Borovitskaya Tower to her father, Nikolskaya Tower to her mother, Kutafya Tower to her grandfather, and Troitskaya Tower to her grandmother. But, during their *council*, the family decided not to eat the Armory Tower: they would leave it aside till the birth of Marfusha's brother. Let him eat it, oh yes, that he should take on knightly strength. But the walls of the Kremlin, the cathedrals, and the bells of Ivan the Great . . . these the family ate themselves, washing them down with Chinese tea . . .

Her eyelids clamping shut, Marfusha sticks the two-headed eagle into her mouth, puts it onto her tongue, and sucks.

She falls into a happy dream.

In which she sees a Sugar Sovereign upon a white horse.

MINSTRELS

THE MIDDLE OF APRIL. PodMoscovie. Night is falling. The ruins of the Kunitsyn Estate, burnt down by oprichniks. The wandering minstrels go through a hole in the high fence and onto the territory of the estate—Sophron, Booger, Vanyusha, and Frolovich. Vanyusha is blind, Frolovich is missing a leg, and Booger has a limp. A herd of stray dogs runs out of the black ruins and begins to bark at the minstrels.

>BOOGER (*picks up a piece of brick and hurls it at the dogs*). Get back, ye nettle seeds!
>VANYUSHA (*stops*). There're dogs here too?
>FROLOVICH (*whistles, waves his crutch at the dogs*). Hey there, doggies!

Still barking, the dogs run off.

>FROLOVICH (*rubs his lower back exhaustedly, looks off to the sides*). Oh Lord, oh God ... Forsooth, 'tis that very same place!
>SOPHRON. That's what I was tellin' ye, bro. I told you ...
>VANYUSHA. Sophronyushka, ye were sayin' somethin' 'bout a copper roof with a weather vane, aye?

SOPHRON. There was such a roof, there was indeed. I swear to God. (*He crosses himself.*) A roof and a tower and granaries and sheds and a kennel. And an apiary with its own orchard. Sixty beehives! There was everything. And wa-a-ay over there was a checkpoint by the gates. That's where the kind man Alyosha let Frolovich and me warm ourselves up. His masters weren't at home so he let us stay over. A kind man.
FROLOVICH. Verily so. He didn't solely let us in, he served us noodles too. And gave us each an apple. They had various different kinds of apples fallin' from the trees that fall . . . But now stands neither guardhouse nor guard. Goodness, Sophronya, such destruction!
SOPHRON. In sooth, such destruction . . .
BOOGER (*blows his nose loudly*). The extortionists burnt it all down.
SOPHRON. They burnt down the guardhouse too.
VANYUSHA. Who?
BOOGER (*irritatedly*). Who, who, Mr. Blue? The oprichniks—who else?
SOPHRON. There's their sign above the gates: WD. Word and Deed.
VANYUSHA. On a stick, huh?
BOOGER (*angrily*). Yeah, on a stick!
VANYUSHA. So what—there's nothing left?
SOPHRON. There ain't shit.
VANYUSHA. And the orchard?
FROLOVICH. What orchard?
VANYUSHA. Well . . . the place where the apples ripened?
FROLOVICH (*taking a closer look*). I mean, the orchard's more or less intact . . . over there, behind the ashes. That's the orchard, I think, right, Sophron?
SOPHRON. Looks like it.

VANYUSHA. I love orchards. They've a glorious scent.
BOOGER. Scent, scent . . . Our legs are achin' and our bellies're drilled through with hunger, and yer talkin' about scent!
SOPHRON. I wouldn't mind chowin' down. Chowin' down and gettin' happy.
FROLOVICH. Soon's we get settled in, we'll set up the kitchen. (*He walks over to the ruins of the house.*) Can it truly be empty?
SOPHRON. Who would be in it? Dogs 'n' crows.
VANYUSHA (*grabbing hold of Booger's shoulder*). Dogs love that which's been burnt down. Keeps 'em warm.
BOOGER. What d'ye mean *warm* . . . They burnt it down in the winter, I think. Ain't nothin' warm 'bout embers.
VANYUSHA. Yes, but people lived there. Where the dogs're sniffin' round now. Warmth always remains where man once lived.
FROLOVICH. We must needs make a fire. Go get some kindling and Vanya 'n' I'll prepare a lil' soup.
VANYUSHA. Are there no apples in the orchard?
BOOGER (*walks through the ruins, collects charred wood*). What kinda apples'd there be in April?
VANYUSHA. When an orchard's abandoned, apples can hide away underneath the snow. Waitin' for spring so that they might drop their seeds into the soil.
BOOGER. They can't wait! (*He laughs.*) Yer actin' all holy, Van!
VANYUSHA. No, my lil' Booger, 'tis not I who am holy. For I pray too little. So's to become holy, y'must needs pray to God for the Holy Spirit t'come down upon ye. When the Holy Spirit comes down, then ye become holy. For a holy person, neither hunger nor cold is frightening, for the Holy Spirit is with them. But I'm freezing and

have great need of a bite to eat. (*He laughs.*) That's how holy I am!

Booger and Sophron bring over a pile of debris. Frolovich takes out a gas lighter, makes a campfire, puts a tripod over it, and hangs a pot from the tripod.

> FROLOVICH (*to Sophron*). There's a snowdrift over by the fence. Go scoop it on up.

Sophron takes the pot, scoops snow into it, then comes back to the campfire.

> VANYUSHA. How can it be there's still snow 'pon the ground?
> SOPHRON. Just 'cause . . . what're ye goan do about it? (*He hangs the pot from the tripod and adjusts the fire.*)
> FROLOVICH (*spreads out an oilcloth in front of the fire*). Well, then, shall we dump it all out?
> BOOGER. Some'll dump and some'll just watch.
> SOPHRON. Enough, Booger. Ye didn't get lucky today, I won't get lucky tomorrow. (*He unties his sack.*)
> FROLOVICH. What was it the deceased Tsao said to ye? Don't fence yerself off. Beg with everyone else. For everyone together gets more than one alone.
> SOPHRON. Ain't that the truth. Tsao was a wise man. But ye, Booger, yer a man of easy thinkin'.
> FROLOVICH. I'm missin' a leg and I still ain't goan go beggin' alone!
> SOPHRON. Even Samson the Stump don't beg alone these days. We live in new and different times! Safety in numbers. And yer always sayin' "me, me, me." Ye ain't even got a sack! (*He laughs.*)

BOOGER (*losing his temper*). Ye think I wanted to get it for myself?! I wanted the best for y'all!
SOPHRON. Yep. And ye lost yer sack because of it.

Frolovich and Sophron laugh.

BOOGER. Why don't ye go—
VANYUSHA (*lays a hand on Booger*). Did they take away yer little sack, my little Booger? Well, God be with it. There are a lot of evil people these days. For evil grows and grows until it's broken by the good. And, for that, one must needs wait . . . Ye can have my sack, my little Booger. I've got deep pockets: I can put alms into them. Take the sack!
SOPHRON. The problem's not his sack, Vanya, but his head. Booger must needs begin to use it.
BOOGER. Ye and Frolovich are so terribly smart. But who was it brought ye pork for Easter? Who was it brought ye two Easter cakes?! Who was it sang for a half chicken from the zemskys in Mytishchi at Epiphany?! Or did ye forget?
SOPHRON. Woah, woah, let's take a minute an' calculate out who sang for what! First ye sang for a half chicken, then ye sang away yer sack.
BOOGER. It ain't even yer sack! No, it ain't!
FROLOVICH. OK, OK, that's enough yappin'. Let's sit down and partake of our repast.

Frolovich and Sophron dump the contents of three sacks out onto the oilcloth.

FROLOVICH. So, we got a buncha chicken bones from The Hen's Golden Eggs. Take yer pick and throw 'em

into the pot. Oh baby! (*He laughs joyfully.*) I managed to scrape together a lot! And without singin' my throat out!
SOPHRON. How ye slid in there, I won't even begin to imagine. There's always a sentry standin' outside.
FROLOVICH. We saw he'd gone off to do his *business*. And, right then, we were singing at the refill station across the way.
VANYUSHA. Yep. About Christ the Child. And no one hustled us along . . .
FROLOVICH. As soon as I noticed the sentry was gone, I seeped through the door. Dove down, looked, and—four plates of chicken carcasses on two tables!
BOOGER. Y'got lucky.
FROLOVICH. While the floor-cloth wench was tinkerin' with her cart, I slid over and got the carcasses into my sack, yep, right into my sack. And nobody raised a cry! I grabbed the bag and out the door. Of me they caught a brief glimpse alone!
SOPHRON. Ye got lucky with the refectorians. Not long ago, I went to the Chinese area on Prechistenka Street and poked around in a xiao sitan's[1] stall, but they noticed me right away, and I got a bolt of electricity right up the ass. The bastards noticed me by my reek.
FROLOVICH. By yer reek. It's all 'cause of yer reek . . .
BOOGER. All of our troubles.
VANYUSHA. Ain't that the truth. We don't smell like ev'ryone else. That's why clean people disdain us. And why dogs are the opposite—they get all cuddly. And bark at clean people.
BOOGER. Forget the damn dogs! Those hounds've never loved me. Not when I walked round as a clean man and

---

[1]. [Chinese] snack shack.

not now. (*He potters through the scraps.*) And what's this?
SOPHRON. A little toy. A boy gave it to me as a gift.
BOOGER. And can we eat the little toy?
SOPHRON. I dunno. Give it here. (*He takes the little toy bun and opens it up; inside is the same bun, only smaller.*)
BUN. Nihao. Nihaoma, shagua?[2]
SOPHRON. Ni shi, shagua.[3] Tsao would know just what to say to ye ... Nay, yon ain't an edible thing. (*He throws the bun into the fire.*)
FROLOVICH. Separate the bread from everything else as usual, guys.
BOOGER. They gave us much bread.
SOPHRON. Mhmm ... These days, they barely give us any money at all.
FROLOVICH. A lot of beggars've moved to Moscow. That's why they don't.
VANYUSHA. And why are there so many beggars these days, Frolushka?
FROLOVICH. Because they're idiots. All of them leap into Moscow thinkin' that the city's just rollin' in cash.
SOPHRON. I already told ye, Van: there are so many beggars in Moscow because they've started burnin' more and more villages down. Back in the day, they burnt zemsky estates alone *and* in Moscow alone. Now, they've started burnin' the villages too so's the zemskys understand that they answer for the subjects on their tracts. Get it?
VANYUSHA. Got it, Sophronyushka.
FROLOVICH. And once their village gets burnt down, they hurry right to Moscow! Of course they've stopped givin' us cash! These days, there're so many beggars on

---

2. [Chinese] Hello. How are you, moron?

3. [Chinese] You're the moron.

Tverskaya that ye can't even push yer way through. Ye think people save up so's to have enough for all of 'em?

VANYUSHA. They flee the flames and come to Moscow because there're lotsa people in Moscow. And they think they can ask all of those people for alms. That's how they think.

SOPHRON. Well, one can always ask. But can ye ever know if yon person's gonna give?

FROLOVICH. Muscovites have hearts of ice. Ye won't even melt 'em with tears. And they could give a shit about our songs.

SOPHRON. That's true. These days, they don't listen to our songs. A year ago, they listened, but now they don't. The late Tsao had it right: one must needs leave Moscow and head to PodMoscovie. There, the people're more compassionate. That's how it shakes out. They don't give ye any money in the country, but shower ye with bread. That's why we're in PodMoscovie, and thanks be to God.

VANYUSHA. Tsao was smart. Y'remember what he'd say to ye, lil' Booger? "Better not to steal, but to ask."

BOOGER (*fussing round the boiling pot*). Yes, I remember, I remember . . . Dang, it boiled up . . . ! It's always safer to ask. But I wanna drink too. And they're not allowed to give us vodka.

SOPHRON. My God, how obsessed ye are with vodka! There hasn't been a day when ye haven't talked about this accursèd vodka.

FROLOVICH. Yer head buzzes and legs go weak from vodka.

VANYUSHA. My deceased dad loved vodka. It's real bitter.

SOPHRON. Bitter and undelicious. How people can drink it . . . is incomprehensible . . .

FROLOVICH. Man puts everything into his mouth.

BOOGER. I love drinking vodka. Especially in the winter. Warmth flows forth into yer veins when ye drink it.
SOPHRON. And all yer money flows away to it. Beastliness shall always remain beastliness. There's nothing to discuss. Well then, brothers, shall we rejoice?
FROLOVICH, VANYUSHA, BOOGER (*preparing spoons and moving toward the pot*). Let us rejoice.

Sophron takes out a rag and unfolds it. Inside of the rag is a packet of *soft* ampoules. There is a *living* image on the packet: flowers suddenly begin to grow on a man's bald head, the man smiles, and out of his mouth fly two gilded Xingfu[4] characters.

FROLOVICH. How many?
SOPHRON (*with a sigh*). Seven.
BOOGER. Won't be enough for two suppers.
VANYUSHA. What do y'mean seven? Weren't there ten?
SOPHRON. We gave three away to the Pharaohs in Perkhushkovo yesterday. Near the tavern. Don't ye remember?
VANYUSHA. Yesterday?
SOPHRON. Yesterday. When ye and Frolovich were singing about Ataman Kudeyar.
FROLOVICH. He must not've seen. The Pharaohs walked over and Sophronya silently gave 'em three without bein' asked. So that they wouldn't bother us. And, sure enough, they rolled right off.
VANYUSHA. Yeah, so I didn't see. But ye didn't say nothin' either.
FROLOVICH. What's the point of vainly wigglin' one's tongue about?

---

4. [Chinese] happiness.

Booger removes the pot from the flame, Sophron lays a piece of wood out in the center of the oilcloth, Booger puts the pot onto the board, and Frolovich takes out and distributes spoons.

> SOPHRON. Well then, bros, shall we throw in five and save two? Or shall we throw in all seven?
> FROLOVICH. Two ain't goan save us tomorrow anyways. We'll regret it.
> BOOGER. We'll regret it.
> SOPHRON. We'll regret it.
> VANYUSHA. Isn't seven an awful lot?
> SOPHRON. It'll be stronger. Just the ticket.
> VANYUSHA. Ye know best, Sophronyushka.

Sophron breaks the ampoules and shakes their contents out into the soup. He then takes out a phial of dark-red liquid and drips seventy drops of it into the pot.

> SOPHRON (*to Booger*). Gimme the sugar.

Booger rummages through his pockets, takes out a cellophane packet, and sees that it's empty.

> SOPHRON. Where's the sugar?
> BOOGER (*rummaging through his pockets*). My God, I didn't tie up the packet . . . it all spilled . . .
> FROLOVICH. Into yer pocket?

Booger turns out his pocket. There's a hole at the bottom of it.

> BOOGER. The sugar's leaked out. Forgive me, brothers.

Frolovich hits Booger with his crutch.

SOPHRON. Ye bastard! How're we gonna chow down now?!
BOOGER. Forgive me, brothers, it wasn't out of spite. Not out of spite. It wasn't out of spite.
FROLOVICH. Ye wretched thing! How are we supposed to believe ye?! Where are we gonna find sugar now?! Well, then, go limp to the station for some sugar! Look alive, ye little nit!
VANYUSHA. I've some sugar.
SOPHRON. What sugar? From whence?
VANYUSHA. Well, I got a sugar tower. Ye remember? The girl gave it to us at the market in Vnukovo. (*He reaches into his pocket and pulls out the tower of a Sugar Kremlin.*) We decided to save it.

Those minstrels who aren't blind gaze upon the tower.

VANYUSHA. Throw it into the soup, Sophronyushka.
SOPHRON. Wouldn't that be a waste? It's so pretty.
VANYUSHA. What waste? I can't see it in any case.

Sophron silently picks up the sugar tower and lowers it down into the soup.

FROLOVICH. No big deal, they'll give us more . . . Y'must needs mix it around so that it breaks up . . . strong sugar . . . (*He mixes the soup.*)
VANYUSHA. A good girl. She was talkin' loud. Maybe she was deaf?
BOOGER. The deaf are unkind. They're all evil, Van. And they don't give nothin'. Once some deafies beat me up on Pushkin Square . . . Give it here, Frolovich, I'll mix it round.

FROLOVICH. Sit back down, deadbeat.
SOPHRON (*looks around*). Woah, it got dark so fast.

There's a pause. The minstrels sit in silence. Frolovich mixes the soup. The bonfire crackles. A dog whines somewhere off in the distance.

FROLOVICH (*fishing out a piece of the tower nearly dissolved in the soup*). Woah! It's workin'. (*He puts the spoon down.*) Let us pray, brothers.

Everyone puts their spoons down onto the oilcloth and stands up.

MINSTRELS. Send us tomorrow that which Ye sent us today, oh Lord.

They cross themselves, sit down, take up their spoons and pieces of bread, and begin to eat the soup. At first, they quickly and eagerly gulp down the broth, then they fish bits of the chicken carcasses out of the pot and gnaw at them slowly, not rushing at all, the bones crunching. Their movements gradually begin to slow. The minstrels smile, wink at each other, mutter something, sway, grab each other by the nose, and laugh. Then they lie down on the ground around the campfire and quickly fall asleep. The dying flame illuminates their faces. The minstrels smile in their sleep. The campfire is extinguished. A little while later, a dog cautiously approaches the sleepers, sniffs at them for a long time, grabs a chicken bone up off of the oilcloth, then runs away.

THE POKER

CAPTAIN OF STATE SECURITY Sevastyanov arrived to work at the Secret Order at around 10:00 am. Having gone up to his office on the fourth floor, he sent out a personal TK-signal to indicate his arrival, *entered* the atmosphere, ate a sandwich with Szechuan-style ham, as well as some Tula gingerbread, drank a cup of "Dragon Shadow"-brand Chinese green tea, watched the news, first on the Russian Net, then on the External Net, prayed to an icon of St. George, picked up a standard steel case containing all the necessary tools for an interrogation, a case nicknamed "the gloomy box" at Lubyanka, called the internal prison, ordered that detainee No. 318 be taken into basement cell No. 40, left his office, locked it, and went down to basement floor No. 5 in the elevator.

Sevastyanov was a short, broad-shouldered forty-year-old man with a balding head and a black-browed, black-mustached face. His black Secret Order uniform with its red hemming, blue shoulder straps, three bars of the Order, golden badge representing 370 years of RSO,[1] steel badge representing "ten years of excellent service," and silver buttons decorated with two-headed eagles

---

1. Russian Secret Order.

suited him. Captain Sevastyanov's boots always shone and never squeaked. He was married and had a twelve-year-old son and a four-year-old daughter.

Having gone down to basement floor No. 5, he walked over to the internal security post and placed his right palm against a shining white square on a steel pedestal. Sevastyanov's pass with his rank, position, and track record rose up before the ensign at the guard post. The ensign pressed a button and the lattice blocking the way moved off to the side. Sevastyanov set off down the concrete hallway, waving the "gloomy box" and whistling the Russian song "I Dreamt of a Garden." When he reached cell No. 40, he turned the lock to the left, opened the door, and went inside. In the twelve-square-meter cell sat two people: a junior sergeant of the escort troops and Smirnov, the man under investigation. The sergeant immediately stood up and saluted Sevastyanov:

"Comrade Captain of State Security, the individual under investigation, Smirnov, has hereby been delivered to you for interrogation."

"You're free to go," Sevastyanov nodded.

The sergeant left the cell and locked the door from the outside. Sevastyanov walked over to the small metal desk with a side underframe, placed the "gloomy box" onto the underframe, sat down in a chair, took out his mobilov, a pack of Fatherland cigarettes, and a lighter, then laid them all out onto the desk. The man under investigation was sitting in a steel chair that was fastened to the concrete floor and had a channel bar as tall as a person instead of a back. The hands of the accused were bound behind him with *soft* handcuffs and lashed around the channel bar. Smirnov was a thin, stooped twenty-eight-year-old with long arms and legs, curly dark-blonde hair, a narrow, bearded face, and large gray eyes. Sitting on a steel chair with his hands behind him, he was staring at his knees.

Sevastyanov tore open the pack of Rodina cigarettes, pulled one out, and lit up. Called up an access-clearance spark on his mobilov. A rectangle opened up on the surface of the desk and the smart machine's keyboard came up out of it. Sevastyanov animated it. A hologram rose up over the desk:

CASE No. 129/200

This was Smirnov's case. Sevastyanov flipped through the semi-translucent pages, smoking and flicking ashes down onto the floor. He put out the cigarette on the edge of the desk, threw it onto the ground, clasped his hands together, and looked at the detainee with a smile on his face:
"Hello, Andrei Andreyevich."
"Hello." Smirnov raised his eyes.
"How are you feeling?"
"I'm fine, thanks."
"Any complaints about the conditions of your detention?"
Smirnov thought for a second and squinted off to the side:
"Wherefore'd you arrest me?"
The investigator sighed, paused:
"I asked you a question, Andrei Andreyevich: have you any complaints about the conditions of your detention?"
"A lotta people in the cell. Verily," the detainee muttered, not raising his eyes.
"A lotta people?" Sevastyanov raised his thick black brows inquiringly.
"Yeah. Twelve spots, but eighteen people. We take turns sleeping."
"Did you sleep poorly?"
"I slept well last night. But the night before . . . I didn't sleep at all."
"Got it," Sevastyanov nodded thoughtfully. "So, you're saying the cell is verily most overcrowded?"

"Yeah."

The investigator paused and spun a thin laser lighter around in his hand.

"And what do you think? Why are there so many detainees in your cell?"

"Not only in our cell. In other people's cells too. Two guys who'd been in other cells joined ours yesterday. They were taking turns sleeping there too. Lebedinsky said that all of the cells are overcrowded."

"Is that so?" Sevastyanov exclaimed in surprise, standing up as he did. "All of the cells are overflowing?"

"Yes." The detainee nodded, looking down at the floor.

The investigator approached him, biting his lip anxiously with his arms folded behind his back, then turned sharply, walked over to the door, and stood there, rocking onto the toes of his perfectly polished boots:

"And what do you think, Andrei Andreyevich: Wherefore are the cells of Lubyanka overflowing?"

"I dunno," the detainee answered quickly.

"Well, do you have any suppositions at all?"

"Wherefore'd you arrest me? Why won't you let me call home?"

Sevastyanov turned around:

"My dear Andrei Andreyevich, I've come here precisely to explain to you wherefore we arrested you. And I shall certainly do so—do so without fail. But you are not answering my utterly inoffensive question: why, in your opinion, are the cells of Lubyanka overflowing?"

"I dunno . . . well . . . there're probably not enough cells and too many people under arrest . . . I dunno . . ." Smirnov mumbled.

"There!" Sevastyanov raised his finger. "Too many people under arrest. And why are there so many people under arrest?"

"I dunno . . . Probably . . . investigators can't keep up . . .

or they work slowly . . . not very many free cells . . . it's an old prison . . ."

The investigator shook his head:

"You're mistaken. The prison was rebuilt and deepened four years ago. There's plenty of space. And we don't work slowly. That's not the reason for this crowdedness, Andrei Andreyevich. The reason is that, as our state blossoms and strengthens, the number of criminals within it does not, unfortunately, shrink. In fact, it's just the opposite. The number grows. Do you know why that is?"

The detainee shook his curly head of hair.

"Do you remember the Sovereign's Easter Address to the people?"

"Yes, of course."

The investigator returned to the desk, found the Sovereign's speech on his mobilov, and called forth a hologram. And in the cell appeared the Sovereign's living face as he addressed his people:

"Barely had Russia emerged forth from the whirlpool of Red Troubles, barely had she risen forth from the fog of the White Troubles, barely had she gotten up off of her knees and walled herself off from the foreign on the outside and the devilish on the inside, when the demonic foreign enemies of our Motherland overwhelmed Russia, enemies both internal and external. Indeed, a grand idea shall also birth great resistance to it. And if external enemies are destined to gnaw at the granite of the Great Russian Wall in impotent malice, then internal enemies shall pour their poison upon us in secret."

Sevastyanov extinguished the hologram:

"You remember, Andrei Andreyich?"

The detainee nodded.

"Internal enemies shall pour their poison upon us in secret," the investigator repeated. "There you have the answer to your question, Andrei Andreyich: *wherefore'd you arrest me?*"

"I'm not an enemy of Russia."

"You're not an enemy of Russia? Then who are you?"

"I'm... I'm a citizen of Russia. A loyal subject of the Sovereign."

"That means you're a friend to Russia?"

"I'm a citizen of Russia."

"What are you harping on about... citizen this, citizen that... We're all citizens of Russia. A murderer is also a citizen of Russia. So is a saboteur. I'm asking you: are you a friend to Russia or an enemy?"

"A friend."

"A friend?"

"A friend." Smirnov nodded, licking his parched lips and shifting his thin shoulders.

"Terrific." Sevastyanov nodded, leafed through Smirnov's case, took a text out of it, made it bigger, and highlighted it in red.

Red lines hovered up in the air of the cell.

"You recognize this?" the investigator nodded.

"No..." Smirnov squinted and lowered his head. "I can't really see it..."

"Lemme help you."

The investigator sat down at the desk and began to read in an even, loud voice:

THE POKER
A Russian folktale

Once upon a time, there was a poker. It stirred up coals in the stove, raked out ash, and shifted logs if they were burning poorly. This poker had stirred up many coals and raked out much ash. It was sick of living by the stove, tired of stirring up hot coals, and bored of raking out gray ash. Thus did the poker decide to run away from home so's to find an easier, cleaner, and more pleasant job too. One evening, as soon as the stove set to burning, the poke stirred up the coals and raked out the ash. Then up and ran away from home. It spent the night in a bunch of nettles and set off along the road in the morning. It walks and looks round as it goes. It looks and—hey!—a cook is coming toward the poker:

"Hello, poker."

"Hello, human."

"Where are you headed?"

"I'm looking for some work."

"Come with me."

"And what will I do with you?"

"You're going to rake coals to pots and pans, then rake them away, watch over the fire so that the roast doesn't burn and so that the soup doesn't boil over, and you're going to clean out the part of the stove where my pies go."

"No, that job isn't for me. I'm to find something easier, cleaner, and more pleasant too."

"Well, then, farewell, poker."

"Farewell, human."

The poker set off further down the road. It looks and—hey!—a steelworker is coming toward the poker:

"Hello, poker."

"Hello, human."

"Where are you headed?"

"I'm looking for some work."

"Come with me.

"And what will I do with you?"

"You're going to forge steel with me: rake coal toward the blast furnace, watch over the fire, punch through the shell that forms over the steel, and help the liquid steel to come out of the blast furnace."

"No, that job isn't for me. I'm to find something easier, cleaner, and more pleasant too."

"Well, then, farewell, poker."

"Farewell, human."

The poker set off further down the road. It looks and—hey!—a major from the Secret Order is coming toward the poker.

"Hello, poker."

"Hello, human."

"Where are you headed?"

"I'm looking for some work."

"Come with me."

"And what will I do with you?"

"You're going to torture the enemies of the people with me: burn their heels, cauterize their balls, and place the brand of the state onto their asses. Clean, easy, and pleasant work."

The poker thought and thought, then agreed. And ever since, it's been working for the Secret Order.

The investigator closed the case, took away the image, pulled a cigarette out from his pack, and lit up:

"What a cute 'Russian folktale.' You recognize it?"

The detainee shook his head.

"Well, then why'd you blush so much? Hmm, Andrei Andreyich? Some people go pale, but you blushed. That's really rather childish . . . Anyways, everyone has their own reaction to the discovery of a lie. 'Tis professionals alone who don't blush and don't go pale, for 'tis they who are doing grand deeds for the state. And you're simply an amateur. And you're doing the deed of an enemy of Russia—a secret and shameful deed. A destructive deed. And your soul, created in the image and likeness of God, opposes yon destructive deed, for thou art destroying not only the Russian state, but your own lost soul as well. Thus have your jowls gone red."

"I didn't write yon tale . . ." Smirnov muttered.

"You didn't only write yon tale, you also distributed it all around your person, to your left and to your right, as if t'were a stinking poison which you might use to spray the world over with your fierce fury," the investigator pronounced, opening the "gloomy box" as he did.

"I didn't write it." Smirnov shrugged, looking down at the floor. "I didn't write yon tale."

"You wrote it, you wrote it. And you wrote it on paper, in the old-fashioned way, you didn't type it up on Mademoiselle

Keyboard. That was rational: For, if you'd posted such a thing on the InterYes, they'd've had you beneath their fingernail in a moment, as though thou wert a pregnant nit. But you scribbled down yon pasquinade on paper. So's to muddle the traces. But we," Sevastyanov pulled a needleless injector out of the "gloomy box," "are experienced tracers. And we've unraveled worse snarls than this before. For how is the hound dog to act, when the beast takes a cunning tact? Forward! He flies forth as an arrow toward its burrow. That's how it is, Sokolov . . . I mean Smirnov."

The investigator put an ampoule into the injector and walked over to the detainee. The detainee had clearly become anxious: his thin knees trembled and knocked together and his curly head was drawn down into his shoulders.

"I didn't do anything, I didn't do anything . . . " Smirnov muttered, hunching over even more and bowing his head toward his long legs.

"You did, you did." Sevastyanov grabbed the man's hair with his left hand. "Here's what interests me, Andrei Andreyich: To whom did you give your tale to read?"

"I didn't write it," Smirnov spoke dully into his knees.

"I'll repeat it again: to whom did you give yon pasquinade to read?"

"I didn't give it to anyone . . . I didn't write it . . . " the voice of the detainee trembled.

Sevastyanov sighed and looked up at the ceiling with its big, flat, matte-colored dome light:

"Listen, in five minutes, you're gonna tell me everything and squeal on everyone. But I'm gonna give you one last chance, as they say in Europe. Name them. And I'll let you back into your cell and your desire to help with the investigation shall be recorded in your case. A relief for you and a relief for me, hmm?"

Smirnov's shoulders began to tremble delicately.

"I'm innocent . . . they put it there . . . I don't even have paper at home . . . I have books alone . . . no paper, I keep no paper . . ."

"Why are you such a drag?" Sevastyanov sighed with resentment in his voice.

"Don't torture me . . . I didn't do anything . . ."

"No one's gonna torture you. You think I'm gonna hang you from the rack and start lashing your balls with a bullwhip? You're mistaken, Smirnov. In Russia, only oprichniks torture people on the rack. Well . . . that's their rule, what're you gonna do? They create Word and Deed out in the open, for fear must needs fall upon all enemies of the state, thus do they behave so brutally. Whereas we, the members of the Secret Order, are men of culture. We don't lash anyone's balls with a whip."

"It wasn't me . . . they put it there . . ." Smirnov mumbled.

"Say it again—my *enemies* planted it there." The investigator yawned.

"They put it there . . . they planted it . . ."

"And did you start planting it on others in your fright?"

"I didn't do anything . . . I don't know anything . . ."

"Goddamn you, you fool."

With a violent motion, Sevastyanov pulled Smirnov's head toward him, inserted the injector into his carotid artery, and depressed its trigger. The crushed *soft* ampoule popped and the injection passed into the detainee's blood. Smirnov's body jerked, then he cried out and froze, as if ossified. His large gray eyes widened and glazed over, having become even larger. His lips parted and froze into a silent question. It was as if he'd been stung by a scorpion both giant and invisible. A slight tremor took control of the detainee's thin figure, which was frozen in a tense pose. Sevastyanov let go of his hair, walked over to the desk, and put the injector back into the "gloomy box." Then he pulled a cigarette out from his pack and lit up.

His mobilov let forth a thin, iridescent ring.

"Captain Sevastyanov here," the investigator answered, putting his cigarette down into the ashtray.

An image of Colonel Samokhvalov rose up over the mobilov: "Nikolai, hello."

"Health be to ye, Comrade Colonel."

"Ah, you're working . . ." the colonel looked around. "OK, I won't bother you."

"You're not bothering me in the slightest, Comrade Colonel."

"I wanted you to help Shmulevich in the matter of the cow. He's most deeply bogged down and there've been no uplifting developments."

"As thou wilt." Sevastyanov smiled. "We'll help."

"Thankee, Kol. Arkhivov demands too much from me, as if I were a Hunan torturer. And this is the third week of wretched failure, may its mother be laid into dry gristle! So, put your mind to work. I'll write up the order."

"Sir, yes, sir, Comrade Colonel."

"Well, health to ye," Samokhvalov winked with a tired smile, then vanished.

The captain picked his cigarette back up, took a drag, and stared fixedly at the frozen detainee. Then he pulled a tiny hammer out of the "gloomy box," began to play with it, finished his cigarette, stubbed out the butt, and approached the detainee.

"Well, how are you, Smirnov?" the captain asked, smoothing out his mustache.

"I . . . I . . . I . . ." came forth from his parted, pale lips.

"Do you understand that you've turned to crystal?"

"I . . . yes . . . I . . ."

"You're made of crystal, Smirnov. Look." The captain lightly tapped at his shoulder with the hammer.

The hammer let forth a thin ring, as if it were being tapped against glass. The captain hit Smirnov's knee with the hammer. The hammer rang out once again. The captain hit the other knee. Then the hand. Then the detainee's pale, sweaty nose.

The hammer let forth another ring.

Horror filled the detainee's eyes to their limit. The tremble left him and he froze, not breathing at all.

"You're our expensive vase." Sevastyanov smiled, looking into the detainee's crazed eyes. "You're our crystal goose. All of you is made of transparent crystal—your legs and your arms and your internal organs. Your liver, your kidneys, your spleen—it's all crystal. Even your rectum—that'll ring too! And your balls'll ring, as if they were Valday bells. You're an astonishing individual, Smirnov!"

The detainee sat motionlessly, as if he were an exhibit at a wax museum.

"Now, you're gonna get a gift."

The investigator returned to the desk and tapped at the keys. A bright, convincing hologram of a muscular dude, naked to the waist and holding a heavy hammer, rose up in the cell with a formidable roar. The dude roared, grimaced, and played with the hammer threateningly.

"Here we go, Vanya," the investigator placed his hand onto the hammerman's mighty shoulder. "Let's smash this *crystalline* intellectual into little bits, hmm? So that he doesn't harm Russia anymore."

"Let's do it!" the hammerman snarled.

"A-a-a . . . no-o-o-o . . . I . . . " came forth faintly from the detainee's mouth.

"What do you mean—no?" Sevastyanov bent over him.

But Ivan was already winding his hammer up with a roar.

"No-o-o-o-o . . . " Smirnov wheezed.

The hammer described an arc with a whistle, then froze a centimeter from the detainee's head.

"Say their names, you fuck!" the investigator hissed, grabbing Smirnov by the ear. "Now!"

"Rudensky . . . Popov . . . the Khokhlovs . . . Bo . . . Boiko . . . " the detainee moved his lips weakly.

"Too few! Too few!"

The hammerman roared once more, winding up with the hammer as he did. The hammer described a circle and once again froze just above the paralyzed detainee.

"Name them! Name them!" the investigator pulled Smirnov by the ear.

"Gorbachevsky . . . Klo . . . Klopin . . . the Monakhovs . . . Bronstein . . . Gol . . . Goldstein . . ."

"Name them!"

"By . . . Bykov . . . Yanko . . . the Nikolaevs . . . the Te . . . Teslers . . . Pavlova . . . Gorkaya . . . Rokhlin . . . Pinkhasov . . . Dyu . . . Dyukova . . . Valerius . . . Bobrinskaya . . . Sumrakov . . . Klopin . . . Bronstein . . . Goldstein . . ."

"You already named those ones. That's enough."

The investigator let go of the detainee's ear, sighed with relief, returned to the desk, sat down, and lit up. Cigarette smoke wafted through Ivan, frozen with the hammer in hand.

"Thanks, Vanya." The investigator winked.

"Glad to help!" Ivan smiled, then vanished.

Smirnov was sitting in the same awkward position, both hunching over and throwing back his head. Sevastyanov clacked over the keys, all of the families Smirnov had named *getting caught up in* the case file, then glowing with orange light.

"Well, that's at least something . . ." The investigator put the case file in order.

He finished his cigarette, took the injector from the "gloomy box," put an ampoule into it, walked over to the detainee, and did an injection in his neck. Smirnov's body relaxed and his head fell to his knees. While Sevastyanov smoked another cigarette, the detainee came to his senses.

"Now then, now then . . ." Sevastyanov clacked over the keys. "Everything's in the stove, as they say."

The detainee lifted up his head:

"Give me . . . something to drink . . . "

"I will," Sevastyanov pressed a button.

A guard came in.

"Bring the detainee some water."

The guard brought the detainee a plastic bottle of Altai spring water and a plastic cup, put them onto the desk, then left. Sevastyanov closed the case, poured water into the cup, walked over to Smirnov, and put the cup to his parched lips. The detainee drew the water into himself greedily, in three gulps.

"More?" Sevastyanov asked.

Smirnov nodded. The investigator filled the cup a second time. Smirnov drank it. Then he drank a third glass too. The bottle was empty. Sevastyanov threw the bottle and the cup into the trash. Glanced at his watch:

"So."

He rubbed at his smoothly shaven cheeks with his palms:

"So then, Andrei Andreyich. It's now clear which great minds you were thinking alike with, as it were. It's clear about the paper too. There remaineth one little question alone."

Smirnov raised his gray, emptied-out eyes to look at the investigator.

"The poker!" Sevastyanov winked at him and stroked his mustache.

Smirnov stared at him blankly.

"The poker," Sevastyanov turned sharply in place, his heel squeaking this time, then stepped over to the desk and pulled a metal drawer out from it.

In the drawer was a poker. Sevastyanov took it and showed it to Smirnov:

"Yours?"

"I dunno."

Sevastyanov walked over and brought the poker up to the detainee's face.

"Yours?"

"I mean, like . . . "

"No 'like's!"

"It's mine . . . "

"That's right, it's yours. The very poker that you described in your little tale. As you write: once upon a time there lived a lil' Mister Poker. It lived for a long time with the derelict Sokolov . . . oops, Smirnov . . . and then it ran away. To us. To the Secret Order. And now, as it turns out, it also serves with us. And we give it a rea-a-a-a-al good salary. So, don't think for a second that it won't get a good pension down the line."

Sevastyanov took a miniature laser out of the "gloomy box," brought it to the tip of the poker, and turned it on. A red beam shone onto the tip and it began to heat up quickly. Sevastyanov moved the ray evenly up and down the top of the poker:

"You're a Russian Orthodox man, Andrei Andreyich, and an educated one too. You should understand this: Every one of us is responsible for everything. For our deeds and for our words. For verily, every deed rests on words. Where the word is, there shalt thou also find deed."

The point of the poker glowed red-hot. The cell began to smell like a forge.

The investigator turned off the laser and put it away into the "gloomy box." Walked over to the detainee, grabbed him by the ankle, and pulled his leg violently upward.

"No-o-o," Smirnov exhaled.

Sevastyanov pressed the point of the poker to the detainee's skinny buttocks. The red incandescent metal instantly burnt through the rough burlap of his prison pants and entered into his flesh with a hiss. Smirnov howled and jerked. But Sevastyanov held his leg firmly as he pressed the poker into him. Once it had stopped hissing, he let Smirnov go. Continuing to howl, Smirnov twisted around and stomped his feet, twitching and shaking his curly head of hair.

Sevastyanov removed the steaming poker, which smelled of shish kebab, then put it back into the drawer, called the guard with a button, closed the smart machine, closed the "gloomy box," picked it up, grabbed his mobilov, and exited the cell.

A guard came down the hallway toward him.

"Take the detainee back to his own cell."

"Sir, yes, sir!" The guard saluted him.

Sevastyanov turned and, swinging the "gloomy box" through the air, cheerfully went down the hallway and into the elevator.

Captain Sevastyanov was working in his office until 13:45, sorting through Smirnov's denunciations and opening new cases about those he'd named. And, as always, far from all of the names spoken by the crystalline detainee had a direct relation to the actual business of spreading this particular bit of sedition. Sevastyanov only opened cases on six of them. On the other hand, though, those last five—Monakhov, Klopin, Yanko, and Mr. and Mrs. Boris and Anna Tesler—truly were enemies of the state and not the "rusks" that some young, lickety-split investigators had learned to mold so zealously of late. Captain Sevastyanov didn't have much regard for such investigators.

Having had lunch in the bright, spacious dining room with murals in the style of late Somov on its wall, Sevastyanov went into the smoking room and, first having drunk a cup of Albanian coffee, lit up a black Indian cigar, trying not to think about his cases. Thoughts of his dacha in Tolstopaltsevo—a construction project that would drag until late autumn—whirled through his head and he began to think about the fact that he would probably have time to move the gate this year, but would definitely not have time to pave the courtyard before they started building the outbuilding in the summer, that the Chinese workers had turned out to be crooks once again, that the vaunted hydrogen generators didn't actually produce that much electricity, that the price for building materials this season had gone up by 150%, that his dacha-neighbor, the Duma clerk Ryabokon, somehow lived too *clearly* within his means, which was strange in and of itself and also couldn't not make one suspicious, that Nina, the little fool, wanted to have a third child, and that his service-provided Kia had set to complaining not solely about oil, but also about gasoline.

Having returned to his office, he called Captain Shmulevich, who came by, then Sevastyanov sat there until 17:44 with that bald and nasal-voiced bore and worked through this *most darkest* cow case. Sixteen months ago, six members of the mystical, anti-Russian sect "Yarosvet" were arrested. Having drawn a map of Russia onto a white cow, they performed a certain magic ritual, dismembered the cow, and began to take pieces of the cow's body to remote regions of the Russian state and feed it to foreigners. The cow's hindquarters were taken to the Far East, boiled, and fed to Japanese settlers, the flank and underbelly were taken to Barnaul, where they were folded into pelmeni and fed to Chinese people, they made borscht from the brisket in Belgorod and fed it to eighteen *dumb fuckin' Ukrainian* overseas traders, they made a meatballs out of the cow's front legs for Belarusian farm laborers in Roslavl, then made kholodets from its head, which, not far from Pskov, they fed to three old Estonian women. All six of the sectarians were arrested, interrogated, then admitted to everything, named their accomplices and abettors, but, nevertheless, a *dark place* still remained in the case: the cow's offal. In this magic ritual of the "dismemberment" of Russia, it played an important role. However, the intestines, stomach, heart, liver, and lungs had disappeared without trace in a miraculous way and no torture was capable of helping the investigation to clarify the situation. It was clear that the six sectarians simply did not know who had taken the dismembered cow's offal, where it had been taken, and for what purpose. Captain Shmulevich, the lead investigator on the cow case, also didn't know, not until the day when a well-known bibliophile and collector of postage stamps, coins, and antique items was arrested in Svyato-Petrograd, the neighbor-lady had reported to the authorities that, along with the stamps, books, and various other junk, he was palming off canned goods to the foreign tourists who visited his shop and, upon detailed examination, they turned out to be self-sealed cans of cow pâté, which had been produced in artisanal fashion in the basement of his house. All of the cans had exactly the same label: "White Cow Beef Pâté." Additionally, yon cans weren't sold, but given to customers for free as a sign of "gratitude for their purchase." In just thirty-eight days, the bibliophile's handicraft henchmen had managed to produce and distribute fifty-nine cans of pâté to foreigners. Additionally, the cans of pâté were given to Western tourists alone, and not to Chinese or Asians. After an eighteen-hour interrogation, the bibliophile admitted that he'd received the orders about the preparation and distribution of the "White Cow" from a certain converted Jew, who'd then disappeared without a trace, before being found all cut up in the city sewer of Svyato-Petrograd—without fingers, teeth, or eyes, and only identified with great difficulty. After the mutilated man's house was searched and the people close to him interrogated, it became clear that, like the bibliophile, the converted Jew didn't have a flicker of knowledge about the secret society "Yarosvet" and was only an intermediary used blindly by Svyato-Petrograd members of the sect. After three months of searching, Shmulevich managed to reach a certain arendator, who, during his interrogation, named an elderly tradesman, a seasoned ice-cutter, a street singer, a kettlebell juggler, a master of the Net, and the watchman of a zoological museum. All five of them were people of very different classes, beliefs, and occupations, which demanded much time and effort from the investigative group led by Shmulevich. He wasn't too clever, but he was meticulous and plodding, and, in his work with the aforementioned five men under investigation, he discovered two important circumstances: they all frequented the same bathhouse and had the same distance-talking service—Alkonost. But the interrogations of the bathhouse attendants and of the employees of Alkonost didn't give them any more definite information. Here, the case of the cow had stopped in its tracks. And it was with this that Shmulevich came to Sevastyanov. Having reflected and read *bushes* of the case's bifurcations, he decided to focus on the main thing: the intestines. The cans of pâté and the stomach didn't interest him *yet*. He spoke with Shmulevich about the guts until dark.

When the liquid clock in Sevastyanov's office poured out 18:00, he stood up from the desk, stretched, and yawned:

"O-a-a-a-a . . . Generally speaking, Vitya, you must needs have a look around Moscow. That's the first thing. And you must needs look for the intestines. That's the second thing."

"Clear as clear can be." Shmulevich nodded as he stood up. "And I must needs look among the bibliophiles."

"Look among the bibliophiles. That's right!" Sevastyanov repeated didactically. "Alright, enough for today. We'll continue tomorrow."

They shook hands and Shmulevich left.

Sevastyanov lulled his smart machine, shook out the overflowing ashtray into the trash, took his black overcoat, blue scarf, and winter-uniform shapka out from his locker, put them on, fastened his mobilov to his belt, then left the office.

It was dank, dark, and slushy on Lubyanka Square. The first wet snow was falling.

"October 22 . . . it's much too early for snow . . . " Sevastyanov thought as he walked over to his car. He put his palm to the door and it squeaked, then opened. He reached into his left pocket for his gloves and, instead of them, found a lump of paper. He pulled it out, unfolded it. And smiled: in blue scratch paper lay a small, two-headed sugar eagle, broken off of the tower of a Sugar Kremlin by Sevastyanov's daughter after she'd received it during Christmas on Red Square. According to family tradition, Sevastyanov's daughter always broke the two-headed eagles, or "lil' eagles" as she called them, off of the towers of the Kremlin and gave them to her dad. There were seven of them in all. This last one had been lying in wait in the left pocket of the captain's overcoat since winter. Sevastyanov thought of the whitish-pink bows in his daughter's short pigtails, her sharpish little bird's nose, and her lively black eyes. He laid the eagle onto his tongue, took thick leather gloves out of his right pocket, got into his car, started the engine, rolled out of the parking lot, and unhurriedly drove through the evening streets of Moscow.

'Yeah . . . winter is here . . . ' he thought, sucking at the eagle.

"What would you care to listen to, Nikolai Ilyich?" the car asked.

"Something old that's to my liking . . . " Sevastyanov answered distractedly.

The car thought for three seconds, then a band began to play suavely and, suddenly, a pleasant masculine baritone, well-known to him since his childhood, began to sing:

> While the country soundly sleeps,
> they don't sleep,
> they don't sleep,
> they don't sleep,
> oh, those middle-rank Chekists.
>
> All across the country, they fight
> their invisible war—
> for honest labor, for world shelter,
> for the memory of fathers and grandfathers,

> for the quiet of our native fields,
> for daughters and for mothers.
>
> And every hour, they go off into battle
> to fight for me and you . . .

This was a famous song, a throwback to a distant 2008, when Kolya Sevastyanov, having successfully graduated from PS120 in Moscow, entered the Economics Department of Moscow State University, rode the subway and jitneys, had dreads during his first year, then shaved his head to the skin, wore enormous pants, made love with Sonya at her parents' dacha in Krekshino, read Elizarov and Beigbeder, listened to Marc Ribot and Gogol Bordello, smoked weed and drank Arsenalnoe beer, watched Vyrypaev and Almodovar, played volleyball and Mortal Kombat, and went to V-2 with Olesya once a month.

Back then, he was living with his mom on Vernadsky Prospect, his parents had separated and his mom worked as an accountant at Shatura, a furniture store, his father, having married someone the same age as Kolya, paid him and his mother 1,500 dollars a month, his mother would put one-dollar bills in the corners of their two-bedroom apartment "to get the money flowing," his grandma sent cured muksun and nelma from Tyumen, his rich-ass friend Alik Muhammedov gave him a dope Kopa bike for his birthday, Sonya had a successful abortion, Kolya had a Marantz stereo, someone very beautifully and rakishly wrote "Never fuck you again!" in English in the entrance to his building, there was a clumsy black inscription on the garages beneath his windows that read "Oligarchs in the Kremlin!", Kolya's little sister got the flu, was lying in bed with a high fever, was delirious, and heard a song—"remember the golden words, my son / bread is the key to everything, bread is the key"—and became terribly afraid, was weeping and saying that everyone's bread was filled with keys now, people and things and books and televisions and cats and pillows—everything was filled with keys, everyone's heads were filled keys, and when they opened their terrible mouths, keys spilled forth . . .

Sevastyanov was driving slowly in a stream of cars, recollecting as he sucked at the two-headed eagle. The singer sang his song in a pleasant, calm, and courageous voice. Sevastyanov could remember this singer as well—he had a smooth, fleshy face, as if it were made of rubber, and wore a black wig. But he'd forgotten his name a long time ago. Perhaps it was also this singer who, in his time, long ago, had also sung about bread being the key to everything.

"Bread is the key to everything . . . " Sevastyanov pronounced and smiled.

> And the whole country is grateful,
> oh, to those middle-rank Chekists.

The song ended.

The sugared eagle on Sevastyanov's tongue cracked pleasantly and broke into three pieces.

A DREAM

O N THE NINTH OF February, two thousand and twenty-eight years after the Birth of Christ, the Sovereigness fell asleep at 6:17 am (Moscow time) in the pink bedchamber of her Kremlin manor house. And had a dream:

Naked, but also wearing shoes with very thin high heels, she walks into the Kremlin through the Spassky Gates. It is a warm, sunny day, a hot day even. The Kremlin is perfectly illuminated. It shines with such whiteness in the sun that the Sovereigness is blinded. But this intense radiance is extremely pleasant: It invigorates her and fills her body with joy. The Sovereigness feels *very good*. In the Kremlin, everything is so, so white. Not just the walls and the buildings, but the familiar cobblestones beneath her feet are also white, sparkling and shimmering in the sun. The cobblestones squeak beneath the Sovereigness's heels, and she continues to walk, feeling herself grow younger with every step she takes, her body filling up with strength and health. She feels her breasts sway with every step, tightening up, becoming more elastic and youthful. She touches her bosom, feeling how her nipples harden wonderfully with each new step. Each step gives her more and more pleasure. The feeling of youth's return fills her body with inexpressible delight. The Sovereigness finds it very pleasant to walk, walk, walk through the empty, white Kremlin, drenched as it is with hot sunlight. She understands that the Kremlin is entirely empty. There's no one here: no sentries, no archers, no Kremlin regiment in the barracks, no boyars, no bursars, no functionaries of any rank, no attendants of bedchambers, no stewards, no groomsmen, no stable keepers, no houndsmen, no executioners, no watchmen, no janitors, no porters, no doormen, no servants, no jesters, no spongers, no henchmen, no priests, no monks, no sextons, no deacons, no lectors, no lectors' assistants, and not even the usual beggars on the blinding parvis of the cathedral square. The Sovereigness walks through the Kremlin, surveying its contours and touching herself. Her heart beats joyfully . . . deafeningly . . . It feels so good that she moans with joy at every step. Her moans become louder and louder and the Sovereigness begins to emit sharp, enthusiastic sounds. Echoing off of the dazzlingly white Kremlin walls, her cries return to her in the form of a bizarre echo. She screams and squeals even more violently. And suddenly discovers an unexpected new possibility within herself, a wondrous gift that has just awoken in her body: her rejuvenated, tightened throat can sing. Oh and how it can sing! Not simply, like everyone else sings, but mightily, high and clean, ably reaching any note. The Sovereigness *tries out* her rejuvenated throat, forcing it to make the most bizarre of sounds. Her throat obeys her utterly. Her voice rings through the Kremlin. The strength and purity of her own voice shocks her. She weeps with joy, but quickly comes to her senses, filled with pride and awareness of her own greatness. Before this, she didn't like singing and nor could she, because of which she doesn't know all of the words to any song or Russian poem set to music. She'd loved it when others sang, though—especially young, handsome men in military uniforms. Treading along the white paving stones, the Sovereigness recalls fragments of songs, operatic arias, and poems set to music, then sings them at the top of her lungs, shaking the walls of the Kremlin with the power and purity of her voice. A fragment of one song gets stuck in her throat for a long time and she begins to sing it continuously, trying on different styles as she does:

> Don't leave, stay with me,
> 'Tis so cozy and bright here,
> With kisses I'll cover thee,
> Thy lips, brow, and ears.

Singing these words, she walks and walks through the white Kremlin, becoming younger and more joyful, she sees great Russian artifacts—the Tsar Bell and the Tsar Cannon—she walks past the Tsar Bell, touching its shining white surface, the Tsar Bell resounds, harmonizing with her song, and the Sovereigness's voice hums and rings inside of the Tsar Bell. She walks further along and notices that even the bluish Kremlin fir trees have become blindingly white, she walks over to them, touches the solid, sparklingly white surface of a fir tree's trimmed paw, then walks over to the Tsar Cannon, sings, sings, and sings, and the enormous maw of the Tsar Cannon responds to her, rings out, and roars forth loud as loud can be. She places her rejuvenated hands onto the white Tsar Cannon and suddenly realizes with great clarity that everything in the Kremlin—the walls, the cathedrals, the Sovereign's manors, the cobblestones, the fir trees, and the Tsar Cannon—is made from especially, from *unbelievably* pure pressed cocaine. It is precisely this unusual, this, as it were, *celestial* cocaine that has rejuvenated her body. She licks the Tsar Cannon, sensing all of the charming might of this substance, and her heart feels as if it might beat right out of her ribcage. The Sovereigness begins to tremble with arousal, arousal that is rising like a wave. Her slender young legs tremble, her elastic breasts sway, and her breath expands her chest to the point of breaking.

She licks and licks the cannon, her legs writhe, her tongue goes sweetly numb, tears flow forth from her eyes, her hands touch her own body, youthfully and enchantedly touch her body, she touches her body with delight, all of its twists, turns, all of its protrusions and elongations, she strokes her warm, silky skin, cherishing its every indentation, then she squeezes her breasts and becomes even more intoxicated. She wants to cum so badly, clinging as she is to this divine substance, but the protrusions of the Tsar Cannon are stiff and uncomfortable. She notices a pyramid of white cannonballs nearby, three balls on the bottom and one on top, enormous balls that the Tsar Cannon used to fire long, long ago. Trembling with impatience, she climbs onto this pyramid, sits down on the topmost ball, squeezes her legs around it, pressing her delightful shaved groin to the sparkling white ball, cool to the touch, grabs onto this enormous ball with her hands, presses herself to it tighter and tighter and tighter and tighter and tighter—then she cums.

The Sovereigness woke up.

Opened her tear-filled eyes. A handmaiden was standing next to her bed.

"What?" the Sovereigness asked hoarsely, lifting up her head, then, with a heavy sigh, tumbling back onto the pillows.

The handmaiden silently wiped the Sovereigness's eyes with a handkerchief.

"Och . . . my God . . . " the Sovereigness pronounced, breathing heavily. "Get it off of me."

The handmaiden pulled the downy duvet off of her. The Sovereign lay there in a semitranslucent pink nightgown, the same color as the room. The Italian greyhound that had been sleeping at her feet got up, yawned, shook itself, wagged its thick tail, and, stretching out, walked across the bed toward its mistress's face. The Sovereigness still lay there breathing heavily. Her large breasts swayed in time with her breath.

The greyhound walked up to her face and began to lick at her nose and lips.

"Go away . . ." the Sovereigness gave the dog a shove.

The greyhound leapt off of the bed and ran through the open door leading into the bathroom. The Sovereigness turned over, still breathing heavily, and tried to sit up, so the handmaiden grabbed hold of her chubby white arm, helping her and placing pink silk pillows behind her back.

The Sovereigness sat up and leaned back against the mound of pillows. She spread her full white legs, lifted up the lace-embroidered hem of her nightgown, ran her hand along her smoothly shaved groin, and brought it up to her face. Her palm was wet. The Sovereigness showed her hand to the handmaiden:

"There."

The handmaiden mournfully shook her fair, neatly combed head of hair, took hold of the Sovereigness's hand, and began to delicately wipe off her palm with a handkerchief.

"And it's all because this is already the third night I'm sleeping alone."

The handmaiden shook her head sympathetically.

"O-o-o-och!" The Sovereigness sighed loudly and looked up at the mural on the ceiling.

In that mural, chubby Cupids were fighting for someone's flaming heart in the clouds.

The Italian greyhound ran back into the bedroom, jumped up onto the bed, and began to lap at its mistress. The Sovereigness embraced it, pressing it to her swaying chest:

"Get me some cognac."

The handmaiden quickly filled a glass sitting on a carved table from a crystal decanter, brought it over along with a golden dish with pineapple that had already been sliced and sprinkled over with powdered sugar. The Sovereigness drank the liquor in a single gulp, put a piece of pineapple into her mouth, then set to chewing, smacking her full lips as she did. The handmaiden stood there with the tray, looking at her mistress with restrained adoration.

"Give me . . . " The Sovereigness put the empty glass back onto the tray.

"Olives?" the handmaiden asked.

"No, no . . . the . . . " The handmaiden took another piece of pineapple and rummaged through the bedroom with her moist black eyes.

"Dost thou desire tobacco to sniff?"

"No, no. I mean . . . the . . . !"

"The mobilov?"

"Yes. Dial up Komyaga for me."

The handmaiden took the golden mobilov in the shape of a fish with large emerald eyes from the tray and dialed. The mobilov emitted an iridescent chime. The fish let forth a hologram from its mouth: Komyaga's sleek, preoccupied face in the cabin of his Merstallion. His hands on the wheel, Komyaga bowed his head with its curled, gilded forelock:

"Good day, oh Sovereigness."

"Where're you?" the Sovereigness asked, chewing the pineapple.

"I've only just flown in from Tyumen, oh Sovereigness. I'm driving along the Kiev Tract."

"Fly here. Like a good little fly."

"Yes, my lady."

The hologram disappeared.

"It's time, isn't it?" Burping, the Sovereigness looked at her handmaiden.

"'Tis time, oh Sovereigness." she replied with quiet delight.

"It's time! It's time!" The Sovereigness turned around, shedding the greyhound from her chest.

The handmaiden presented her arm, the Sovereigness leaned onto it and stood up. Shook the thick black rings of hair scattered across her shoulders. Stretched out her plump body, moaned, grimaced, then grabbed at her waist. Stepped over to the curtained window, touched the pink curtains with a single finger. The curtains parted obediently.

Through the window, the Sovereigness saw the square with its bluish fir trees covered in snow, the Cathedral of the Archangel, part of the cathedral square with its beggars and pigeons, archers in red overcoats with luminous blue halberds, sentries with maces, begging monks with iron bags for food offerings, and the holy fool Savoska with a cudgel. A little ways off, around the white corner of the Cathedral of the Assumption, she could see the black cast iron of the Tsar Cannon. Next to it, against a background of white snow, were the black cannonballs. The Sovereigness remembered the smooth white chill of the cannonball and stroked her warm belly with her palm.

"It's time," she pronounced almost inaudibly, then clicked her fingernail against the window's bulletproof glass.

CHOW TIME

A LOUD, HARSHLY IRIDESCENT signal, irritating in its blind mercilessness and repulsive to the human ear, came forth from the round gray loudspeaker that had been heated up by the midday sun and frightened away the dragonflies that had landed on it and were already mating, then spread through the hot July air of Eastern Siberia, awakening the eternal silence of hills and sky, drowning out the monotonous sounds of working masons, the creak of pulleys, the mumbling of the brigadier, the humming of midges kept out of the working area by an ultrasonic perimeter, sailed toward hills sparsely covered with coniferous trees, bounced off of them, then immediately returned, only to bounce off of a second surface—that of the Wall being erected, a smooth white stripe crawling through the hills and disappearing behind them into the uneven blue horizon.

"Ptooey, ye damned Kikimora . . . why don't ye just . . . " San Sanych wiped off his damp forehead, tried to spit in the direction of the column with the piercing speaker atop it, but there turned out to be no spit in his dry mouth.

He pulled a narrow plastic bottle of water out of the knee pocket of his boilersuit, pushed the soft cork of self-generating rubber out of the bottle, and greedily put it to his dry lips. The warm water gurgled into his throat, his Adam's apple covered over in gray bristles twitching in a way that seemed almost painful.

"Break time, oh Orthodox brothers!" The strapping, stooped, and narrow-shouldered Savoska put his trowel into a plastic tub of mortar, straightened up with a moan, rubbed at his lower back, then stretched out on the scaffolding. "Ain't that nice!"

Working below on the pulley block and hauling up white foam-concrete blocks, Bocharov and Sanyok immediately stopped the pulley. A basket of blocks was suspended in the air. Bocharov squinted, looking up at the Wall and shielding his eyes with his thick, swarthy hand:

"Ye ain't takin' no more?"

"Lower it back down!" the lame, hawk-nosed, always pissed-off Zilberstein, who went by the nickname of Horseshoe and was Savoska's partner, spat down to them. "Work ain't a wolf and chow time ain't no laowai!"[1]

"Inch'allah! Is it already twelve?" The toothless, shaven-headed, and broad-foreheaded Timur displayed his teeth joyfully.

"Sure ain't one yet, boys." The sinewy, big-nosed Savchenko grinned exhaustedly and began to shake the sticky mortar from his hands and into the bucket, looking up into the clear, cloudless sky as he did. "But I ain't seein' no *archangels*. Where've they got to?"

And, as if on command, from behind a ridge of distant, bluish-green hills appeared three points of color. The sound of helicopters soon became audible.

"They're comin', my man." The quiet, stumpy, white-bodied, white-haired Petrov lowered a foam-concrete block onto the freshly laid masonry, scooped up the mortar that had been squeezed out with his trowel, dropped it into a tub, then set to

---

1. [Chinese] an old foreigner or intruder: (more generally) a pejorative word for foreigners.

cleaning his trowel on the edges of the block. "Glory be to ye, Lord Almighty—we've made it to lunch . . . "

"Time t'chow down, may yer mother stick 'er snout where it ain't wanted . . . " Savoska pulled off his gloves, gray with mortar, and laid them over a crossbar.

"Hey, brigadier! What're we s'posed to do with the mortar?" The shaven-headed, big-boned, big-eyed Salman threw down a cigarette butt and scratched at the mediastinum of his collarbones beneath a silver security collar.

"Leave it!" Slonov the brigadier, unhandsome in appearance, short, but loud-voiced, lean, with an eternally sweating duck nose and quick eyes, used his quick, knotty, always restless fingers to take his blue convicts' cap off of his balding head, wiped off his sweaty bald spot, then squinted incredulously at the approaching helicopters.

As always, one flew directly to them and two flew to either side of them—one to Chekmazov's brigade on the left and one to the hunchbacked joker Provotorov's wards on the right.

The helicopter was coming closer. It was painted dark green, but, on its side, next to a golden two-headed eagle, the inscription WALL-EAST-182 stood out in striking white.

"Chow time, jailbirds!" a loudspeaker pronounced loudly, then went quiet.

Slonov's brigade slid down from the Wall by way of the scaffolding made of red plastic pipes and soon reached the ground:

"Pick up yer hooves, Savoska . . . "

"Looks like Provotorov's guys're goan get their chow before us again, San Sanych."

"Bless their little souls."

"Damn 'em, don't bless 'em! Gimme a lil' water . . . "

"Here's yer drink, mischief-maker."

"Who's got a surplus of tobacco, oh Orthodox brothers?"

"I wonder if we goan get meat."

"If only the Lord saw fit to put a cloud in the sky . . . "
"Ye just stew in yer juice, it's goan snow tonight."
"Separa-a-a-ation, oh separa-a-a-ation . . . "
"Stuff it, ye bent Horseshoe."

The helicopter landed.

Its green door opened, a ladder descended, then two freedmen in dirty white robes carrying two two-liter thermoses, briquettes of bread, and a package of disposable dishes and utensils made from rice flour came down it. And right behind them—two escort troops with the folded-up "Tanya" and the camp executioner Matyukha with his narrow pail. The brigade fell silent. The small, stumpy Matyukha jumped down from the ladder and winked at the brigade:

"Hey there, handy fellas!"

He was fair haired, with a thick neck and a flat, rumpled, browless, very freckled face, the slits of his eyes almost impossible to make out.

"We waited long enough, motherf'er . . . " Horseshoe muttered, then spat angrily between his yellow, gingivitic teeth and onto the mossy ground.

"We've got a salty seasoning for your lunch!" Matyukha reached out and nodded to the escort troops. "Lay it out, guys."

The escort troops began to lay out "Tanya."

Petrov pulled the cap off of his white-haired head and crossed himself:

"May Ye strengthen and carry through, oh Lord . . . "

With a tired grin, San Sanych scratched at his wrinkled forehead:

"Mhmm . . . there's yer eight-two percent, Gramma . . . "

The escort troops laid out "Tanya," green and ceramico-metallic, tightened its joints with screws, and undid its belts. The freedmen crouched beneath a canopy with their thermoses. Leaning out of his cockpit, the pilot was smoking and watching.

Matyukha pulled his mobilov out of his belt and connected

it to the loudspeaker nearby. And the round gray speaker, which had only just let forth the signal for "chow time," began to broadcast the voice of Major Semyonov, the head of the educational sector of Camp No. 182, this brigade's *native* camp, which included forty-two barracks between two hills—Smooth Hill and Reclinin' Hill—and was almost two hundred and fifty versts from where they were now:

"For the failure to execute the Six-Day Plan for the erection of the eastern section of the Great Russian Wall, Brigade No. 17 is sentenced to selective flogging with salted rods."

The brigade began to stir forth from the paralysis that had overtaken it.

"Selective . . . " Petrov sighed quietly. "Glory be to ye, oh Lord, that it shan't be all of us . . . "

"Don't worry, yer goan get yers," Horseshoe spat.

"Eighty-two percent's sure's hell better than *seventy*-two." Sanyok laughed stupidly.

Matyukha threw a box of matches to Slonov the brigadier, leaned over toward the pail, and began to unscrew the lid:

"Here we go."

The brigadier pulled out the matches, broke three out of the ten, and handed them back to Matyukha. Matyukha turned away, then immediately turned back to them, displaying to them the ten match heads sandwiched between his fingers with professional speed.

They began to draw lots. Savoska, Salman, and Petrov drew the broken matches. The unlucky ones all reacted to their *lot* in different ways: Savoska scratched at an old tattoo from the Putin era on his chest, grinned, stuck the match between his teeth, and squinted at Matyukha:

"Home run!"

Salman immediately became gloomy, darkly muttering something in Chechen, then threw the match away from his person, stuck his strong hands into his pockets, and, whistling silently, but still evilly, crushed at the marbly-green moss with his boot, which was covered in gray cement.

Upon drawing the broken match, Petrov gasped, stuck out his lower lip, crossed himself, and, clutching the match in his white-skinned fist, began to mutter to himself:

"Oh Lord, save and protect me, oh Lord, save and protect me, oh Lord, save and protect me . . . "

Having put all of the unbroken matches back into the box, Matyukha pulled a birch rod as thick as a man's little finger out of the pail—it had been stripped of leaves and soaked in saline solution. Wiping the moisture off of it, he ably waved the rod, clearly used to doing so, and sliced through the hot air:

"First one come lie down."

The chosen ones exchanged a look. According to camp tradition, no one ever hurried to be first. Matyukha knew this and didn't rush them, waiting as he let down the rod and rested it next to his foot in professional fashion.

"Hang in there, brothers." The brigadier cheered them up in his traditional way, restlessly fiddling with the thumbs of his swarthy hands.

Matyukha kept silent. He was a veteran executioner and torturer with six years of experience and had long ceased repeating common sayings of camp executioners—sayings like "first to lie down, first to stand up," "protect your ass, you'll lose your head," "as friends, the whip and the ass are close, to serve the state they both have chose," and "the whip shall keep you well, protect you from fengshibing[2] as if by a spell."

"What we waitin' for?" Savoska sighed, glancing at Petrov, who was still babbling, then winking at Slonov. "'m I the one's gotta get stamped first, Brigadier?"

---

2. [Chinese] rheumatisms.

"There ye go, Savoska, don't be shy." Slonov nodded.

Savoska waddled over to "Tanya," unbuttoned his trousers, lowered his blue underpants, crossed himself, and lay down quickly. The escort troops immediately belted his arms and legs to the table. Matyukha rolled up Savoska's t-shirt and pulled down his underpants further, exposing his muscular legs, then straightened up, and, without winding up almost at all, loudly and strongly cast the rod out over Savoska's elastic bottom, streaked with the scars of prior floggings.

"Fuckin' one!" Savoska grimaced, pressing his cheek to the green headrest shining in the sun.

Matyukha whipped him again.

"Fuckin' two!" Savoska counted.

The whip whistled against his buttocks.

"Fuckin' three!"

Lilac stripes appeared across his buttocks. Matyukha whipped easily and strongly, making no extraneous motions, doing his work in business-like fashion, and with each blow showing that he really did earn his bread as a camp executioner, as well as his northern bonus. He was also counting the blows, but only to himself. Only amateur executioners who take up a bullwhip, a seven-tailed lash, or a salted rod by the whim of circumstance count their blows aloud. A true executioner should fulfill his duty in silence, so that nothing might distract the punishee from their bodily punishment or the witnesses from the instructive contemplation of that same act.

Each of the punishees was to receive thirty standard blows from the salted rod. If the rod were to break, the punisher would immediately stop. But only an inexperienced or unscrupulous executioner would break their rod. Matyukha, on the other hand, was experienced and conscientious in his work—his rods broke almost never.

"Fuckin' sixteen! Fuckin' seventeen! Fuckin' eighteen!" Savoska counted loudly, clenching his fists and smirking at the brigade with great effort.

The black rod noisily slashed at his firm, tight ass, the lilac stripes became red, then crimson on the buttocks, before they finally began to let forth fast-flowing blood. His legs were bent into strange positions, his back ossified, and his head trembled with the strain. All of Savoska was clenched, as if he were a fist—he was squeezing himself, letting no pain into his body, fighting with it in his own way. Anyone who's ever experienced the lash of a camp rod, anyone who's ever been laid out on "Tanya," anyone who's ever counted whistling blows . . . each of them will have their own way of suffering through it. Savoska conquered the pain by tensing his whole body, overcame it with the tenacity of his muscles. It was obvious that he'd met with the rod more than once and that he knew how to negotiate with it.

"Fuckin' twenty-six! Fuckin' twenty-seven! Fuckin' twenty-eight!"

Savoska's face turned red, he was snarling with his last strength, gnashing his teeth, the short, clingy whirls of hair on his head trembling.

"Hang in there, hang in there," Slonov encouraged him.

"Fuckin' thirty!" Savoska whipped out and the smile blew off of his face.

He went limp and his legs twitched weakly. The escort troops unbelted him. Without rushing, Savoska stood up, grabbed his underpants and trousers, then showed his buttocks to the escort troops:

"There's a Repin paintin' for ye, huh?"

"Get back to your place, prisoner," a broad-cheeked escort troop answered calmly from beneath his felt hat.

Buttoning up his pants, Savoska walked over to the brigade.

"Well done!" The brigadier slapped him on the back.

Throwing away the used rod, Matyukha briefly shook his right hand in his habitual way, allowing it to relax, then stuck it into the pail's narrow mouth, grabbed a new rod, and shook it off. The salty drops scattered, sparkling in the sun.

"Oh Lord, give me strength . . . " Petrov muttered, his flaxen-haired head retreating into his broad shoulders, pudgy like a woman's.

Salman spat and walked decisively over to "Tanya," untying the rope around his trousers as he walked. The escort troops grabbed him, laid him out, and belted him down. Salman's flat, dark, hairy behind was also scarred. But not as densely as Savoska's.

"Bismillah rahmani rahim . . . " Salman muttered as he turned away from the still brigade.

Matyukha measured him up, then drew the lash across his buttocks. Salman began to growl.

"Hang in there, dzhigit!" Horseshoe shouted with a half-smile.

The executioner whipped him just as quickly and easily as he'd whipped Savoska, but still without rushing. The Chechen growled, but didn't flinch at the blows. His thin, sinewy body seemed to be entirely stuck to "Tanya," fused with it even. Salman replied to each of the rod's whistles and blows with a growl. He looked out over the hills as he growled.

"There ye go!" San Sanych scratched at his gray-bristled chin approvingly.

"Yer not gonna break Salman with a rod." Bocharov watched gloomily.

"That's right, he's smoke-cured . . . " Savoska nodded.

Six kites, hovering smoothly and floating in a deep, cloudless sky flew over the Wall—out of Russia and into China.

Salman's growling didn't become any louder or angrier; it continued to accompany every blow as he remained completely motionless atop "Tanya." Matyukha finished flogging him and threw the rod over his shoulder. They unbelted Salman, he stood up, pulled up his pants, and began to mutter viciously in Chechen.

Everyone glanced at Petrov. He shuddered, as if everyone had hit him at once, then doomily dragged his heavy body toward "Tanya."

"Don't worry, Petruccio, Matyukha's got a light hand!" Savoska calmed him down.

"Get a lil' tired before ye get goin', huh Matyukh?" San Sanych grinned evilly.

"Cease conversing, jailbirds," one of the escort troops said.

Pulling his fair-haired head into his shoulders, Petrov was walking as if he were carrying a basket of foam-concrete blocks upon his shoulders. Matyukha was waiting, licking his sweaty lips, and holding the rod down at his feet.

Petrov sat down on "Tanya," then awkwardly lay down on his side, as if this were the lower bunk of a long-distance train cabin, extended out his chubby legs, and began to roll over onto his stomach.

"Lie down, what are ye flounderin' around for?" one of the troops grabbed his arm and belted it down.

The other belted down his thick ankles.

"And the pants?" Matyukha squinted unhappily. "I'm supposed to pull them down?"

Grunting and turning his pale face off to the side, Petrov slid his unbelted arm under his stomach, undid the rope around his pants, and, wriggling his seal-like body, began to pull down his pants and underwear with great difficulty. Matyukha unhappily jerked them down and rolled up his navy-blue t-shirt. Petrov's big white butt had also been whipped before, but not as frequently as Savoska's or Salman's.

And Matyukha hadn't yet managed to even-handedly wind up with the rod when Petrov began to howl into "Tanya":

"Gu-u-u-uilty! Ach, I'm gu-u-u-uilty!"

Matyukha sonorously cast the black rod across the big, round white butt. The butt trembled, but its master remained motionless, his face jammed into the green ceramic-metallic headrest, which had grown hot in the sun:

"Gu-u-u-uilty! Ach, yes, gu-u-u-uilty!"

"Ye ain't guilty, ye motherfucker," Horseshoe muttered.

One escort troop shook his finger at him. The other looked at the butt shuddering with the blows.

"Gu-u-u-uilty! Ach, yes, I'm gu-u-u-uilty!" Petrov howled.

Matyukha was unappeased by this repentance, seeming to become even more angry: he began to lash less frequently, but harder, keeping his arm held aloft before each blow as if he were measuring something, then striking with an enormous wind-up. Petrov attempted to draw up his chubby legs, his butt trembling like dough:

"Oh, I'm gu-u-u-uilty! It's me-e-e who's gu-u-u-uilty!" He yelled into the headrest so violently that his white neck quickly went pink, then red. His burnt, shortly trimmed fair hair trembled on the back of his neck with a gentle tremor.

"Our Petruccio's a sensitive one," San Sanych muttered, glancing up at the sky.

The six kites, having flown over the Great Wall of Russia and into Chinese territory, split up: four of them remained where they were and soared in place, while the other two, squealing and languidly attacking each other, returned to Russia.

When he had been lashed more than twenty times, Petrov switched up his repentant theme:

"By all the sa-a-a-aints! By all the sa-a-a-aints! All the sa-a-a-aints!"

"He wants to piss," the simple-minded Sanyok confidently nodded his unbeautiful head.

Petrov's legs thrashed around, the nape of his neck shaking delicately, his head jammed more violently into the headrest, his face squished . . . it was only his butt that took on the full measure of the trembling. The lilac stripes from the first blows began to intersect with red stripes produced by stronger blows and the sun sparkled in the tiny droplets of sweat beetling out onto the surface of his buttocks.

During the final blows, Petrov roared like a stag and it was difficult to make out what he was saying. He had clearly annoyed Matyukha, who was investing more and more strength into his blows. The rod broke on the twenty-eighth.

"Ptooey, what a hunk of meat . . . " Matyukha spat on Petrov's butt, threw the splintered rod behind him, and shook his right hand.

Petrov was still roaring and the sweaty back of his red neck was trembling. The escort troops unbelted him. He calmed down immediately, toppled down off of "Tanya" and onto the ground, raised himself up, then, pulling up his pants, ran over to the brigade. Matyukha screwed the pail of solution shut and nodded to the escort troops. They gathered up "Tanya." Then Matyukha quickly and gloomily glanced at the brigade:

"Bon appétit."

"Thankee," the brigadier replied in the traditional way.

The executioner and the escort troops carrying "Tanya" set off over to the helicopter. Having left the thermoses, bread, and dishes they'd brought on the table beneath the canopy, the freedmen followed after the escort troops. The five of them disappeared into the dark-green vehicle, the ladder rose up, the door shut, the blades came to life, and, a minute later, WALL-EAST-182 had risen up into the air, turned briskly, and flown north. Only Brigade No. 17, the table beneath the canopy, chairs, a tank of drinking water, and a large security pole with a large electronic clock, five security cameras, and a round, gray loudspeaker remained in the zone.

"You have sixteen minutes for chow time, jailbirds!" the loudspeaker announced.

The simple minded Sanyok took off his faded blue cap and rushed over to the canopy:

"Well, well, chow time's been eaten away by floggin' once again."

"Fourteen whole minutes gone!" The big-lipped Bocharov swayed after him like a camel.

"What'd ye think'd happen, y'wolverines?" Horseshoe limped and squinted into the sun.

The brigade unfolded the chairs and sat down around the table. Savoska and Salman sat down on their plastic chairs as if nothing had happened. Petrov, grimacing and groaning, sat down, felt at his knees, and leaned onto them with his big, white hands. San Sanych unwrapped a packet of soup dishes pressed from rice pulp. Horseshoe unwrapped a packet of spoons.

"Who's pourin'?" Savchenko muttered in his Ukrainian-inflected Russian, scratching at himself and turning his head from side to side.

"I will, I will." Timur opened the thermos of soup, unfastened the ladle from it, and began to pour it into the soup dishes.

"Barley?" Horseshoe tugged at his nose. "That's good."

As always, Slonov unwrapped the briquette of sliced gray bread himself and distributed it to the brigade. Once Timur had finished pouring the soup and closed the empty thermos, everyone stood up. Slonov crossed himself and began to speak:

"We thank Thee, oh Lord, for Thou hast filled all of us with Thy earthly blessings, deprive us not also of the blessings of Thy Heavenly Kingdom, but as Thou came to be in the midst of Thy disciples, oh Savior, give peace to them, come to us, and save us."

He crossed the entire table. Everyone, with the exception of Timur and Salman, also crossed themselves. The whole of Brigade No. 17 sat down and attacked their food. The soup was immediately slurped up and the dishes and spoons crunched into right afterward: they were only given three pieces of bread for lunch, so the pressed dishes and utensils were a nice addition. Having eaten the dishes and the spoons, they unwrapped and distributed the plates and the forks, which were also very gray, having been pressed from Chinese rice pulp. Timur opened the second thermos and announced:

"Meat with rice."

The brigade grumbled approvingly. They got meat on Tuesdays, Thursdays, and Sundays. Today was a Thursday. On the other days of the week, they got barley, millet, or rice porridge with rapeseed oil after the soup.

The second course was laid out onto the plates and eaten just as quickly and silently. They also ate the plates, but put the forks away into their pockets; it was customary to take those away to the construction site and chew at them while they worked. They called this practice "fork swallowing."

While crunching on his plate, Slonov glanced at his watch:

"Nine more minutes. Well, who's gonna weave us somethin' cheerful today?"

Everyone exchanged a look.

"Let me!" Savoska smiled readily, as brightly as if he hadn't been lashed at all.

"That's enough out of ye—ye weave us tales too often!" Horseshoe straightened him out.

"Didn't you tell us a tale just yesterday?" Sanyok expressed his surprise.

"Wha'? Ye didn't think it was funny?" Savoska snapped back.

"About the oprichnik and the maiden? 'Twas funny enough."

"Then why'd ye open yer great maw, shabi[3]?"

"Ye weave just fine, Savos, but other people want to as well."

"I don't mind if Savoska would or if it'd be someone new..."

"Bocharov should weave us a tale. That'll cheer us up!"

"Ha ha ha!"

"Maybe Petruccio instead! Hey, Petruccio? By all the sa-a-a-ints, right?"

---

3. [Chinese] asshole.

"Let me be, for Christ's sake . . . "

"That's enough gabbin', the time's flyin', Orthodox brothers."

San Sanych wiped off his face, sweaty from the hasty eating, with his cap, then put it back onto his little, gray head:

"Here ye go, lads, how 'bout I weave y'all a true tale."

"Why don't ye, San Sanych," the brigadier approved.

"So then," San Sanych began, resting his swarthy fists with traces of mortar around the nails onto the table. "'Twas the year of our Lord one thousand nine hundred and eighty-six."

"That's when I was born," the gloomy Petrov suddenly mumbled.

"Don't interrupt. So, I had just turned twenty. Which means I had served in the army, become a senior sergeant, returned to Bryansk, started work at a factory as a milling machine operator . . . And fuck, I started to work my ass off so much, so motherfuckin'—"

"Don't swear." Slonov grabbed his arm.

San Sanych glanced at the security camera, then continued:

"I began to work very hard, I fit in with everyone so yanli de,[4] I made so much progress in a year that they elected me as Komsorg of the Komsomol, then, one day, a party organizer came up to me: Come on, Buzulutsky, time for us to let you into the party and for you to start to climb the ranks. Well, what do I care? Let me in, I say, to the party."

"Into what party?" Bocharov asked.

"The Communist Party . . . "

"And what kind of party was that?"

"It doesn't matter, motherfucker, what're ye interruptin' 'im for?" Horseshoe gave Bocharov a shove.

"So," San Sanych clasped his hands together. "This party secretary, Barybin, he got attached to me, as if he were my dad.

---

4. [Chinese] diligently.

His son had drowned when he was a schoolboy and he became sorta like a mentor to me: He'd invite me over, give me tea, soulful conversations would ensue . . . Generally speaking, the top brass took me under their wing. And, he says, get ready, Sanyok, for, by my dick, the party is serious business, read a little Lenin, a little Marx . . . "

"Are those writers?" Petrov asked.

"Those are the main people responsible for the Red Troubles, that clear?" Slonov clarified harshly. "Enough interruptions!"

"So. I go to the factory library right away, got me some Lenin and Marx, locked myself up at my aunty's—I was living with her back then, she worked quality control at the same factory, the Bryansk Machinery Factory. My parents had gotten divorced, my mom had gone north with her new husband, and my dad and I had a fu . . . I mean, a really bad, bad relationship. Yep. And Barybin knew that too. So. And then, for whatever reason, I got prostatitis that winter. Maybe 'cause I got a cold, who the hell knows. My dick had already caught a cold in the army once, we were doing exercises in the winter, setting up a pontoon bridge, fuckin' frosty, twenty degrees below, everyone got sick. And after that it gets hard for me to piss—the base of my dick kinda aches, fuckin' cramps, weakness . . . And, now, it was happening again. I went to the doctor, he's a friend of Aunty's, so she hooked me up, and he gave me sick leave for a week. And he gives me some pills to take and I'm also s'posed to go to him the next day for a prostate massage. The way he explained it to me was, 'if only you had a wife, she could massage your prostate herself, but you don't, so you're gonna have to come to me.' So, it's all fine, I'm reading Marx and Lenin, getting ready, watching dianshi,[5] and, at three o'clock, I made my way through all of Bryansk to that doctor for a prostate massage. And he shoves his finger up my

---

5. [Chinese] television.

ass. Once, twice, three times . . . And after the third time, I got sick of it, y'know, a long journey, gotta take two buses, wait for them, basically I'd had a fu . . . I mean, yeah, I was sick of it. So I thought, 'maybe I can give myself a prostate massage.' I found the hammer Aunty used to tenderize meat, it had a real smooth handle, made of steel. Then, I got undressed."

"Was your aunt home?" Sanyok asked cautiously.

"No, she was at work. I got undressed, took off absolutely everything so's it'd be more convenient, smeared the handle of the hammer with margarine, bent over, and shoved the hammer up my ass. And right away I could feel that it was going well. The handle was as smooth as a finger, even if it was cold. So I bent over like this, grabbed onto the head, and started to massage my prostate with the handle. I got the hang of it quickly. So yeah, it's fine, it's good, I'm massaging and massaging, getting all happy that I don't have to cross the whole city to do this, that I can do it on my own, and I'll get better, I'll piss normally, and I don't need a doctor, I'll sit at home and watch dianshi. And at the height of my joy, without taking the hammer out of my ass, I reached for the turntable and started to play Toto Cutugno's 'Felicita,' turned it up real loud, and started to massage my prostate to the music. When, suddenly, holy fuckin' shit—"

Slonov grabbed him by the arm.

"Yeah, yeah, forgive me, Orthodox brothers . . . So, suddenly I see my aunt standing in the hallway. And our factory party organizer Barybin standin' next to her."

Slonov, Horseshoe, Savchenko, Bocharov, and Savoska laughed. Timur, Salman, Sanyok, and Petrov didn't laugh.

"Barybin had let my aunt go home early so that he could come visit me with her. She'd said that I was sick. And they're standing there in their winter clothes, their eyes just fixed on me. And I'm standing there naked looking right back at them with a hammer in my ass and 'Felicita' blaring out behind me."

Sanyok and Salman laughed. Timur stared blankly at San Sanych. Petrov nibbled gloomily at his lower lip.

"In short, the party secretary turned around and went right back out the door!"

Everyone except for Petrov laughed.

"Not a bad tale." Slonov gave his approval, reached into his pocket, and pulled out something wrapped in a clean handkerchief.

Unwrapped the handkerchief. A Sugar Spasskaya Tower was inside of it. Its base had been nibbled at, but its peak with the chimes and the two-headed eagle was intact. Half a month ago, the brigadier had received a package from his wife in Tver containing two pairs of woolen socks, a scarf, garlic, crackers, and a Sugar Kremlin with the Borovitskaya Tower broken off of it. Slonov's daughter had received this Sugar Kremlin during Christmas. She and her mother had eaten Borovitskaya Tower, then she'd decided to send the rest of it to her father in faraway Eastern Siberia. The package was in transit for five months. When he received it, Slonov immediately broke up the Kremlin, gave the walls, inner cathedrals, and buildings to the foremen and the Bell of Ivan the Great to Tomilets, the camp cook. Slonov had eaten the Kutafya, Nikolskaya, and the Armory Towers himself, sucking them before he went to sleep. He'd also given the Troitskaya Tower to his old camp sidekick Volodya Park, a Korean. But, as for the Spasskaya Tower, he'd decided "to designate it as the humor fund": every day after chow time, someone from the brigade had to tell a funny story—as they said in the camp, "weave a proper tale." If the tale was *humorous*, Slonov gave its teller a bite of the Spasskaya Tower.

"Have a bite, San Sanych," the brigadier held out the tower, "but from the bottom alone."

San Sanych took hold of the tower with both hands, turned it around so's to measure it up, then took a bite from its bottom with some difficulty. The sugar was *strong*.

The brigadier took the tower back from him, wrapped it in the handkerchief, then put it into his pocket. And right away, as if on command, the gray loudspeaker came to life:

"Chow time is over! Get up and occupy your working positions, jailbirds!"

The brigade stood up and wandered over to the Wall. Slonov, Horseshoe, Savoska, and Bocharov lit up.

"Hey, San Sanych, did the stinkers from the Party let you in after that?" Savchenko asked.

"They let me in." San Sanych sucked at the sugar. "But . . . mmm . . . only . . . mmm . . . I didn't . . . really climb the ranks."

"Why's that?" Sucking at his "Russia" cigarette, Slonov looked gloomily at the three unopened cubic packages of foam-concrete bricks, each of them taller than a man's height.

Each of the packages had an identical *living* label: a tanned, muscular mason, deftly wielding a trowel, laying a foam-concrete block onto the wall, taking up a second block in his left hand, tossing it up, catching it, then winking mischievously with his right eye. A golden spark flew forth from the eye and dissolved into a semicircle of iridescent letters taking up the entire label: WE'RE GONNA BUILD A GREAT RUSSIAN WALL!

"Well, for whatever reason . . . mmm . . . it just didn't work out for me back then . . . " San Sanych rolled a piece of the Sugar Spasskaya Tower through his sparsely toothed mouth with enormous pleasure. "I got married. Then divorced. Then the Red Troubles ended. And the Party ceased to be."

"Then the White Troubles got started up, right?" Savoska asked.

"Exactly . . . mmm . . . then the White Troubles got started up . . . "

"Was that when the Three-Toed Foe entered Moscow in a tank?" Sanyok asked cautiously.

"Exactly!" reaching the Wall, San Sanych began to pull on his gloves.

"Ye remember all of it. Really remember." Salman shook his head. "Yer an old man."

"The fuck I'm old! Ye just try and catch me!" San Sanych laughed and began to climb quickly up the scaffolding.

The brigade returned to their places. Savchenko and Timur went reluctantly over to the big trough with the remnants of the mortar.

"Brigadier, ye think we can mix up some fresh mortar or do we gotta use this stuff?" Savchenko asked.

"Mix up some fresh mortar." The brigadier nodded, then climbed the Wall.

Having ended up on the scaffolding next to San Sanych, Petrov had a question:

"What's a party secretary anyways?"

"A junguan,"[6] San Sanych replied unthinkingly, taking up his trowel as he did.

---

6. [Chinese] boss.

PETRUSHKA

THE LILLIPUTIAN PYOTR SAMUILOVICH Boreyko, who served as a jester in the Kremlin Chamber of Japery, returned home well past 2:00 am after Friday's concert for the Inner Kremlin Circle. The japers' big red bus, which, as usual, was taking the Lilliputians home for the night after a performance, brought him right up to the entrance of his nine-story brick building on Malaya Gruzinskaya.

The driver opened the door and announced:

"Petrusha the Green—your stop!"

Slumbering in the backseat, Petrusha woke up, slid down to the ground, then walked unhurriedly to the door. In the semidarkness of the bus's interior, in seats that seemed disproportionately big for the size of their occupants, another twenty-six Lilliputians were also slumbering. They were all wearing their japer's costumes, makeup, jester's caps, and hats. And all of them, without exception, were sleeping. Having walked down the aisle past sleeping baba yagas, wood goblins, Wassermänner, kikimoras, and witches, Petrusha extended his little hand toward the driver and began to speak in a hoarse, creakily high little voice:

"Take care, Volod."

The driver closed his tattooed fingers around Petrusha's little hand:

"Sleep tight."

Petrusha swooped boldly down the bus steps and jumped onto the asphalt, wet from the light but incessant rain. The door closed and the bus drove away. Petrusha began to walk up another set of stone stairs leading to the entrance of his building. He was wearing the costume of *Petrusha the Green*: a three-pointed green hat with bells, a green caftan with enormous buttons, iridescent green pants, and short green boots with curled toes. Petrusha's face was also green and embellished with red freckles and a big scarlet nose. Over Petrusha's shoulder dangled a green balalaika, which sparkled brightly even at night.

There were three more Petrushas asleep in the departing bus: the Red, the Blue, and the Gold.

Petrusha pulled out a plastic key and put it to the lock of the scratched-up and scribbled-over door. The door squeaked and opened up. The Lilliputian stepped into the dimly lit stairwell. It wasn't too clean in here, but there were also no traces of vandalism or arson; three years ago, the Road Administration had bought it from boyars. Petrusha pressed the elevator button, but there was no response.

"Ptooey, you lil' kvass-ass!" Petrusha creaked out his usual curse, remembering that it wasn't Friday but Saturday and that, by order of the city council, not a single elevator was to rise or fall in Mother Moscow on the weekends. Economization! A foreign word with a Greek root... A real Russian would say "frugality."

Petrusha made it to the sixth floor on foot. Stepping up to each stair was a serious endeavor, Petrusha banking from side to side wildly as he did. His bells rang out in time with his climb, the green balalaika wiggling behind his back. And it was thus that he swingingly overcame all five floors of stairs, walked over to Door No. 52, and put the same rectangular key to it. The door sang out, "Ah, who's come down from the lil' mountain?", then opened up.

Immediately, a light came on in the apartment and a large silvery-beige robot named Egorr rolled out to meet him:

"Hello, Pyotr Samuilovich!"

"Yo, Egorro," Petrusha pronounced exhaustedly, leaning against a low coat rack and catching his breath after the long climb.

The robot drew came right over to him, then its beige, plastic belly opened up and shone forth: Inside of the robot was a glass of vodka. And the "March of the Toreadors" from *Carmen* began to play. Four years ago, this had become Petrusha's tradition after every nighttime performance in the Kremlin.

Having caught his breath, Petrusha took the glass out of the robot's belly, clinked the glass against its silver groin, drank the vodka, then put the glass back. Took off the balalaika and gave it to the robot. Leaning against the coat rack, he took off his boots. Then took off the outfit of Petrusha the Green and hung everything over Egorr's arms. Rumbling away, the robot set off over to the wardrobe.

Dressed in his black underpants alone, Petrusha stretched out wearily, yawned, then slapped his feet into the bathroom. The faucet was already making a racket in here, filling the tub with foamy water. To his great delight, Petrusha noticed that the robot hadn't added "An Apple Dream" to the water, as Petrusha had grown very sick of it, but "A Tale of the Seven Seas." He took off his underpants, tumbled over the side of the tub, and floundered into the water.

The foam smelled of the sea. Petrusha immediately sank down into it. The warm water seething around his small, tired body was delightful. The vodka he'd drunk bloomed into a hot flower in his stomach.

"Toothsome . . ." Petrusha exhaled and closed his eyes.

Egorr came into the bathroom with a lit Fatherland cigarette. Without opening his eyes, Petrusha parted his crimson-painted lips. The robot put the cigarette between them, turned around, then froze with an ashtray in hand. Petrusha took a long drag with great pleasure, then blew the smoke out between his bright lips. The foam trembled unhappily when it encountered the smoke. Petrusha took another drag and lowed. The robot took the cigarette from him. With a groan of pleasure, Petrusha grabbed his scarlet nose, unfastened it, and threw it down onto the ground. Then he began to wash the makeup from his face.

Having washed all of it off, he again opened his little mouth with its thin, pale lips. The robot put the cigarette back. The water ceased flowing. The jester was smoking, lying in the bath in a state of total relaxation, and looking up at the dark-blue ceiling with brightly shining stars glued onto it. Everything had gone smoothly during the performance, he had japed and danced dashingly and easily as he always did, making sparks fly by twirling as a "spindle," but also walking as a "poker," a "duck," a "blizzard," a "grouse," a "pike," a "samovar," a "roly-poly toy," and, when he had to, an "American" *dropping* his ass dancingly. The entire Inner Circle gathered together in the Faceted Chamber clapped and whistled approvingly—Prince Boris Yurievich Oboluev even threw coins to Petrusha twice.

"Two gold coins and one silver . . . ten rubles . . . " he muttered, trying to remember as he looked up at the stars.

"What do you desire?" the robot asked.

"Nothing." Petrusha knocked ashes into the foam. "Actually, a little more vodka."

"Sir, yes, sir." The robot's belly opened up.

Petrusha took the glass from the robot, overturned it into his mouth, and gave it back to the robot.

"Oof . . . damn good . . . " he muttered, catching his breath and taking a drag from his cigarette.

"All's well that ends well," the robot spoke up.

"Exactly." Petrusha closed his eyes and leaned back onto a

plastic headrest. "Find me something to eat. Just don't warm it up."

"Sir, yes, sir."

The robot left. Petrusha finished his cigarette and spat the butt into the foam. Stood up, turned on the shower. Strong jets of water beat down from a wide head up above. Petrusha hunched over and crossed his hands over his genitals. Then straightened up, lifted his head, and placed his face under the jets. He felt incredibly good, his fatigue flowing away with the water.

"There we go." He turned off the shower and climbed out of the bath.

He took his terry cloth robe from a low hook, put it on, climbed the wooden ladder in front of the sink, and looked at himself in the mirror: a broad face with small, swollen eyes, plus a snub nose and a small, stubborn mouth. He took a comb from the shelf and pushed back his sparse, sandy hair.

"There we go," he repeated and stuck out his sharp little tongue with its white coating. "Be well, Petrusha!"

Climbed down the ladder swingingly and went into the living room. There, Egorr had almost finished setting the table.

"How's it going?" Petrusha slapped his warm palm—incredibly pale after the bath—across Egorr's eternally cold plastic butt.

"As well as soot is white," he replied, setting out the appetizers.

"Refresh my drink!"

"Sir, yes, sir."

Petrusha took a glass out from Egorr, drank half of it, stuck his fork into a pickled saffron milk cap mushroom, put it into his mouth, and began to chew. Then he finished the glass, grabbed a pickled cucumber with his hand, sat down at the table, and crunched into the pickle. In front of him was a plate of boiled and smoked sausages cut up by the robot, a bowl of eggplant puree, and a not very neatly opened can of sprats in tomato sauce. At the center of the table stood a Sugar Kremlin. Petrusha had already eaten all of the two-headed eagles and some portion of the walls.

"Any news?" he asked.

"No news," Egorr replied.

"That's good." Petrusha nodded, took a piece of black bread, then eagerly pounced on the food.

He ate quickly and with obvious effort, as if he were working; his head trembled and the muscles of his face worked violently beneath its pale, unhealthy skin, ruined by the constant application of makeup.

"Refresh my drink!" he ordered with his mouth full.

The robot's belly swung dutifully open.

Having drunk a fourth glass, Petrusha immediately became very tipsy and began to wobble around in his chair. The movements of his hands became imprecise, he knocked over the can of sprats, breaking off a piece of bread and using it to mop up the spilled sauce.

"Because of the fo-o-o-orest, we say, 'twas because of the mo-o-o-ountains," he began to sing, winking at the robot.

"Uncle Ego-o-o-orr was on his wa-a-ay ou-u-ut," the robot immediately sang out in response.

"He left on a gra-a-a-ay ca-a-a-art," the Lilliputian sang as he hiccuped.

"Pulled cre-e-e-eakily by his ho-o-o-orse," the robot sang.

"Ne-e-e-e-e-e-eigh," they sang together, imitating the sound a horse makes.

Petrusha laughed, tilting back and dropping his fork. Clutching a bit of bread that had been dipped in sauce in his hand, he laughed creakily as he swayed. The robot just stood there, its blue eyes blinking.

"Refresh my drink!" Petrusha shook his head.

Its plastic belly opened up. Petrusha took the glass, had a drink, then put it cautiously down onto the table:

"There we go . . . "
He shifted the untethered gaze of his little eyes onto the robot: "What's the plural of glass?"
"Smithereens!" the robot replied.
"Well done." Petrusha nodded. "And how's it going?"
"As well as ash is white!"
"Well done!" Petrusha knocked his fist against the table.
The half-full glass fell over.
"Ptooey, you lil' kvass-ass . . . refresh my drink!"
The robot swung open. A tiny hand took a glass of vodka out from its belly. Petrusha's untethered gaze noticed the Sugar Kremlin.
"So."
He climbed up onto the chair, stood up, and reached out for the Sugar Kremlin, almost lying down on the table. Having reached it, he broke off a merlon from the Kremlin battlements, put it into his mouth, slid back down, then smacked his palm against the plate of sausage. Swung back into the chair and crunched loudly into the sugar:
"And how's . . . mmm . . . are we doin'?"
"As well as ash is white."
Petrusha crushed the merlon from the Kremlin battlements between his teeth.
"Y'know what, Egorro?" He thought for a moment. "Gimme the . . . "
"What do you desire?"
"Gimme Ritulya."
In the room arose a low-quality hologram of a very young Lilliputian sitting in a garden in a rocking chair. The Lilliputian rocked, smiling and fanning herself with a fan that seemed enormous in her miniature hands.
"Turn away!" Petrusha ordered the robot.
The robot turned away.

With glass in hand, Petrusha slid down from his chair, walked over to the hologram and sat down awkwardly next to it upon the soft material covering the floor, spilling his vodka as he did.

"Hello, Ritulya," he creaked. "Hello, my dear."

The little woman continued to sway and smile. Sometimes, she brought the fan to her face, covering it and winking.

"Ritul. The same thing again today... We japed without you. My sixty-second performance. Without you," Petrusha muttered haltingly. "The sixty-second! And without you. Hmm? That's how it is. And everyone misses you. It's frightening. Everyone! Nastya, Borka, Cucumber, Marinka. And that... new one... Samsonchik ... the water goblin. Everyone. Everyone. And I love you terribly. Terribly! And I'll wait for you. Forever. And there's not much, this... Not long. A year and a half. It'll fly away real quick. You won't notice. Where you are. You won't even notice. They'll fly away like birds. Just a moment, then they're gone. And your sentence will be over. And we'll have it all, this... Good. We've got loads of money now, Ritulya. In sooth I say to you: loads of money. Today the prince, this... Obolyov. Hurled two gold pieces. Hurled 'em right at my face! Hmm?! That was all. And the last time they threw me silver... just... well. Here's what. Frightening! They throw and throw... And Sergei Sergeyich said ... Exactly! That we'll get a bit more dough after the New Year. A bonus. Then I'll already have this... A hundred twenty. In gold. Per month. And they threw even more. Hmm?! We'll live like kings, Ritulya. Be healthy there, this... Ritochka. To you."

He drank, furrowed his brow, then sighed. Carefully placed the empty glass onto the floor. Looked at Rita rocking there.

"You know... this... Ritul. Our Vitenka is here. He japed in secret. This. For members of the Secret Order. Hmm?! And an oprichnik was there. Violently intoxicated. Drank too much. And he liked Vitka so much that he threw him three gold coins. Immediately! And then... this... Even got him up onto his lap.

Ne-e-e-eigh! Made him drink wine. And said can we . . . this . . . That we'll perform for the oprichniks. Because! The oprichniks didn't used to love Lilliputians. And now . . . this . . . Love. Hmm? There. Maybe. What? He'll agree to that. With Bavila. That's it. And we'll set to jigging for the oprichniks. And everything will be very good. Everything! And he was paying. Vitenka. So, there. And our Vitenka, this . . . He's verily most quick. And he asked the members of the Secret Order flat out. On the nose: when will you re-ex-am-ine the case of the Krem-lin Lill-i-pu-tians?! On the nose. Hmm?! Vitenka! And the other guy was listening. Seriously. And he was seriously . . . this . . . He replies: soon! That's right. Seriously replied: so-o-on! So-o-on! And that means there will be . . . this . . . Reopening. And then—amnesty. And all of you, all sixteen of you, will be set fre-e-e! There!"

Petrusha squinted his eyes, swollen with drink, makeup, and fatigue, as he looked upon the rocking Rita. She was fanning herself, hiding her little face behind the fan, and winking at him, just as before.

"Amnesty," Petrusha pronounced and licked his little lips. "Hold on . . . I'm really . . . this . . . I was saying. I was saying it to you! Already! Yes? Hold on . . . Egorr!"

"Yes."

"Have I told Ritulya about the amnesty?"

"You have."

"When?"

"On August 12, August 28, September 3, September 17, September 19, October 4."

Petrusha thought for a moment.

Rita was rocking, fanning, smiling, and winking.

"What is it with you? Why're you laughing? Idiot."

He took his empty glass and hurled it at the hologram. The glass flew through Rita's smiling head, bounced off of the wall, and fell to the ground. The glass was made of transparent self-generating plastic. The robot immediately scooted over, picked the glass up, and put it back into its belly.

"Cunt!" Petrusha cried out, looking furiously at Rita.

Rita winked at him from behind the fan.

"Hold on . . . " Petrusha curled his lips in a state of agitation, having just remembered something. "Hold on, hold on . . . Egorr!"

"Yes."

"I wanted to! Quickly! This! This! Cap!"

Egorr rolled over to the wardrobe, opened it, and pulled out Petrusha's green three-pointed jester's cap.

"Quickly! Give it here!"

With the cap in hand, the robot rolled over to Petrusha.

"Quicker, you lil' kvass ass! Look alive!"

Staggering, Petrusha grabbed the cap from him, jammed it onto his head, took off his robe, and stood there naked.

"Get me the Most High!" he cried out.

Rita's hologram immediately disappeared and another arose: the Sovereign sitting in the Imperial Box of the Bolshoi Theater.

"Health to ye, Sovereign Vasily Nikolaich!" Petrusha screamed and tried to do his "samovar" move but fell over.

"Health . . . health ye to be . . . "

He twisted around on the ground, then rose up swayingly. Bowed to the Sovereign, saluted him, then began to mumble:

"I present a little gift to Thy Imperial Grace: a gift of swampy rottenness, of copper mortar, of a horse's glans, of cat anuses, of a lame dog, of a hungry hooker, of a sick uncle, of a chunk of meat, of damp weather, of a smashed face, of torn clothes, of a slithering reptile, of nuclear collapse, of a rotten porch, of a branded young stud, of a thin bast basket, and of me too, if only just a little bit."

He bent over and placed his dry little buttocks right in front of the Sovereign's calm face:

"Egorr! The fuse!!"

The robot raised its middle lighter-finger to Petrusha's buttocks and a flame flashed out of it. Petrusha broke wind loudly. The gas came out greenish-yellow. The quick flame ate the Sovereign's head, then was extinguished. A hole appeared in the hologram. The Sovereign was sitting in the box as before, but without his head or a piece of his left shoulder.

Petrusha straightened up staggeringly, moved away from the hologram, then glanced back at it:

"Well, there."

His terribly swollen eye slits cheerfully took in the damage done to the Sovereign:

"Toothsome! Right, Egorr?"

"Just so."

"Well then, this . . . show me the last one."

Next to the first hologram arose another identical to it, but smaller. In this hologram, the Sovereign had neither neck nor chin.

"Woah, you see that?!" Petrusha walked over to the robot and wrapped his arm around its faceted thigh. "That time, the fart went low. And this . . . I was weak back then, hmm? A weak farter, hmm?"

"Just so."

"And today? How was I? Dope! Hmm? Egorr?"

"Just so."

Petrusha and the robot stood looking at the holograms. Petrusha's head leaned against the robot's narrow waist, the bells on his cap ringing and swinging constantly.

"Refresh my drink!" Petrusha ordered.

And, reaching out his hand, he took a glass out of the robot, brought it up to his mouth, spilling as he did, then tried to drink, but stopped, moved the glass into his left hand, and flipped off the hologram with his right:

"That's for you!"

He elbowed the robot.

"Egorr!"

The robot extended a silver metal finger out from its fist and proffered it toward the holograms:

"This is for Thee, Sovereign Vasily Nikolaevich."

Two middle fingers stood for a long time in the empty air: one a strict shade of silver up above and the other pinkish-white and oscillating down below.

Petrusha got tired first and let down his hand.

"Well done!" He slapped the robot across the buttocks, drank, then threw the glass behind his back.

The robot immediately turned around, picked it up, and put it away into itself.

"This . . . " Petrusha scratched at his bare, hairless chest. "This must . . . "

His swollen eye slits looked around the living room.

"Egorr!"

"What do you desire?"

"This . . . " Petrusha's short-fingered little hands restlessly fumbled across his chest. "This . . . I . . . "

"What do you desire?" The robot looked at him.

"How is this . . . " The Lilliputian was about to recall in a state of great torment, then suddenly sat on the carpet and sprawled out onto his back, but immediately got back up and shook his head.

The bells rang out. Robot looked at master. Master looked silently at robot, his fingers and toes wiggling.

"Who . . . are you?" Petrusha asked, his tongue barely moving.

"I'm Egorr the Robot," the robot replied.

"And how's . . . it going?"

"As well as ash is white."

"And . . . you . . . this . . . well . . ."

"What do you desire?"

"Who . . . are you?"

"I'm Egorr the Robot."

Petrusha lifted his hand, reached out for the robot, moved his lips mutely, then suddenly collapsed backward and fell silent. The robot rolled closer to him, got down onto its knees, bent over slowly, took Petrusha into its arms, straightened its body, then stood up. Rolled over to the bedroom. Petrusha was asleep in his arms, his little mouth wide open. The robot put him down into the unmade bed, then tucked him in. Took the cap off of his head and rolled into the living room. Put the cap away in the wardrobe. Cleared the table. Turned off the holograms. Turned off the light. Rolled over to the wall. Switched into sleep mode. Its blue eyes were extinguished.

A TAVERN

THE HAPPY MOSCOVIA PUBLIC house on the corner of Neglinnaya and Maly Kiselny, belonging to the converted Jew Abram Ivanovich Mamona, was already *full up* with a diverse public by eight in the evening.

Whom doesn't one meet here! *Smoked* zemskys from the disfavored Trubnaya Street and all adjacent lanes, *wet* mercenaries from the labor exchange, tselovalniki from the mortgage offices of Samoteka, upperclassmen from Vocational School No. 78 (VS78), students from the architectural institute, Chinamen from the Troitsky Market, retired clowns and acrobats from the circus on Tsvetnoy Boulevard, shadow-play actors ruined by drink, merchants from neighboring shops, street-walking hookers, *mollusks*, executioners, *retards*, sbiten sellers, kalach hawkers, and good ole' drunks.

The immense, smoky basement hall of the tavern, always reeking of vodka breath, beer, dried fish, and various other human fumes, is strictly divided by estate and occupation: for example, here, next to the concrete column covered in the splinters of painted poems and stuck with *living* pictures, the students make a ruckus with the artisans, a little further off, the circus people "suck down beers with trailers," talkative Chinamen goof off behind a curtain of luminous self-generating fiber, in the corner, next to the shabby air conditioner, giggly tradeswomen "knock back" rowanberry vodka, having finished their shifts in their shops, next to them drink sbiten sellers, kalach hawkers, and peddlers of cheap chow, while in a narrow "vestibule," painted prostitutes slurp down a shot of cranberry vodka before they go back out to the boulevard, and, in the furthest corner, at four tables shifted and clamped together with steel braces (with Mamona's personal permission), local executioners gradually come together for their preferred "Bloody Mashas."

The executioners' table is special in Mamona's tavern: Nobody except for executioners and subexecutioners has the right to sit at it. The tavern's patrons know this, and, even on Fridays when the tavern is jam-packed, the executioners' table always waits emptily for them—even the drunkest sbiten seller with his tradeswoman from the "Land of Ants" wouldn't dare to sit at it.

Right now, there are six people at the executioners' table: the executioners Matvei Samopal-Trubnikov, Yuzya Lubyansky, and Shka Ivanov, and their subexecutioners Vanka, Sable and Mishanya. Samopal-Trubnikov lashes on Trubnaya Square, Yuzya—on Lubyanskaya, and Shka Ivanov—far from here, on Pytnitskaya. The oldest and most experienced of all of them is Matvei. He's already been lashing for nine years and has lashed a grand total of, according to him, almost eighty thousand asses. Matvei is portly, broad shouldered, with a full beard. As soon as he drinks a couple of Mashenkas, he immediately sets to boasting.

"Whom have I not lashed," he speaks slowly, in a bass tone, sipping from his glass. "The disfavored Solodilin princes, four generals from the Joint Staff, the chairman of the Smart Chamber, the Voronina sisters (countesses, I might add) for the defilement of young Prince Dolgorukov, the Sovereign's cowherd Mironov for criminal indifference to animals . . . Every year, round about a hundred wellborn asses pass 'neath my whip."

Of the three executioners, Matvei is the most *fearsome*—he lashes with a whip. He has a respectful attitude toward that whip and often repeats his favorite saying: "The whip ain't no angel, it don't take your soul, but it do tell the truth!" Yuzya Lubyansky and Shka Ivanov are *light* executioners, imprinting the Sovereign's Word and Deed onto the bottoms of their subjects with salted rods. Their favorite saying is "the rod shall sharpen the mind and the spirit find." They're younger than Matvei and love to mock and make digs at their *authoritative* companion.

"So, Matyush, you really aren't blinded by yon radiantly high-ranking asses?" Shka Ivanov asks and winks at Yuzya through his round glasses.

"Have no fear, gents, I shan't go blind. I shan't even dislocate my arm, as you do. I swing rarely, but aptly. My swing is worth ten of yours."

"'Tis true, you're in greater demand and the *posterior* resentment toward you is stronger!" Yuzya smiles. "I mean to say: We just swing quick, then go our separate ways. And the simple people feel no resentment toward us. These aren't high-ranking asses we're whippin', y'see!"

"For us and for the asses, the main thing is—be quick as can be!" Sable interjects.

"But an ass ain't just an *ass*," Matvei disagrees. "Some asses feel like takin' communion when you whip 'em."

"And some asses don't even deserve the loogies we spit on 'em," Shka Ivanov nods. "Few worthy asses are left in this world, oh my brothers."

"Worthy asses reside only in lil' girls' schools." The subexecutioner Mishanya grins slyly. "Hot damn, I mean, hot damn, how it feels to lash a girlie's lil' ass! Just five strokes and yer ten years younger!"

"You must needs *execute* the sentence honestly, without self-interest, don't y'get that?" Matvei explains to him.

"How could I not *get it*!" Mishanya sneers smugly, making quotation marks with his fingers.

"They're able to lash without self-interest in the camps alone," Yuzya objects. "I'm not a robot who can carry out Sovereignly business without love. I must needs love the rod *and* the ass. That makes it so that there's no contradiction in my soul."

"I love my whip, can't argue with that." Matvei strokes his beard. "But I love it *immaculately*."

"We also love our rods immaculately, Matyusha," Yuzya reasons. "There're no sadists among us."

"The rod and the whip, as if 'twere the Alpha and the Omega," Vanka puts in.

"The whip has one set of metaphysics and the rod has another . . ." Shka Ivanov takes a sip from his glass.

A notorious beggar from Trubnaya Square tumbles into the tavern—this is Nikitka the Foolish. He crosses himself and bows:

"Health an' well-bein' to all the Lord's creatures!"

They know and love him in the Happy Moscovia. There are immediately offers to Nikitka from all sides:

"Come an' join us, y'practical fella!"

"Have a lil' circus beer, Nikitka!"

"Jump on over here, y'little flea!"

But Nikitka has his own *design*: on Wednesdays and Saturdays, he doesn't sit with anyone, but makes the rounds of the tavern, showing *living* pictures and drinking just a little bit—then it's back to Trubnaya Square.

"Sit and drink, oh log that's come ashore!" Matvei calls him over loudly.

"It has not been ordained by the Virgin to sit for long on a Lenten day." Nikitka hobbles over to them, exposes the smart machine hanging from his dirty chest, and animates it. "Have ye seen how our Sovereigness occupies herself at night?"

The smarty blows forth a luminous bubble: the Sovereigness

smearing herself with blue ointment in her bedchamber, turning into a blue fox, then running into the Kremlin kennel. And, there, she gives herself to the hounds.

"We've seen, Nikitka, we've seen." Shka Ivanov grins. "*Mold* us somethin' newer."

"Newer? Have ye heard about the beautiful woman in the Kremlin who has three poods of shit lurking in her gut, when she bends over to bow, a half pood breaks off, then she continues on her way like a peacock and two more accumulate! Can ye guess who it is?"

"The Sovereign's daughter-in-law."

"Soon, Ilya the Prophet shall destroy both of them with lightning for whorishness! He'll burn yon stinkers with heavenly flame!"

"He won't burn them," Matvei yawns. "Just as our Sovereigness has fucked, so shall she continue to fuck."

"Solely not with hounds, but with guardsmen."

"'Twould be better for you to *mold* us the Sovereign's son, Nikitka. There's been no *foolish* news about him for a long time!"

Nikitka walks over to the table, knocking over a glass of vodka and sniffing at his sleeve as he walks:

"The son of the Sovereign is sick with the sin of the sodomites."

"That so?" The executioners light up.

"But not by his own will."

"How then?"

"He's been infected with sodomy by the design of the external enemies of the Russian State."

"And who infected him?"

"The Serbian ambassador Zoran Baranovich."

"He's old friends with the Sovereign. What're you millin' on about? They go huntin' together."

"Baranovich's been bought by the Trans-Oceanic Sodomitic Plutocracy."

"And how did he infect the Sovereign's son?"

"The day after the Apple Feast of the Savior, the Sovereign set up a fishing expedition on Lake Pleshcheyevo. After they went fishing, they went to the banya. There, Baranovich sprinkled a potion into the Sovereign's son's kvass. And the son was inflamed. And Baranovich initiated him into the bowels of the sodomitic way."

"Paved a secret path, if you will!" Mishanya grins.

"These days, the plutocrats set their agents forth on yon path all too often. Verily—once a week!"

"And the evidence?" Matvei strokes his beard.

"It'll come out!" Nikitka slaps his dirty hand across his smartypants. "Enough, I've no time!"

He walks away from the executioners' table and walks over to the circus table. Here, they're always expecting him:

"Take a sip, Nikitka!"

"Disdain us not, Mr. Down-and-Out!"

"Pour yourself a drink, dear one!"

Nikitka takes a glass from the circus people, drinks, then takes a bite of pasty. And begins his report:

"Yesterday, the groom's wife gave birth to triplets in the jockeys' alcove."

"And?"

"And all three of them had foals' heads."

"A-ha ha ha!"

While the circus people are still a-ha-ha-ha'ing, Nikitka has already made it over to the students. They give him Zhiguli beer. Nikitka takes a sip from the mug:

"Have ye heard the news about the cerebral clay? The Chinamen have made one that works not for robots alone, but for humans too."

"Now, that's gotta be a lie, Nikitka!"

Verily! Verily I speak! They've conducted secret experiments with yon clay in our Siberia: they pumped it into the heads of muzhiks in the village of Karpilovka with syringes, but all too much of it; they hadn't calculated correctly."

"And?"

"And so, yon muzhiks had written a proposal to the Sovereign by the morning: 'How to Properly Arrange the Russian Countryside.'"

"And what was in yon proposal?"

"They supposed that the Sovereign must needs attach a steel pecker to every peasant so's they can plow the land without any *obstacle*! Here, take a look for yerselves!"

Nikitka shows them his *foolish* pictures. The students giggle and clink mugs with Nikitka. But he doesn't linger—already hobbling over to the Chinamen he is.

"Wanshang hao[1], you heavenly things!"

And now, a drunken clerk from the Treasury Chamber whose basso voice matured practically overnight tumbles into the tavern. He crosses himself to all four corners of the room and begins to sing:

> And in the capital city, in Moscow,
> Three homeless dogs were off to drink their fill
> of water right round noon.
> One dog was white,
> Another was black,
> The third was red.
> They came to the Moscow river,
> Found themselves a quiet place,
> Right round noon.
>
> The white dog drank—and the water went white.
> The black dog drank—and the water went black.
> The red dog drank—and the water went red.

---

1. [Chinese] Good evening.

The earth shook and the sun disappeared,
Lobnoye Mesto entirely collapsed,
Collapsed and broke apart,
Sprinkling forth scarlet blood,
And from the heavens, a thunderous voice rang out:
"He who was an executioner, shall now be the victim!
The hour of retribution, oh it is approaching!"

They applaud the former clerk, bring him a drink, call him over to their tables, and sit him down.

With noise and laughter, Tanechka and Dunechka, two inseparable flower girls from Trubnaya, rush into the tavern. As soon as they've sold their forget-me-nots, the girls immediately rush for and pounce on their favorite cranberry vodka. Tanechka is statue-like and corpulent. Dunechka is bendy—and twisty too. The regulars call out to them right away:

"Where's your entry ticket, girlies!"

Tanechka and Dunechka understand. They open their mouths, stick out their forked tongues, and make them vibrate. The regulars clap, whistle, and let 'em in. One of the students makes a witty remark:

"You should show us your *lower* tongues—we've already seen your upper ones!"

Volodka Nightingale, a circus entr'acte clown, appears. He joins his people, drinks, gets wasted fast, and starts up an old conversation: when are they going to *spank him*—which is to say: kick him out of the circus? He comes in weeping and justifying himself:

"I'm the best entr'acte clown! The be-e-e-e-est! How could they?!"

The circus people try to sooth him:

"Stop shittin' yourself, Vova, they won't dare!"

"Won't dare! Ach, how they'll da-a-a-are!" Nightingale bleats, letting forth a tear.

A panting *mollusk* in a luminous quilted jacket with a "People and Will" icon pinned to it runs into the Happy Moscovia, runs over to his people, drinks a glass of *sledgehammer* in a single gulp, then reports:

"They took some *hardos* on Tverskaya again."

"Who'd they take?"

"Kaspar, Kasyan, and Lemon."

"All of them? Whaddaya mean?!"

"I said what I meant is what I mean!"

"Crookedly?"

"No, honestly."

"In the 45th?"

"Where else?!"

"We're gonna have to bribe 'em again."

"Yeah, we will. Trifle with the beavers."

One of the tipsy students decides to break into verse. With mug of beer in hand, the curly-headed poet stands up on a chair and begins to declaim:

> Pale-visaged youths' forearms,
> I kiss for nights and nights on end.
> I dream of love causing harm,
> Onto my chest your white honey you spend.
>
> A youth, oh so swiftly undressed,
> Moans with pain . . . well, what of it?
> Soon you shall be crucified again at my behest,
> Shall to the cross of my tremulous body submit.

The curly-haired student's comrades clap for him and put cherry jam into his mug of beer. That's been a tradition among Moscow students for a long time—flavoring beer with jam. In the student tongue, this is referred to as "adding the comely." Moreover, each academic institution has its own tradition of which "comely" to add: university students put raspberry jam into the beer, polytechnic students—marmalade, mathematical students—gooseberry jam, metal experts and machine tool builders—apple jam, economists—strawberry jam, oil and gas experts—plum jam, and road builders—strawberry jam.

One of the craftsmen is telling a joke:

"So, Father Onufriy enters the classroom: 'Children, what's two times two?' Vanechka Dicky puts up his hand. Father Onufriy: 'Dicky!' Vanechka stands up: 'Father, two times two is twenty-six.' Father Onufriy: 'Sit down, Dicky. That was very bad. Two times two is four. In an extreme case five, or six, or seven, or eight, or even twelve at the end of the day. But never twenty-six, you knot-headed moron!'"

"We've known that one for a year plus!" one of the architecture students pinches his nose. "Listen to this new one, *homie*. Father Onufriy enters the classroom: 'Children, I have a question for you: did God create man for the sake of labor or pleasure?' Vanya Dicky raises his hand. Father Onufriy: 'Dicky!' 'For the sake of labor, Father.' 'Justify your answer!' 'Well, Father, God gave man ten fingers and only one dick.' 'Goodness gracious, Dicky, you answered correctly, but justified your answer most shamefully!'"

"Ha ha ha!"

Between two false windows filled in with *living* Russian landscapes (in the leftern—it's winter and a coachman is riding a troika, in the right one—it's summer, the birch trees are stirring, and the maidens are doing a roundelay dance), the tselovalniki are sitting with the tradeswomen, drinking rowanberry vodka and tea they chase with bites from a Sugar Kremlin. Today is the tselovalnik Andrei Petrovich's name day, and he didn't hesitate to smash his son's Sugar Kremlin for the occasion:

"Help yourself, comrades! I have two more just like it at home!"

"Ai-i-i, thank you, Andrei Petrovich! How you honor us!"

The tselovalnik is content, his bald spot gleams, his glasses sparkle, and his crimped mustache quivers. Basanya, Pot, Sergunya, and Dimulya, also tselovalniki, are drinking and partying with him, along with their lil' *business-like* girlfriend. The Sugar Kremlin crunches between their teeth.

A certain Purgenyan rolls and tumbles into the tobacco smoke of the tavern; they say he's a famous inflater of cheeks and passer of state winds, a pair of *blisters*—Zyuga and Zhirya—beat each other on the forehead with Caspian roaches, the retired police warden Gryzlo shuffles a deck of marked cards, the circus people, the bender of horseshoes Medvedko, and the magician Pu I Tin sip *carbonated* kvass, the *round* janitor Luzhkovets laughs from deep down inside of his bowels, and the *sweetie* Grishka Vets nods sadly, bent over his carrot juice.

With howls and ululations, the famous Moscow klikusha Parkhanovna runs into the tavern. She's big-bellied, bandy-legged, with a potato nose, lardy locks that tremble over her acned forehead, an icon of Yuri Gagarin shining forth above her bosom, and a gilded trowel gleaming out from under a girdle round her stomach. Parkhanovna stands in the middle of the tavern, crosses herself with two hands, and shouts as loud as she can:

"The sixth empire!! The sixth empire!!"

"Go eat something!" The craftsmen calm her down.

In the *sinister* corner where sit the zemsky councilmen who've been *smoked* by oprichniks, the Mukhalko family, all balalaika players, flails about. These are nimble and resourceful people, they know how to cheer others up and squeeze money out of 'em. They say that the family once worked as Kremlin jesters but got *spanked* out of there for whatever reason. Their soloist, who goes by the nickname Greased Mustache, sings and plays well and can *drop it* when he dances, but the main thing is his songs are always soulful and his eyes in the wet place. And our people respects both song *and* tears. And now—look!—Greased Mustache has rolled over to the *smoked* ones: strummed his balalaika, stamped, clapped, and winked to his four-eyed friends. So they burst into song:

> The shaggy twerp off into the protestant church,
> The gray rat off into the grain sacks,
> And the noble daughter beneath oprichniks at night totters,
> Follow her generous spirit she must.

> So forward! let us follow the oprichniks' errant torpedo,
> Into tower rooms where voices set to tremble,
> And digits stroke with lo-o-onged-for woe
> The bodies that blush and cannot dissemble!

> And toward the torpedo's base, off to meet fate,
> With trembling tongue . . . mmm . . . God be with you,
> That is how one must be, not fear any strait,
> If you want to remain alive, this is how you must screw.

The disfavored zemsky approves of this bit of seditiousness, chucks some copper coins into Greasy's hat. And Greasy accepts them with tears:

"God be with you, darlings, God be with you, precious ones!"

But the regulars of Mamona's tavern aren't kind to everyone.

Now, for example, the door swings open and the sinisterly squat, unshaven, red-eyed, rude bowl of city-square *zatirka* Levontius walks in. Wheezes out:

"Well, hello!"

"Well, go get fucked!" the response comes to him.

Levontius gnashes his teeth, his eyes sparkle red, he turns around and walks out. Not everyone, oh far from everyone is welcome in the Happy Moscovia!

As soon as the *living* clock strikes midnight, Mamona himself appears. He's short, plump, bearded, balding, cross-eyed, and crafty. He bows to the guests, welcoming them, slowly walking through his establishment, and asking everyone his usual questions:

"Is all in good order, dear guests?"

"All is in good order, Abram Ivanovich!" they respond to him all together.

"No roughhousing?"

"We shan't allow it, Abram Ivanovich!"

"No one offending anyone else?"

"We shan't let them, Abram Ivanovich!"

Mamona nods, squints slyly, then walks out. But the Happy Moscovia continues drinking, whirring, and seething until three in the morning. Barely has the clock struck 3:00 when the floorcloths come out to give everyone their checks, then the floorcloths leave, giving way to the broad-shouldered Ingush bouncers, who hurry the public that's had its fun to the exit with electric brooms.

And, invariably, the doors of the Happy Moscovia close at precisely 3:12 so's to swing open once again at 6:00 the next evening: Welcome, dear guests!

THE QUEUE

"WHERE'S THE LINE END, Orthodox people?"

"Right here, I think, but there was also a woman in a blue fur behind me."

"So, 'twould seem I'm behind her?"

"'Twould seem so. Take your place behind me, my dear man."

"You're gonna be here for a bit?"

"But, of course!"

"I wanted to go off for a minute, a single minute alone . . . "

"First you must needs wait for her, then God be with you, go where you want. Otherwise, I'll be left to explain all of this coming and going. If it continues, I suppose I'll sprain my tongue! Just wait. She swore she'd be back right away. I think she went round the corner to a shop."

"Alas, nothing to be done. I'll wait. Have you been waiting here for a long time, daddy-o?"

"For half an hour."

"And do you know how much they're givin' out?"

"Damned if I know, Lord forgive my cursing . . . I didn't yet ask. Hey, beardy, you know how much they're givin' out?"

"I don't know today. I heard they were giving two per person yesterday."

"Two?"

"Mhmm. And they were giving three on Thursday. Three on Thursday and two yesterday."

"That ain't much. No real point in standin' . . ."

"You just have to stand in two lines, my dear man. People from the provinces sometimes save their spots in three."

"Three?"

"But, of course. Three."

"But that means standing in line all day!"

"What are you talkin' about? They'll get us outta here real quick."

"I somehow doubt it, daddy-o. We're just standin' still, we haven't budged."

"Yeah, all the people who went away just bundled back in. Hence—we haven't budged . . . And here's the woman."

"Wasn't I behind you?"

"Just so, ma'am. And this young man is behind you."

"Yep, I'm behind you."

"Wonderful. Have we moved?"

"As far as I can tell—not much."

"I wonder if we'll be through by two."

"Maybe we will. And maybe we won't."

"I asked to be let out of work until after lunch. My God, why are so many people running over?"

"The Kremlin Wreck, what else?"

"Oh yeah . . ."

"'Tis once a year alone they give out such a nice lil' gift. You've a beautiful fur."

"Thankee."

"I've seen similar furs in Moscow. Self-generating and light-colored, I think? And yours is blue. Most uncommon!"

"Someone bought this coat for me in Moscow."

"That's what I thought. Woah, look at it eat snow!"

"It got hungry in the warm, stands to reason."
"And what do such blue furs find tastier—snow or rain?"
"Snow, of course. Look how it's stretching out . . . yes, eat, my dear, eat . . . "
"I know that self-generating furs can be most gluttonous with rain too. But what a color . . . "
"Mine likes snow more. I get warm as soon as it eats a bit. And when there's a heavy snowfall, I get hot, most verily."
"Oh yeah, a beautiful fur. And its owner is even more beautiful."
"Enough of that."
"Your eyes are exactly the color of the coat. Are they yours?"
"Nope. Disappointed?"
"Not at all. Tell me, could I have seen you recently in Vyatka . . . during Shrovetide?"
"Nope. The last time I went to Vyatka was in December."
"Really? You weren't standing on the right side of the cathedral? By St. Parascheva? You weren't defending the snow fortress?"
"You're a joker. We have our own snow fortress here."
"Wherefore d'you laugh? I'm sure I saw you in Vyatka."
"During Shrovetide, my husband and I went to my aunt's in Glazov."
"To such a backwater? Wherefore?"
"To eat pork. My aunt has thirty-six pigs."
"You got a nice aunt. They sharecroppers?"
"No no, she and my uncle work their own land."
"I guess they pay tribute then?"
"Yep. It's more profitable that way."
"Of course. Better to pay tribute than to sharecrop. So, you had a lil' bit of pork there?"
"Oh, yes. My aunt has Chinese pigs, zhu-dalishi, marbled meat, so tasty. I gained twelve pounds."
"Plumpness suits you."
"Ach, what're you sayin' . . . Well, seems we're kinda movin'."

"Is there still fish in the Cheptsa too?"

"Not sure. I don't know a thing about fish."

"So 'twould seem you feast on pork alone in Glazov?"

"Ohh, yes! I love it when it's baked with garlic."

"How about the ham?"

"Yep! And Aunty also had a most overpowering love for baking pork sausages in the stove . . . she'd put 'em in a pan with offal fat, potatoes, and turnips . . . "

"I'm begging you, you need not continue, I'm startin' to drool!"

"Well, well, looks like we've moved . . . and our lil' line has been set into motion."

"Everything got faster once you arrived. You're the line's blue muse."

"You're such a joker. How can your wife stand you?"

"I'm spouseless."

"That can't be."

"It can."

"Such a sightly man without a wife. That just doesn't happen."

"We split up in the fall."

"You got divorced?"

"Divorced."

"Quickly?"

"It took three months. Ended up having to grease some palms."

"Well, that's understandable."

"Now, we're free from each other."

"Do you have any kids?"

"My daughter stayed with her mother."

"You miss her, I'd guess?"

"Of course. A daughter's like a splinter in the heart. Y'just can't pull it out."

"You know . . . hold on, what's your name?"

"Trofim Ilyich."

"Most pleasant to meet you—I'm Vera Konstantinovna."

"A beautiful name. It suits your figure."

"So then, Trofim Ilyich, I'll tell you my heartfelt conviction: I'm a great opponent of divorce."

"My wife had a lover."

"'Tis a great sin, of course. But the Lord teaches us to forgive the trespasses of our neighbors. Your ex-wife . . . did she repent?"

"She repented. She went to Optina to pray for forgiveness."

"And did you punish her?"

"Yes. I took her to the police station twice."

"Did they whip her there?"

"Yes."

"And that wasn't enough for you?"

"That's not the point, Vera Konstantinovna."

"What's the point, then?"

"The point is that . . . hey, old man, y'need not shove!"

"Who's shovin'?"

"You're shoving."

"It's that they're all pushin' in over there."

"Shove off, for God's sake, and stop pushing . . . And so, most venerable Vera Konstantinovna, the point is that I lost my faith in her after that. And then I fell in love with another woman myself. True, nothing came of that. But I was no longer able to commit myself to relations with my wife."

"Were you completely estranged from each other?"

"Yes."

"Estrangement is a sin."

"I know. But after all of that, we were sleeping *asunder*."

"And what about your confessor? Couldn't he do anything to save your family?"

"Our confessor was kind beyond measure. He imposed obeisances on my wife . . . time spent kneeling in buckwheat . . . But the thing that occurred to me was that he didn't really condemn my wife all that harshly. His kindness was innate, hence it was unlimited, for, verily, it had been fermented, erected, and laid out on a foundation of Christian *philokalia*. He would always speechify: 'For there is no sin so great that God cannot forgive it!'"

"And, verily, that is so."

"Should my wife have begged forgiveness for her sin in the Optina Monastery, that would mean she was forgiven?"

"She was."

"But I couldn't forgive her."

"That was your sin."

"It is, it is. But I still can't forgive her."

"You know, Trofim Ilyich, it seems to me that you just didn't flog your spouse enough."

"I'm no great fan of the lash."

"You need not have taken your wife to the station to go beneath the rods of others; you might have lashed her yourself, in the *comme il faut* way. My husband never takes me to the station."

"Does he whip you often?"

"Once a week. On Saturdays."

"That's often. Is there any reason why?"

"Well . . . you know . . . some small sin always presents itself. But, between us, there is a reason wherefore."

"Ha ha ha! You're most open!"

"Sin is oh-so-sweet as they say. I'm a weak woman and the unclean one is oh-so-skilled at catching us in his nets."

"It stands to reason. If you don't sin, you can't repent."

"Ain't that the truth!"

"But, speaking honestly, once a week . . . yon is somehow . . . most painfully often!"

"It's nothing, I'm used to it."

"And your body, if you'll forgive, is also used to it?"

"'Tisn't too easy to gore me. And there are good potions available. Tinctures too."

"And you don't hold any grudge against your husband?"

"What do you mean! To beat is to love! And he doesn't exactly work me over like a drunkard—he plies his rod precisely as was laid down in the Domostroy. My mom even got jealous of me: In her troublesome times, whipping wives was forbidden because Russia was a godless country. Mom always says, 'If only your deceased father had been able to lash me every Saturday, we'd be living in a three-story house right now!'"

"No, I'm not against whipping on principle, but everything must needs be done deliberately . . . "

"Everything must needs be done as was laid out, Trofim Ilyich. Our woman's business is to obey our husbands. My husband is detail-oriented, unhurried . . . A homemaker. And he whips in the same way—correctly and without haste."

"Mhmm . . . well, you've puzzled me, Vera Konstantinovna."

"How so? Because my husband doesn't take me to get whipped by a torturer down at the station? You're the one who's puzzled me. Oy, how quickly we've started to move! Finally! And so shall I make it back before lunch."

"We'll make it . . . with you here, I'm sure we'll make it in time. Ooh, what a smooth fur . . . Verily, I must say that self-generating furs are something special."

"You like it? Give it a stroke, the coat likes it."

"Real tender . . . "

"It likes you too."

"You know, I almost feel as if you and I were old friends."

"That so?"

"No, don't laugh."

"I'm not laughing at you. I just feel good."

"It's true, I've seen you somewhere. Where do you work?"

"At Dobrynya's Horsery."

"You a creator?"

"No, a converter."

"Of smarties?"

"Precisely. A converter of those darling smarties."

"I never would've thought that such a beauty could work with smartypantses."

"You thought I was just a housewife? No, no . . . oven forks aren't my thing."

"So, who works the stove in your house?"

"Mom, two grandmas, and a scullery maid. And, on the weekends, a lackey comes to help too."

"It's good when one's relatives are among the living."

"Don't you have any?"

"My dad was killed in Abkhazia by a Georgian bullet back when I was a kid. And Mom ran off with a Chinaman."

"She left you?"

"Pretty much. I spent my boyhood and adolescence with my grandma."

"I'd imagine your grandma indulged you a lot."

"You're not wrong. But she knew how to punish me too. She had a heavy hand."

"You're a hapless orphan, then."

"I'm *happy*."

"I've already noticed."

"We've nearly reached our goal, Vera Konstantinovna. Only nine people remain ahead of us! That's how fast things turned around with you here!"

"Tell me, please, are you buying a Kremlin Wreck for your daughter?"

"For who else? And you?"

"For my kids."

"And you have . . ."

"Three of 'em."

"Spectacular! It's clear you have a wealthy husband. I could've guessed from the fur."

"Yes, we're hardly poor, thanks be to You, oh Lord. My hubby's a merchant."
"What does he trade in?"
"In shine in the winter and in scooters in the summer."
"Both profitable businesses."
"We can't complain. And how do you earn your daily bread?"
"You'll never guess."
"It occurs to me that you're probably a man of state and not a businessman."
"Nope. Neither state nor business."
"A man of the church?"
"Also no."
"A tax farmer?"
"Nope."
"A sharecropper?"
"Oof, what a thing to think . . . "
"Can it be you're a sponger?"
"You must think rather poorly of me."
"An indentured servant?"
"Now we're talkin'! Thanks for that!"
"A mercenary?"
"For verily, as Ivan the Terrible *never* said, I am a peaceful man."
"A freedman?"
"God forbid!"
"I'm gonna break my teeth on you . . . a singed one?"
"Not yet."
"What are you then?"
"A healer."
"Oy, how charming! Do you cast spells?"
"That too. But it occurs to me that it's you who's cast a spell on me today and not the other way round. Plus your spells are stronger than mine."

"Do you have an office or do you do house calls?"
"I guess you could say I do house calls."
"For a long time?"
"Since I was a kid. My mom and grandma were both healers."
"They passed the trade onto you?"
"Precisely so. Grandma did."
"Tell me ... oy, they're shoving again ... what on earth ... look, he's cutting the line!"
"Hey there, y'watery bald spot! What d'ya think you're doin'?"
"Get him outta here! Get him out! Don't allow this, good Orthodox people!"
"We were standin' here before!"
"No way! I would remember your ugly mug!"
"Hey now! Get your hands offa me!"
"I'll show you 'get your hands offa me'! Get outta here!"
"My God! They're still shoving! I'm sure they were never here!"
"Come on, make room!"
"I'm not gonna make room! Woah, you see that?!"
"My knocker's bigger than yours! Woah there!"
"Hey, now ... "
"I'm gonna ... "
"Ach, you bastard ... "
"Hey, hey, enough of that!"
"What are you lookin' at, gentlemen?"
"A whole shitty village's pushin' in! Don't let 'em!"
"They're really askin' for it! The bastards!"
"Get out-t-t-ta here!"
"I'll show you! I'll ... "
"Outta here! Outta here!"
"Ach, you dick ... I'll ... "
"I'm gonna fuck your spine in half!"
"You'll only fuck yourself, Zemstvo cocksucker!"

"You sharecroppin' shitstain . . . erm . . . erm . . . this one's for you!"
"I'll . . . I'll . . ."
"Fu . . . bastard!"
"Ach, you fuckin'. . . ."
"Gentlemen! Gentlemen!!!"
"Enough, Orthodox men!"
"Step back, for Christ's sake!"
"Don't let 'em go, Mr. Merchant! There's a brawl!"
"They're swearing! Dial the warden!"
"Don't let 'em go!"
"I'll . . . cocksucker . . ."
"Take that . . ."
"Like that, huh? Like that?! Like that?"
"Shove 'em out of line! Shove 'em to the dogs!"
"Ah . . . there! Well? Woah . . . well? More? C'm'ere! C'm'ere!"
"I'll . . . I'll . . ."
"Where to . . . bastard . . . where to . . . where to! Where to!"
"Help!!!"
"Don't let anybody go! Stop sellin'!"
"Such bastards, huh?"
"Look, the warden's coming!"
"Arrest 'em!"
"The fucks!"
"They were swearin'!"
"CITIZENS OF PERM, BE QUIET! STOP SHOVING! STAND STILL AS PRESCRIBED!"
"Get 'em outta here!"
"They're cuttin' in!"
"They were swearing! I recorded it! I wrote it all down, Warden!"
"CITIZENS OF PERM, BE QUIET! WE'LL BE TAKING THE TROUBLEMAKERS DOWN TO THE STATION!"
"Move, lady, keep your mouth shut!"

"I was behind you, what're you doing?"
"No, I was there . . . hey there, c'mon, lemme go . . ."
"Get in line, Orthodox people!"
"But where . . . ? Ah . . . there we are . . . "
"May I make a report, Warden? They were swearin'!"
"MAINTAIN ORDER, CITIZENS OF PERM!"
"Vera Konstantinovna!"
"Oy . . . they shoved me away from you!"
"Come here! Let 'er through, beardy!"
"Oy, how horrible!"
"Is your fur alright?"
"My darling's alright!"
"And you?"
"I'm alright too!"
"Thank God! Come on—come forward! And you shove off! You were behind us!"
"Hmm, give me everything available."
"Walls alone remain."
"What about towers?"
"The Tower Wreck is sold out."
"How could that be?"
"Walls alone, lady. Y'want any?"
"Gosh . . . what did I wait for . . . and why didn't you say anything?!"
"Will you have any walls or not? If not—keep movin' and don't delay others."
"Such beastliness!"
"Take the walls, Vera Konstantinovna, take the walls!"
"Yes, but . . ."
"Ma'am, take the walls or get thee the heck hence!"
"Don't hold us Orthodox people up!"
"Well, I'll take the walls then . . . "
"Just two packets per person."

"My God! We're being swindled!"

"At least give 'er three!"

"I don't have the right to. That'll be four silver rubles or one golden ruble."

"What an outrage! What the heck was the point of waiting?!"

"I'll take the same. But can you break my ten-ruble coin?"

"Yeah . . . here's your change."

"I'LL SHOW YOU HOW TO CUT IN! I'LL SHOW YOU HOW TO CUT IN! COME ON, EVERYONE MOVE AWAY FROM THE LINE!"

"They were swearing!"

"Let's get outta here."

"They're not gonna let us through . . ."

"Excuse us."

"Thankee . . . my God, such beastliness!"

"MOVE AWAY FROM THE LINE! GIMME YOUR REPORT, GRANDMA!"

"Here it is, sonny!"

"Let's go . . ."

"Beastliness! Beastliness!"

"Don't be so upset."

"No, but they verily stated it in the bubble the day before yesterday: the Kremlin Wreck—walls and towers—you get to choose and prices will vary! And here we have a few walls alone . . . gosh darn it! And for two silver rubles!"

"They gave the towers to their own people—clear as clear can be."

"Such beastliness! Shall we report them?"

"We'd be wasting our own time alone."

"I have three children! What am I to do—tear open the packaging?"

"Yep, tear it open and divide 'em up."

"But they're so beautiful! And all the pieces have the proper form! Two perfect pieces! I'm supposed to smash them?!"

"Into smithereens. Or not. Here's an idea, my darling Vera

Konstantinovna: Take this packet from me as a token of our new friendship."

"What are you saying? Impossible!"

"Not another word! I have but one daughter. A single packet is plenty."

"No, I mean, I don't have—"

"Enough. It's yours."

"Then I'm going to pay you two—"

"By no means!"

"But I can't just take it, Trofim Ilyich!"

"I've already forgotten it existed."

"And I—no! I'm in debt to you."

"Good. Should you be in my debt, promise that you'll come out with me for a cup of tea."

"I can't right now, I must needs return to work."

"What about this evening?"

"This evening . . . yeah. After eight."

"Fantastic! Where d'you live?"

"Over there—by the fish market."

"That's right in the center! You're a real *Permian*!"

"Yep!"

"So. Shall I come by and pick you up?"

"God forbid! My husband is a jealous man."

"Then I suggest we meet at Hot Cross Bun."

"A nice lil' place."

"What time works best for you?"

"Hmm . . . at a quarter past eight."

"Wonderful! You won't forget?"

"What are you saying? I'm in your debt!"

"It pays to pay one's debts!"

"Ain't that the truth! Oy . . . it's already two! Alright, I gotta run! See you this evening, Trofim Ilyich!"

"See you this evening, Vera Konstantinovna!"

A LETTER

H ELLO, KIND SISTER, YOU who are so dear to my heart and endlessly precious to me, oh my Sofya Borisovna! Tis your twin sister Praskovya Borisovna writing to you.

Six years have passed since you left us, my darling, since you fluttered out of the family nest like a little birdie, already six years since Mom, our brother Vanya, and I have been living miserably without the presence of your radiant smile, without your little voice ringing out like a Valdai Bell, without your kind, outgoing, truth-loving, and ever-joyful heart, without your tender little soul, pure and God-fearing as it is, and without your sisterly and daughterly care and prayer. We've been praying without you for six years already, in the morning and in the evening, we go to church without you, we take communion without you, we confess to Father Yuri without you, we fast, then break our fast without you, we celebrate holy days without you, dear Sonechka, but we also pray for you as a whole family, pray hotly for you, for our darling birdie Sonechka, for our blue-wingèd turtledove who has flown off to distant lands, and I personally pray for you every night when I'm falling asleep, when I'm lying all snug in my bed, lying there and thinking about my dearest Sonechka, and I recite three prayers: "Mother of God, Holy Virgin, Rejoice," "Living to Serve the Most High," and "For Travelers." For, verily, Mom and Dad and I believe that you and Tso are going to get sick of living in far-off Khabarovsk, then you'll return here to your native Izvarino.

My darling little sister! I didn't think, I wouldn't have guessed, that living without you, without my little sister, would be so difficult and complicated, that my life would be entirely different—so independent and focused. It's not like I'm entirely independent, it's more like they took me, Praskovya, and threw me into a pool called Life when I was a girl, and this little girl Praskovya of PodMoscovie grew used to swimming in the pool with her darling little sister alone, holding her by the hand, helping her while also being helped herself, and, though Praskovya herself had learned how to swim, she hadn't struck out on her own yet, and now, she was swimming out and out and out, like a little birch twig, it seems it's not going to sink for now, but there's also fear, Sonechka, fear, like a gray wolf, always eyeing you from the woods, eyeing and spying, and it won't let you go, and Praskovya from PodMoscovie is swimming and swimming in the sea (or is it an ocean?) called Life, and though this is already the seventh year she's been swimming alone, it's still so frightening for her to be swimming alone in yon ocean, there, my darling little sister, that's what's been going on!

You and I were always together, Sonechka—when we were lying for so long in Mommy's womb, then, following our happy birth into God's world, when we were lying side by side in the cradle, and when the late Father Sophron dipped us into the font, baptizing us into the Christian faith, and when we took our first sacrament from his hands in a silver spoon, and when we grew up bit by bit in Mom and Dad's house, and when we would frolic in our yard, in the garden, in the cabbage patch, on the grass, beneath the apple blossoms and the cherry blossoms, by our beloved gooseberry bush, from which Mom would boil up such delicious jams, and when we started school, and when we were sitting at our desks together, when we learned arithmetic, when we learned to domesticate a smart machine, when we ran little races, when we played hide-and-seek, when we gathered flowers and leaves and caught butterflies, when we were embroidering celestial birds onto cushions, and when we were making Mom and Dad proud with our success in school. We were together after school too, Sonyushka, after we graduated, when we became women of marriageable age, when we sewed our dowry, when we went to dances, when we waited and waited to find fiancés... And you were chosen first, you, the white swan, taken into the heart of the kind gentleman Tso Ge, who picked you up with his little white hands and took you away to his distant native land, to far-off Khabarovsk. And your little sister, Praskovya of PodMoscovie, was left alone, oh so alone! That's how it was!

You're the more beautiful one, even though we're twins. You were the first to be shot in the heart with one of love's arrows. And thank God! I'm so happy for you, so happy that my little heart opens up and blossoms with the scarlet shade of Sisterly Love.

Don't be angry that I'm describing all of this so sensitively, Sonya. I'm just doing it for fun—being bookish! I'm actually writing on paper! My smarty is helping me. You know how I like to write with others' words. It turns out more beautiful and more heartfelt. On my own, all I can manage is "hello" and 'goodbye." And I'm doing all of this so that you start to hiccup a little more often on my account over there, Sonya, otherwise you're just living off the fat of the land, basking with beautiful Tso on Chinese sheets, smooching, stuffing yourselves with sweet pork and pineapples, drinking *our* beloved plum wine, having forgotten, forgotten, forgotten about everyone and everything. And Praskovya sobs out all of her tears into our old pillows embroidered with tit-birds, sobs like a white whale.

I'm kidding! I don't sob.

Everything's good here, sister, business is good: Stepfather's trading, Mom's in charge of the house, Vanka runs off to his parish school, Trezorka yaps, and I sit on my thumbs. I visit the Ponomarevs, the Abramovs, Riska Milman and the fool Ozerov. For me, nothing shapely has come into being nor anything stunning come to pass. Vera and Nadia Ponomarev are running after Chinese military men, Masha Abramova is getting ready to enter the Women's Upper School, Raisa's sick all the time, something to do with her pancreas, but the doctors can't figure out exactly what. Ozerov's gone totally crazy—he goes everywhere with his smart machine, gives "gifts," and plays the fool enough to give one the heebie-jeebies: he shoved his way into the Solntsevo school on the night of a reunion, *ate* something for courage, hit on a tenth grader, invited her to dance, had his smarty stuck to his chest underneath his shirt as always, and he's dancing, I mean, really dancing, then he starts to blow multicolored bubbles with *stuffing*—monkeys, wood goblins, poltergeists... then the tenth graders set to screaming. They carried him out underneath their arms like the debaucher and troublemaker he is. And he's not that young anymore—the bonehead's thirty-two, but breezes still blow through his empty head. Can you imagine, at Candlemass, he, Rudakov, and Ashkiyants all gathered in the beer hall at the station and convinced some artisans to go beat up the Solntsevo gooks with them. But the gooks met 'em with nunchucks and Ashkiyants got his head broken in two places and Rudakov got his ear torn.

That's how the livin' is out here, Sonya! And the whoopin'!

There's one bit of news alone about the house construction: The second terrace finally got finished. It turned out wide and spacious, enough to have a dance upon it! Now, in the summer, we'll have breakfast on the little terrace, but be able to dine with guests on the big terrace. Mom planted lilac and jasmine all around it and wild grapes to grow up its pillars. It'll be pretty! When you and Tso come, you'll get to smooch on a new terrace surrounded by lilacs!

And generally speaking, between us girls, you're a wet towel of a person. For you, writing a letter to your darling sister would be . . . I don't even know . . . a great feat! You can't get yourself to write more often than once a month—can't manage to deign to! Yeah, and when you write, it's as if you were just ticking a box: hello, Praskovya, fare thee well, Praskovya, hello, Praskovya . . . I can't begin to imagine what happened to you. For the first three years you were away, you at least wrote detailed letters, gave me thorough *data dumps*. But now—hello, fare thee well. It's strange, sister. It's not the family way. Back in the day, you and I laid everything out to one other, said everything, didn't hide anything—what was in our hearts and in our heads and in our souls, and there were no mysteries or secrets at all, nothing was hidden, and there was nothing to hide, and if there was something to hide, we still didn't hide it, of course not, everything was in the sisterly way, the family way, we hid things from others, but laid everything out to one another. And now here's how you behave—hello, dear sister Praskovya . . . fare thee well. Can it be that love has sucked you up so completely that your family feelings have utterly disappeared? Or has family hustle and bustle overcome you to such a degree that it keeps your hands from ever reaching the keys? Should it be the latter, you're a wet towel three times over. And should it be the former . . . No, Sonya, please understand, I have no plans to slide into your sweet pineapple life, I'm no foolish maiden, I understand—it's family business, insular business . . . as was written once and for all time regarding all newlyweds: "and may man be cleaved to wife." A law's a law. "Family life is a secret between two beings," that's what Father Yuri says at every wedding when he drinks to the newlyweds. You have your secrets, of course, who doesn't have them? You do too—and thank God. Here, Mashka Abramovna's sister made known that her husband was forcing her to commit the sin of sodomy... sometimes, it happens. I'm not asking you about your secrets and I need not know them, each family has their own. Perhaps you don't even have secrets—if so, also thank God. That's not what this is about, Sonya. I'm not expecting any secrets from you, no details of newly wedded life, but simply a heartfelt conversation—sisterly, good, and warm—one in which everything comes from the heart and from the soul, like, as it was before. So that my sister, in distant, cross-eyed Khabarovsk is at least close to my heart. I need nothing else! What more am I to desire—you got married, fluttered away, my darling sister, you married based on love, on intentions, on coincidence of circumstance, and everything turned out terribly well, and thank God, may He bring you love and resolve all your squabbles, I'm happy for you and I pray for you so, so fervently, I pray that you stay together forever and never split up, that you finally have kids, I always think well of you, I direct mental greetings to you, and love you at a distance. But how can it be you've so completely forgotten your sister? That's bad, Sonechka. It's unchristian.

Well, God alone shall judge you. I think this loving frenzy of yours shall pass, you'll have a good laugh, you'll soften up, then you'll start to write to your little sister right away—from your heart to mine. After six years I think you can cool off and calm down a little, hmm? Cool to him already, Sonechka, and perforce you'll begin to remember me. Or you'll remember something cheerful, how cheerfully you and I lived with no knowledge of grief. For there's much to remember, isn't that so, Sonyushka? Do you remember how a *raspberry chuckle* got into our mouths and we almost drowned in the Pakhra during Apple Feast of the Savior? How, afterwards, you were crying, then laughing, then throwing grass at me? And I was laughing so much I let one loose into my undies! Or how we put one over on Sashka Mamulov about the helicopter, how he went to Boris Nikitich to denounce us that evening, but then got shown the door? And Vovchenko—"Girls, do you have flies in both your ears?" And the salty cake? How furious Marfa was? Her nose even set to sweating! How we had to kneel in dried peas in the bastardly history teacher's class? "Ivan Kalita—that ain't no Kekou-Kele!"[1] Remember good ole Pyotr Khristoforovich in God's Law? He's still teaching today, hasn't gone off anywhere, a bachelor with neither spouse nor family. And remember our dolls? Katerinka's still alive and dancin' the "mistress," still talkin'. But Malvinka bit the dust—something to do with her brain clay. She can do nothing more than open her eyes and smile. And remember how, after tea, she used to yell out, "Xiexie, haoch-h-h-h-i-i-i!"[2] Basically, Sonechka, they're both just lying in Grandma's dresser, Malvinka and Katerinka are, they're sleeping on a bed of mothballs, sleeping and dreaming technicolor dreams about you and me.

Oh Sonya, just now, writing this letter, I suddenly remembered: how you and I went to gaze upon the new Kremlin! And you know why I remembered? Here's why! I'm knockin' away on Mademoiselle Keyboard as I'm suckin' at the last of a Sugar Kremlin tower! On Christmas Day, our Vanka went with Seryozha Vorontsov and Nikita Bacha to Red Square in Moscow. And each of them brought back a Sugar Kremlin. Mom decided to save the turrets until Easter so's to decorate the Easter cake, but she broke up the walls and put them into the sugar bowl. And now, instead of sugar, we put the walls of the Kremlin into our tea! So, I suddenly remembered. Somehow, I had completely forgotten about it, but, just right now, I suddenly remembered! Remembered as brightly as if it were right out of a movie! You're to blame, of

---

1. [Chinese] Coca-Cola.
2. [Chinese] Thank you—delicious!

course, who else? You forced me to! Do you remember too? Remember? We had just turned twelve and our deceased dad gave us the news in the morning: they'd painted the Kremlin white overnight at the Sovereign's command. I remember that was on a Saturday. And, already on Sunday, we were off to Moscow. And do you remember you saw a smashed ice cream on the ground in the subway and said, "Look what the Muscovites dropped!" And back then I didn't understand what "Muscovites" had to do with anything! Then we joined the crowd and started walking, walking through the subway with halting little steps, it was frightening even, what if we can't get out of here? I'd never seen such a crowd before. And I asked our deceased dad, "Is the subway always so crowded?" And he replied that it wasn't us alone who wanted to see the new Kremlin. And finally we got out at Tretyakovskaya Station and there the crowd was even bigger, everyone leaping and leaping, Dad holding us by the hands, and us clinging to him. We got up onto the embankment. And, there, you and I saw the White Kremlin, remember? It was standing on the opposite bank of the Moscow River. So very white! The people around it were shouting and gasping, Dad was crossing himself and bowing to the Kremlin. Then the sun suddenly rolls out from behind the clouds and sprays forth its rays onto the white-stoned Kremlin, oh how it shined—enough to burn the eyes! I remember that very well. And it also became painful for you to look at the Kremlin, you say: "Sonya, we should've brought dark glasses." And Dad laughed at you and said, "One cannot look upon beauty with dark glasses, daughter." And, as I gazed upon the Kremlin, I felt I was truly *seeing* it and everything in my head began to shine, as if 'twere filled up with yon unearthly light about which our priest loved to speak. Everything just shines forth and sings in my head and I want to look at the Kremlin more and more. And my little eyes don't hurt at all anymore. And I look, look, look and it's so, so white, and yon whiteness just sucks up my eyes, it shines in the sun, and angels are singing in my head, it feels so sweet, so good, the sky is blue, the clouds have parted, the sun beats down, the Kremlin shines, it sucks up my eyes, I forget about everything, and I look, look, look, and it's just so sweet to look at the white-stoned Kremlin, so sweet I don't stir, I don't wish to stir, I grip my father's hand, and, with all my heart, I want my dad not to stir either, not to speak, and for you not to trifle with me, and for everyone around us to stand as still as stones, so's to look alone to look and look and look and look, for everything to stop, and I would just stand and watch, just praying my eyes wouldn't close or get tired, and my eyes didn't tear up at all and didn't get tired, they just opened wider, and looked and looked and looked, as if I didn't must needs do anything else, I must needs look alone, look, look and stand, look at the Kremlin and stand still, stand well and correctly so's not to frighten or disturb anything. And I look at our White Kremlin alone, look with eyes wide open, so that it'll stay put and not go off anywhere, won't vanish, but'll just stand in the *main place* forever and ever, in the place where the big, main business happens, the place to where everyone has come, everyone has their place, everyone has gathered together to do everything properly and well, to be all together, to decide and resolve everything together for all time, forever and ever, so long as no one disturbs it, so long as the Kremlin stands in its main place and we can look at it properly, look with eyes wide open, in such a way that the soul trembles, that the soul shines forth, shines forth with golden light, grand light, Kremlin light, light that makes everyone feel good, everyone shall feel good, so good that we must needs have nothing else, nothing else we don't must needs have, just to look and rejoice, let your soul be cheerful, drink in the white Kremlin with your eyes, and you must needs have nothing else, and all proper people shall also be standing next to you, properly standing, honestly standing and rejoicing, standing with eyes wide open, with good eyes and in those eyes shall everyone have their own Kremlin thousands of millions of Kremlins in the proper people's eyes, the people that knows how to properly glorify and do everything properly and well and know how to look diligently at our dear and holy Kremlin and must needs have nothing else only to stand in place and that nothing disturb the looking just must needs watch quietly and calmly so's not to frighten or disturb anything without straining the eyes but just that that eyes look calmly look look and everything shall be calm and good and everyone shall feel good and all people shall be happy forever and ever should they solely learn to look properly at the White Kremlin and they must needs have nothing else anything else is above all not good solely to look and look look and look so that their eyes don't shut nobody should do that the eyes must be open and good properly open so that everything in them is good and the White Kremlin stands in everyone's eyes in the eyes of all honest people such that the soul is beside itself with joy that delight and the right way of seeing and people that they stand peacefully calmly and don't move at all so that all is good and that the sun doesn't set and keeps shining and the Kremlin shines and shines forth in every eye and every eye has its own White Kremlin that it shines and shines yes that it shines so that people understands more and accepts that accepts and knows that so that people have no more questions and all people understand that happiness is here and it's never going away they must needs look and look upon the Kremlin alone and there won't be anything bad there won't be anything hidden everything shall be good and clear everything shall shine forth with white light and everyone shall feel so good and we shall be standing in a timid crowd and shall do good and the great Kremlin shall shine forth for us and we are all entirely happy when all is good and the White Kremlin and a white day when the people closest to us have come to look upon the eternal White Kremlin then all is good so it shall be that we shall all see the Kremlin and all eyes shall be open and the people shall see everything after standing there purposefully and all of us shall feel good and if all eyes open and immediately see the Kremlin they shall become calm and immediately begin to love the Kremlin only that everyone stands up in a row and sees the Kremlin right away and that the dead rebel against their state so's to see the White Kremlin and we'll go to Red Square to see the White Kremlin and we'll all see that it's wonderful that the White Kremlin is very kind and our splendid White Kremlin shall shine forth eternally upon us and we shall all live without worry or care if we might look upon the White Kremlin alone and everyone shall look intently upon the most white White Kremlin and then weep serenely and kiss our White Kremlin and everyone's hearts shall overflow when they look upon the White Kremlin and it shall stand there for all time our golden-domed White Kremlin and we shall knit ourselves together around it so's to protect our White Kremlin and all of us shall be saved forever and ever along with it and the White Kremlin shall be with us when all people gather together and set out to look upon the Kremlin they shall be saved from all calamities when they see the White Kremlin and all of us shall be so calm when we see the White Kremlin and we shall stand in harmonious rows so's to see the White Kremlin and everyone around shall knit themselves together all at once so's to see the White Kremlin and we shall touch our beloved White Kremlin with each eye and it shall shine forth upon us strongly our beloved White Kremlin and we shall all look lavishly upon the great White Kremlin and whatever happens to us we shall see the White Kremlin so that the heart beats sweetly we shall all look upon the White Kremlin we shall all stand without even flinching so's to look upon the White Kremlin and we shan't ever forget our golden-domed White Kremlin.

    I'm guilty I'm guilty I'm guilty I'm guilty I'm guilty I'm guilty

I'm guilty I'm guilty.

Forgive me in the name of all the saints forgive me in the name of all the saints forgive me in the name of all the saints forgive me for in the name of all the saints forgive me in the name of all the saints forgive me in the name of all the saints forgive me in the name of all the saints forgive me in the name of all the saints forgive me in the name of all the saints forgive me in the name of all the saints forgive me in the name of all the saints forgive me in the name of all the saints forgive me in the name of all the saints forgive me in the name of all the saints forgive me in the name of all the saints.

I'll never do it again I'll never do it again I'll never do it again I'll never do it again I'll never do it again I'll never do it again I'll never do it again I'll never do it again I'll never do it again I'll never do it again I'll never do it again I'll never do it again I'll never do it again I'll never do it again I'll never do it again I'll never do it again I'll never do it again I'll never do it again.

AT THE FACTORY

AFANASY NOSOV, THE OVERSEER of the packaging workshop, heard the signal for their lunch break in the smoking room.

"Well then..." he muttered, quickly taking a drag from the "Fatherland" cigarette he'd just lit, then placing it into a large metal vessel filled with sand and cigarette butts atop a tall tripod.

There were three more factory workers in the smoking room: Petrov, an adjuster, Dobrenko, a release director, and Kosorotov, the foreman of the casting workshop.

"Dang, seems like Egorych got hungry." Kosorotov grinned.

"Hunger's a bitch..." Nosov spat heavily into the sand.

"A bastard too." The cross-eyed, big-eared Petrov squinted.

Nosov left the smoking room.

Walking down the bright corridor, he turned a corner, went down a staircase, then stepped onto the ribbed belt of the moving walkway.

"Quicker!" he ordered, and the floor began to move at its maximum speed. *Living* posters with smiling workers, both male and female, doing their work were stuck to the walls.

The floor brought Nosov to his workshop. He walked off of the belt and looked around. In the enormous bright space of the shop, among the accumulated mounds of gilded packaging that had been bundled into cubes, six female workers stuck out in blue.

"Six, thirteen, eight, half a hundred. Turn off the supply!" Nosov ordered loudly, and all six of the packaging conveyor belts stopped.

Nosov moved down a wide aisle.

The packaging paws pipped as they shut down. The girls pulled down their shutters and hung the paws in green frames.

"Afanasy Egorych, the ribbons are running out again!" Titova cried out.

"We'll fix that!" Nosov walked down the aisle, looking around.

"Egorych, my squirt[1] got jammed up!" the elderly Maksakova cried out with a laugh. "I'd like to feed him!"

As he walked, Nosov got connected with the squirt adjuster:

"Vit, after lunch, stop by our shop. One squirt got jammed up."

"We'll get it goin' again," the adjuster replied as he chewed.

The workers came out into the aisle. Nosov walked over to them:

"Today, rushing is most unnecessary: The first workshop's ground to a halt."

"What the heck happened?" Dolgikh took off her white gloves.

"'Twould seem their smarty shorted out again."

"Didn't take long for it to give!" The simple-minded Mizina was surprised to hear this.

"Refect unhurriedly." Nosov yawned nervously.

"Thankee, oh benefactor!" Maksakova smiled, exposing her new teeth, then immediately waved to her fellow workers. "Let's go, my beauties!"

The women headed for the exit.

---

1. Cleaning robot.

"Pogosova, has yours been slipping up a lot?" Nosov asked.

"I guess." Pogosova stopped.

"Stay back a sec." Nosov's unhappy gaze made its way through the workshop, then shifted upward.

Beneath a smoothly flexing ceiling of white plastic, an enormous hologram of a Sugar Kremlin hovered and rotated.

Pogosova walked over, pulling off her gloves.

"How is it?" Nosov asked.

"Oh, it's fine," smiled the tall, broad-shouldered, and broad-cheeked Pogosova.

"Fine doesn't mean anything. I'm asking you how the work's going."

"Good."

"Now we're talkin'. But does it slip up often?"

"I guess." Pogosova looked at him smilingly.

"Don't let these slipups accumulate, Pogosova!" Nosov said strictly. "As soon as it slips, whistle up to me."

"Clear as clear can be." Pogosova smiled.

"If I'm not there, bother the adjusters about it."

"Of course. That too."

"The adjusters exist in order to be bothered. That clear?"

"Clear as clear can be."

"Don't keep quiet. We're not just packin' noodles here." He nodded toward the rotating hologram. "It's the Sovereign's order. The whole country has their eyes on us."

"Clear as clear can be." Pogosova smiled.

"Come with me." He turned and walked quickly down the aisle.

Pogosova went after Nosov, catching up easily. She was a head taller than him.

They left the workshop and stepped onto the belt of the moving walkway.

"Quicker!" Nosov ordered the belt angrily.

The belt began to move faster.

"Why are the ribbons always running out with Titukha?" He spread his hands out in bewilderment. "What's she doin' . . . eatin' 'em?!"

"I dunno." Pogosova fixed her light-colored hair, which had popped out from beneath her blue kerchief.

"Why do you and Mizina and Granny always have some stored away? And she's always running out!"

"Probably doesn't store much away."

"What do you mean 'store away'?! I give you all identical amounts!"

"I dunno."

"I *dunno* either! Who knows, then?"

Pogosova shrugged her broad shoulders.

"Could it be she's stealing them?"

"I dunno. What would she be doing with them?"

"Who the hell knows!"

"And how could she get them out of the factory?"

"She couldn't. Everything has an atomic signature. Where would she be taking them?"

"I dunno."

"This Titukha's a nuisance!" Nosov waved his hand angrily, then stepped off of the belt.

Pogosova followed him.

Nosov walked over to a big door inscribed with the word WRECK and pressed a key to it. The door moved off to the side. A light flashed on in the space behind the door. Nosov and Pogosova walked in. The door shut behind them. A long room with no windows was entirely lined with trays of broken Sugar Kremlins. The room was filled from floor to ceiling. There was a narrow passageway between the Kremlins. Nosov moved down the passage. Pogosova followed him, almost touching the sugared bits towering up in the trays with her shoulders as she moved.

Nosov turned behind a column of trays. Pogosova turned after him. Before them was a dead end. All around were piled-up containers filled with sugared Kremlin Wrecks. In the corner was also a roll of transparent wrap.

"There..." Nosov got up onto the roll and turned Pogosova's back to him.

Pogosova lifted up her blue skirt and white underwear, holding them with one hand, bent over, leaned down onto a tray, and pressed her cheek into the Wreck. Pogosova had beautiful buttocks, smooth and white. Nosov undid his black pants and pulled down his long black underwear. His swarthy penis popped out. Nosov sprayed Outpost prophylactic spray onto it, then quickly entered Pogosova.

"Oy," she pronounced, then took a deep breath.

"There..." Nosov muttered and, grabbing onto Pogosova with his hands, began to thrust quickly.

Pogosova stood there silently.

"There, there, there..." Nosov gasped in time with his thrusts.

The black cap on his head trembled, shifting back toward the nape of his neck.

Pogosova reached out toward a broken Borovitskaya Tower with her tongue.

"There, there, there..." Nosov muttered, thrusting even more quickly.

Pogosova licked the tower.

"And there, and there, and there, and there..." Nosov hissed.

Pogosova licked the tower. Her big green eyes wandered aimlessly over the sugared Wreck.

"And there, and there, and the-e-e-e-ere!" Nosov wheezed and twitched, his hands still clutching onto Pogosova.

"E-r-r-m-m..." Pogosova grimaced, still licking the tower.

Nosov sighed heavily and laid his head onto Pogosova's back. A minute passed.

Pogosova continued to unhurriedly lick the tower.

"There . . . " Nosov raised his head with a sigh, pulled out of Pogosova, pulled up his underwear and pants, then stepped off of the roll of wrap.

Pogosova straightened up and spread her legs. Nosov's sperm began to pour out of her, dripping down onto the floor. Pogosova waited for a moment, then wiped at her crotch with her hand and wiped her hand off on the sugared Wreck.

"There . . . well, there . . . " Nosov, now red of cheek, shook his head contritely, breathing heavily and buttoning his pants.

Pogosova turned to him. Looked at him with her perpetual smile.

Nosov fastened his belt and pulled his cap up from the nape of his neck. Took a deep breath and stroked his mustache. Reached into his pocket and took out a silver ruble. Handed it to Pogosova. She took it and put it into the little pocket of her blue jacket.

"Let's go . . . " Nosov coughed, then moved down the aisle.

Pogosova followed after him.

They left the room. Nosov locked the door. They walked down the hallway toward the moving walkway leading to the cafeteria. A few workers were standing on its belt. Nosov and Pogosova got onto the belt. Smiling, Pogosova watched the walls and posters floating by:

"I wanted to ask."

"What?" Nosov squinted at her.

"Why do they write the Wrecks off right away when they could fix them?"

"How would we fix them? They're cast whole from molten sugar!"

"Well, OK, but, if a single battlement breaks off of the wall, the entire Kremlin gets written off right away."

"Yes, that's as it should be."

"Is it that hard to glue the battlement back on?"

Nosov grinned wearily:

"What're you gonna glue it with, dunderhead?"

"With the same sugar it's made from."

"Impossible. Yon sugar can be cast at a single temperature alone—it sets immediately after. There's no way to make it molten again."

"Yeah?"

"Yeah."

Pogosova sighed:

"I feel bad about the wasted work. A single battlement goes and you lose an entire Kremlin.

"A Kremlin . . . it needs to be *whole*."

"Whole?"

"Whole."

"Why?"

"What do you mean *why*? It's to do with the Sovereign, dunderhead! That there not be a single crack! Nor a single chip! Not one single blemish. That clear?"

"Yep." Pogosova looked at him.

"You're not that young anymore and you still ask such questions. How old are you?"

"Eighteen."

"Eighteen! When I was eighteen, I was in the long-range combat troops—I knew what was what. This is your third month with us, yeah?"

"Fourth."

"Woah . . . your fourth! Everything should already be as clear to you as two times two."

"Everything *is* clear to me. I just feel bad about the Kremlin Wrecks."

Grinning wearily, Nosov shook his head:

"You just won't get it through your head! *Wholeness*! Don't you see?"

"OK." She smiled.

He looked away and waved his hand:

"Talking with you's a nuisance. Go away, Pogosova—go eat!"

Pogosova nodded.

Nosov sighed, stepped off of the belt, then set off for the smoking room of the first workshop with a spring in his step.

Pogosova stayed on the belt, gazing forward with her big green eyes.

CINEMA

"LIGHTS, CAMERA . . ." THE DIRECTOR said quietly, but distinctly.

Speakers amplified his voice, which resounded through the birch grove lit up by the setting sun.

"Camera rolling!" the camera pronounced.

"Action!" the director said louder.

A girl in a light summer dress with two long braids clicked the clapperboard:

"Scene 38, take 3."

"Ivan!" the director ordered.

A young man of attractive appearance in a beige nankeen suit, a white kosovorotka with an embroidered collar, and box calf leather boots walked over to a birch tree, got down onto his knees, hugged it, and pressed his face to its trunk:

"Forgive me, Russia, forgive me, Mother Russia . . ." he muttered in a breaking voice.

The director raised his index finger.

A cuckoo cuckooed in the grove.

"One, two, three, four . . ." the young man began to count.

The director bent his finger. The cuckoo fell silent.

The young man sat down, his back against the tree, sighed heavily, fumbled over his chest with his hand, then unbuttoned his kosovorotka violently:

"My God . . . Can it really be my native land shall carry me for four more years? Carry me, feed me, and love me?"

He froze with his gaze stuck on one point in space. Swallowed.

"And it shan't catch fire beneath my feet?!"

He covered his face with his hands, a ring on each of them, and shook his head. Helplessly lowered his hands. Sighed:

"No. You shan't catch fire, oh Russian earth! For you love all of us, all Russians, without discrimination. Those who care for you and those who betray you."

The director raised his hand, squeezed it into a fist, then spread his fingers.

A thin gray-haired man in dark glasses, a cocoa-colored jacket, a T-shirt with the inscription COLORADO 2028, a cane, tight white pants, and big, shaggy "chameleon" sneakers made of viviparous plastic came out from behind the single aspen in the birch grove, an old, dried-out, and hollow tree.

"Why dost thou grieve, Ivanushka?" the man pronounced with a slight American accent.

The young man shuddered, recoiled, and covered himself with his hands:

"Get back . . . get back . . ."

"You need not fear. 'Tis I." The man came closer and touched the young man's shoulder with his cane.

"You scared me, dammit . . ." The young man stroked his chest with his hand and sighed heavily.

"But I'm not a devil," the man said.

"You're worse." The young man squinted at him.

The man took out a cigarette case, opened it, and proffered it to the seated man:

"Would you like a cigarette, my dear?" he asked in English.

"I'm not enchanted by your devilish tinctures," the young man muttered.

"Since when?"

The young man measured up the American with a prickly look:

"From today onward."

The American took off his dark glasses. Their eyes met. There was a long, tense pause; their gazes clashed.

The director gave two thumbs up, shook his fists, and, ecstatically, but also silently, repeated "Yes! Yes! Yes!" beating his fist against the leg of the female screenwriter sitting next to him. Not looking away from the monitor, she grabbed the director's fist and kissed it. A wave of approving fidgets swept through the film crew.

"What's with you, Ivan?" the American pronounced, putting away his cigarette case.

"Here's what." The young man stood up decisively.

He turned out to be taller than the American.

"I'm putting an end to our meetings," Ivan pronounced sternly.

The American squinted:

"Wherein lies the reason?"

"The reason is that I don't wish to work for you anymore."

The cuckoo cuckooed in the grove. The cameraman sitting behind the camera jerked his head, hissed, and spat. The screenwriter covered her face with her hands. The director jumped up out of his chair and shook his fists, screaming silently:

"What the fuck is this?"

The film crew began to stir. The cuckoo stopped cuckooing.

Biting his lips angrily, the director straightened his glasses, sat down in his chair, sighed heavily, and shook his head. The screenwriter shook her head and squeezed her lips together tightly. The cameraman began to hiss monosyllabically:

"Sab-o-teur!"

The American put on his dark glasses:

"Wherefore? Can it be we don't pay you enough?"

"I have no more need of your money. I don't wish to see the beastly snake thou art ever again. You have drunk altogether too much of my blood and driven me to criminal acts. Whereas my soul has never been sold to you, oh ye adversaries of man! Not before and not now! My soul is free! Get behind me, Satan! You can take back your gifts!"

The young man took the rings from his fingers and threw them down at the feet of the American.

"And, finally, I'd like to caution you and your entire embassy: Should you not leave me alone, I'll report on you to the Secret Order!"

There was a pause. The director once again gave a triumphant thumbs up.

The American squatted down and found the rings in the grass.

"So, you've remembered your soul, then, Vanya?"

"'Twould seem so!" The young man turned resolutely away, trying to leave.

But the American hooked his cane onto the young man's shoulder:

"And while you were doing yon things, you didn't care to remember your soul?"

A miniature smart machine appeared in the American's hand. The American animated it and a hologram rose up in the clearing: the young man in the uniform of a captain of the Russian Air Force going into a bathroom, taking something out of a briefcase, quickly putting it under the toilet, standing there for a little while, then flushing the toilet as he sings the Fyodor Miller poem set to music—"I don't care whether I suffer or enjoy"—and leaving the bathroom.

"I don't believe they would rejoice most enthusiastically over yon video in your Secret Order, Vanyusha."

Ivan gazed upon the American with hate in his eyes:

"I'll denounce myself before you can!"

The American froze. The hologram vanished.

"I'm gonna go to the Secret Order right now and confess to everything!"

"You think they'll pardon you?"

"Pardon me or not—that's not for me to judge. But I'm going to tear your insidious network apart! With yon act, I can help my native land! 'Haps they shan't be altogether most wrathful with me!"

Ivan started to walk away.

"And they won't be altogether *most wrathful* about this either?"

Another hologram arose in the clearing: a room in a hotel, shrill American jazz sounds out, Ivan is standing there naked and totally drunk, he's leaning onto a table absolutely overflowing with foreign food and drink, holding a jar of Nutella in his hands, scooping the chocolate goop out of the jar with his finger and eating it. At the same time, a beautiful half-black man with a cigar between his teeth is performing anal intercourse on him from behind. On the man's shoulder is the standard tattoo of all American paratroopers: a skull with a parachute behind it.

Seeing the hologram, Ivan stopped dead in his tracks.

"My sweet Russian boy!" The man laughed lustily and blew smoke into the nape of Ivan's holographic neck.

A spark passed across the hologram. The screenwriter shuddered, but the director squeezed her wrist, raised a finger, and whispered:

"That's how it's meant to be."

Ivan gazed upon the hologram with crazed eyes.

"You'll confess to yon acts as well?" The American came right up to Ivan.

Ivan stood there frozen.

The American shoved him. Ivan fell impotently into the grass.

The American turned off the hologram, squatted down, and began to stroke Ivan:

"Don't be a fool, Vanya. There's no path back for you."

He took out the cigarette case, pulled a cigarette out of it, put it between Ivan's lips, and lit it:

"We're in the same boat. And only death is capable of knocking yon boat over. And you don't want to die, hmm?"

Ivan sat up, his eyes fixed upon the ground. The American lit his own cigarette, tossing the rings up and down in his palm.

"You're still young. Everything lies ahead. Which is why 'twould be better not to hurl our gifts around. They're not made of glass, you know."

He put the rings back onto Ivan's impotent fingers.

"We have another gift in store for you, you know."

The American took a little golden ring with a diamond on it out of his pocket and put it onto Ivan's little finger.

"Now, you don't have a sapphire and a moonstone alone—a diamond shall also shine forth from your hand. And a diamond, my dear Ivanushka, is the stone of all stones. For 'tis like no other earthly stone, but a fragment of a heavenly sphere that fell to earth. Here, take a look."

The American brought Ivan's hand up to his face. Ivan took a hungry drag from his cigarette, jumped up, and began to walk. The camera followed him silently on a dolly.

The American put his arm around Ivan's waist and set off alongside him.

"And a touch more." The American pulled a leather coin purse out of his pocket and dropped it into his hand. "A hundred pieces of gold."

Ivan stopped sharply.

The director stood up, adjusted his glasses in a state of great arousal, and raised his clenched fist.

"A hundred pieces of gold, Vanya!" The American took Ivan's hand and put the purse into it.

Ivan took another hungry drag, dropped the cigarette, then asked hoarsely:

"What do you need?"

The American looked attentively at him through his dark glasses:

"What we need, Vanya, is the secret number that provides access to the internal workings of the cargo aircrafts that carry atomic weapons and make special flights over the northern borders of your state."

Ivan dropped impotently down into the grass and shook his head:

"No. I shan't do yon thing."

The American laughed softly, put his hand onto Ivan's head, and began to speak, looking ominously into the sunset:

"You'll do everything that I command."

There was a torturous pause.

"Cut!!!" the director cried out, then ran over to the actors.

"Cut! Cut! Cut!" He ran over and embraced them.

Crossing herself sweepingly, the screenwriter rushed over to them.

"Cut! Cut! Motherlover . . . " The director kissed, pummeled, and squeezed the actors. "Cut, my darlings! Cut, my bad boys!"

The tall, angular screenwriter with her eternally childish face walked over wearing a tight dress, embraced "Ivan," and pressed herself to him:

"My God . . . my heart nearly jumped out of my chest . . . "

"Satisfied?" the "American" asked, taking off his glasses.

The director hit him on the shoulder with his fist:

"Genius!"

"The real issue is something got into my boot!" Laughing with relief, "Ivan" stuck his finger into his boot. "The little pest's moving around . . . it tickles too . . . Just my luck!"

"My little ass! My precious little ass!" The director embraced "Ivan."

"So . . . really . . . not bad?"

"Ten outta ten! Ten outta ten!"

"We managed to do it with the sunset too!" The squat gray-bearded cameraman walked over.

"With the sunset! With the sunset, motherlover!" The director frantically spun his close-cropped head, constantly adjusting his glasses as he did. "Look at the sunset! Another minute and it'll be gone! Then we'd've shat the bed and been *motherfucked*!"

"Egor, don't swear, I'm begging you!" The screenwriter embraced him.

"We got it done with the sunset! Don't you see, Doshka?!" The director shook her by her angular shoulders.

"A minute and a half before the sun went away," his assistant interjected.

"Woah! A minute and a half! And the sun'd've been gone!"

"Get me a chair so I can take my boot off!" "Ivan" cried out.

"Chair to the set!" the director's assistant cried out.

"That cuckoo really made us shit ourselves, huh?" The "American" lit up smilingly.

"A-a-a-h!" the director recalled noisily. "Get me the sound guy!"

"I'm here, Egor Mikhailych!" A stooped-over, modestly dressed young man walked over. "Forgive me most generously, it broke away once—"

"Once! One mistake won't a faggot make, huh?!" the director cried out, turning red. "Get the hell outta here! You're not working tomorrow!"

"Please forgive me—it was like someone'd jinxed it."

"Don't blame this on anyone else! Get the hell out!" The director shoved him and looked around. "OK! That's it for today!"

"Can we start serving food, Egor Mikhailych?" a plump woman asked.

"Of course! You must!"

"Re-fec-tion, Orthodox people!" she cried out, cupping her hands around her mouth.

"That's it, that's it, that's it!" The director clapped, nodding at the actors. "Head on over to the tent!"

They walked away from the set and entered a green tent, which had been erected in a clearing surrounded by birch trees. The actors sat down in chairs and two makeup artists began to undress them and remove their makeup. The director took a twelve-year-old bottle of Dewar's scotch whiskey out of his briefcase and began to quickly pour it into everyone's plastic cups:

"Quickly, quickly, quickly . . ."

"Are you gonna watch, Egor Mikhailych?" The assistant cameraman glanced into the tent.

"In a bit!" The director hid the bottle of whiskey from his sight and cried out. "Tanya! Don't let anyone in!"

The screenwriter took the bottle from him:

"Let me cover over our sin . . ."

She put the bottle back into the briefcase, slid it under the table, took a bottle of Pshenichnaya vodka out from the refrigerator, and set it onto the table.

"You lettin' beardies in?" The cameraman stuck his head into the tent.

"Georgich, c'mon in!" The director handed him a cup.

Everyone except for the makeup artists took a cup.

"To us!" the director pronounced, fixing his glasses as he did.

Everyone drank.

The director took out a pack of "Russia" cigarettes and opened it. Hands stretched out for cigarettes.

"Well, there. Time to relax . . ." The director lit up.

"You know, I didn't believe we'd manage to shoot it today," the screenwriter took a hungry drag from her cigarette.

"I didn't either." The cameraman grinned.

"For some reason, I did," "Ivan" said.

"The third take!" The reddening director shook his round head. "A mystery, motherlover! The third take's always good! What does yon fact signify?!"

"The Holy Trinity," the cameraman scratched his beard.

"It's fate, Egorushka." The screenwriter smiled.

"Avdosha, my joy!" The director grabbed her by her long arm. "Let us drink to our Avdosha! As Jean Gabin once said, when making sinny, first you must needs have a good script, and second you must needs have a good script, and third you must needs have a good script! That and nothing more!"

"I don't agree." The cameraman shook his head.

"I don't agre-e-e-e-e!" the director mimicked him. "Keep the drinks coming!"

The cameraman reached under the table for the scotch.

"Can I have some vodka?" the "American" asked, wiping his face with a wet paper towel.

"Of course." The screenwriter poured him a cup of vodka.

The cameraman poured whiskey for everyone else.

One makeup artist took the "American's" empty cup of scotch, then sniffed and licked at it:

"A most strange odor."

The director raised his cup:

"Avdosha, to you! Let's drink!"

The director sighed, then immediately took a drag from his cigarette:

"Having that table was a really dope idea, the table filled with . . . everything! Terrific!"

"I've got heartburn from the Nutella." "Ivan" grinned. "How can they eat yon bit of beastliness?"

"They won't let it through with the ass-fucking." The cameraman noisily blew smoke.

"Don't jinx it, motherfucker!" the director cried out.

"You need not think about that, Vasya." The screenwriter touched the cameraman's shoulder.

"I'm not thinking, I'm just talking."

"Maybe they'll let it through and maybe they won't." The director poured the rest of the scotch and threw the empty bottle beneath the table. "I'm not Fedya the Bald, of course not, but I do have the right to a strong statement. I have the ri-i-i-ight! That clear?! And *they* know that!"

"They know, they know . . . " Everyone nodded as they took a cup.

"And you guys have outdone yourselves today!" The director slapped the actors across the shoulders. "To you!"

They drank.

"Oof! For some reason, I'm already drunk," the director smiled.

"You're tired, Egorushka." The screenwriter embraced him. "Go over to your automobile and have a nap."

"No." The director licked his lips, fixed his glasses, and thought for a moment. "I'll tell you what, Georgich. Let's go take a gander after all, brother."

"Let's go." The cameraman spread out his big hands.

The director embraced him and they left the tent.

"I wanna take a gander too." "Ivan" put out his cigarette as he got up.

"And where you go, brother, I go too. Oh my boyos, oh my boyos, oh my bowlegged boyos." The "American" deftly and quickly slapped himself across the knees.

They left. The makeup artists followed them out.

The screenwriter was left alone in the tent. Smoking her cigarette and sipping whiskey from a cup, she paced excitedly through the small square space. Stopped before the refrigerator. There was an upside-down duralight box on top of it. The screenwriter lifted it up. The box was covering a Sugar Kremlin. It had already been largely eaten away by the crew. The screenwriter broke off the crosses from the Cathedral of the Archangel and dropped them into her cup of whiskey. She mixed it around by moving her hand in a circular motion, then finished it in a single gulp.

Exhaled, inhaled, then put her narrow palm to her mouth. Threw the cup onto the ground and stepped on it with her shoe:

"Toward victory alone!"

Then left the tent with long strides.

UNDERGROUND

Having reached Belyaevo station, Arisha made her way out of the train together with the crowd of those who had come from the center of the capital, then, moving slowly along with the human stream, walked over to the exit from the underground. She pushed through the metal turnstiles, used her shoulder to push open a scratched-up door inscribed with the word EXIT, and ended up in an underpass. It was dirty, gloomy, and crowded here: People barreled around in an impulsive mass after their workdays, beggars sat in the corners shaking orange mugs, those who'd lost everything in fires—"burnt ones"—rattled copper coins and howled out their immutable "Mercy, not sacrifice!", shaven-bearded *mollusks* sang hysterically, hucksters sold hot kalachs and the evening edition of the *living* newspaper *Renaissance*, two drunk ragamuffins scrapped with a brightly dressed and made-up Chinaman, and a shaggy stray dog barked at them. Having shoved through the crowd, Arisha went up the trash-covered steps and out of the stinky underpass, breathing in the fresh spring air with great delight.

Up here in Moscow, it was the 12 of May and the clock above the "U" at the entranceway to the underpass showed 6:21.

Arisha straightened the kerchief on her head, pulled down

her chintz dress, and checked whether the wallet, travel badge, and long-distance talker were all in place in the girdle on her belt. Confirming that they were, she sighed with relief and quickly walked past the stalls of a market and toward Konstantin Leontiev Street.

At nineteen years of age, Arisha was tall, thin, and had a calm, but not particularly beautiful face, as well as friendly, intelligent chestnut-colored eyes.

Having pushed through the queues outside four standard-product stalls, she skirted round a large group of Uzbeks squatting with bits of rebar in their hands just in front of four enormous dumpsters with *living* images of a dragon swallowing the sun next to "chuangwei"[1] characters, passed by a tavern, then went up to a recently burnt-down five-story building—the Buslay Trade Fellowship. The typical sign of the oprichniks hung from the soot-black building: a dog's head and a sweep surrounded by a red circle.

Arisha walked around the building that smelled of burnt, treading through firebrands and broken glass in her ankle boots, then noticed Leontiev Street ahead of her with its seven-story block-style apartment buildings, and set off toward them. In the courtyard of Building No. 3, a gray-bearded sharpener was sitting on a bench and smoking. Next to him was a whetstone atop a tripod. Arisha walked over to the sharpener:

"Are you able to sharpen small scissors, Mister?"

"I can sharpen anything, my beauty."

Arisha took a small pair of nail scissors out of her wallet and handed them to the old man. He rotated the scissors in his corned fingers:

"Eight kopecks."

"OK," Arisha nodded.

---

1. [Chinese] bedcurtain.

The sharpener secured the scissors into the sharpener and turned it on. Laser beams flashed red and hissed along the blades of the scissors. Arisha shook the copper coins forth from her wallet and into her palm, found a five-kopeck piece and three pennies, then handed them to the old man:

"Thankee, mister."

"Glory be to Christ, girlie."

The old man accepted the copper coins and handed Arisha the hot scissors. Putting the scissors away into her wallet and her wallet into her girdle, Arisha heard someone else speak:

"Yo, Gramps."

"Hey, fella."

A guy was standing next to them—he seemed to be a craftsman.

"My fiancée sent me out. Wanted me to sharpen some little scissors. Think you can manage?"

"Sure thing!"

"What'll it cost me?"

"Eight kopecks."

"Super expensive . . . ah well—nothin' to be done." The guy reached into his pocket.

Agitated and blushing, Arisha walked away, looked up at the apartment building, then hurried toward a series of doors. Made it to the first one and pressed the buzzer for Apartment No. 8.

"Yes," a woman's voice quickly replied.

"I'm here about the ad," Arisha said, trying to suppress her agitation. "About the flower seedlings."

"Come in."

The door squeaked, Arisha entered a dark, dirty staircase, and found a door marked with a number eight on the first floor. The door opened up and a middle-aged woman's face appeared:

"What is it you want?"

"Dahlias."

"Come in."

Arisha entered the scantily lit, poor, but tidy apartment. The woman led Arisha into a room entirely filled with old books.

"I'm listening," the woman pronounced as she stood before Arisha.

She was thin, with a pale, calmly attentive, and slightly sad face, wearing a long, dully colored dark-green dress and old-fashioned high-heeled shoes.

"Porfiry Ivanovich sent me," Arisha pronounced, still agitated and looking at an antique brooch on the woman's chest.

"Who are you?" the woman asked.

"Arina Lobodina, the daughter of a scrivener of the Regional Land Council. Two years ago, my father was arrested, and he hanged himself in jail. My mom and brothers were exiled to Mariinsk. They've been there for a year."

"Decree 8-26?" a short man with long hair slightly touched with gray and a thin, hairless face asked as he silently came out from behind a bookshelf.

"Yes," Arisha replied quickly, trying to remain calm. "Back then, they were purging all of the land councils. Where we are in Bolshevo, they burnt down eighteen buildings."

The man examined Arisha attentively:

"Mariinsk. Where's that?"

"Just north of Chulym."

He nodded and ran his tongue over his dry, weathered lips:

"I haven't been. Have you ever visited?"

"Twice." Arisha nodded. "The third time, they didn't let me through. At the station, a representative of the Good Younguns put me back onto the return train and stuck a *snake* onto my back."

The man and woman exchanged an understanding look.

"What's your job?" the woman asked.

Arisha pulled out the long-distance talker from her girdle, turned it on, and called forth her *labor card*: a small hologram indicating her dates and places of work arose.

"A plasterer at Zagoryansky Pillars," the man read. "Did they burn your place down too?"

"Right after Dad's arrest," Arisha nodded. "They burnt out two floors in our stairwell and three in the neighboring stairwell."

"Where do you live?" The woman walked over to the curtained window and peeked through the translucent curtain covered with blooming lilies.

"Sometimes with Grandma in Schelkovo and sometimes at a dorm in Zagoryanka."

"How did you find Porfiry Ivanovich?" the man asked, taking out a pack of "Russia" cigarettes and lighting up.

"Some burnt ones I know at the market told me—gave me a jackdaw."

The man nodded and took a hard drag from his cigarette:

"You owe us one *new* ruble."

Arisha took a preprepared ruble of the second coinage with the Sovereign's profile emblazoned onto it out from her girdle and handed it to the man. He took it and put it into his pocket.

The doorbell rang. The man raised his finger. The woman went to open it.

"Hello, it's us—we've come for the flower seedlings," Arisha heard.

It was the voice of the young craftsman who'd gotten his scissors sharpened after her. The man opened one of the bookshelves and made a sign to Arisha to follow him. They went through the shelf and into a neighboring room, which led to the hallway. There wasn't anyone in the hallway anymore; the woman had immediately taken the guy into the library room. The man opened the front door:

"Go up to the attic and quietly knock on the door twice. When they open up, say 'protein.' That clear?"

Arisha nodded, left, went up to the seventh floor in the old, dirty elevator, got out, looked around, walked over to the stinky attic staircase, covered with layers and layers of cigarette butts, then cautiously climbed up to the tin-plated attic door. Contorted her finger into a hook and knocked cautiously on the door: once, twice. The door opened quickly and silently.

"Protein," Arisha pronounced.

A thick-bearded, broad-shouldered man nodded silently to her and stepped aside, thereby inviting her in. She entered the large, poorly lit space of the attic.

"Go straight," the bearded man told her.

Arisha walked along the concrete floor covered with tar and saw a group of people in front of her sitting right on top of it. She walked over to them. They looked at her.

"Twenty-five," a plump woman with a scar on her face pronounced. "Come sit, deary."

Arisha looked around quickly, then sat silently next to a shaven-headed man.

"Why're you late?" the man asked gloomily.

"I . . . dunno." Arisha shrugged.

"First time?" the girl sitting behind her asked.

"Yes." Arisha turned around.

"She's new," the girl explained to the man.

"New, old . . . what's the difference . . . " he grumbled, then fell silent.

Everyone was sitting without speaking. Arisha looked at those seated around her. In general, these people were poorly or modestly dressed, but not of the lower classes.

"Burnt ones," she guessed.

Soon, the craftsman guy came in too.

"Twenty-six." The plump woman nodded. "Sit down, handsome."

The guy sat close to Arisha. Arisha looked at him. He winked at her without smiling.

A few more minutes passed and two more people came in—a girl guiding a limping old man, who was also leaning onto a crutch, by the arm.

"Quorum!" the bearded man pronounced loudly as he followed them in, then the seated people began to stir excitedly.

The bearded man and the girl helped the old man to sit down on the ground. Breathing heavily, the old man extended his legs and laid the crutch across them.

"Get started, Nadezhda," the bearded man pronounced, sitting down next to the old man.

The plump woman with the scar across her face pulled a small, metallic case out from under her, opened it, then stood up. Arisha noticed there was an English inscription on it:

VENGEANCE-28

The woman took a pill out of the case and handed it to the man sitting next to her:

"Eat up, handsome."

The man opened his mouth readily and the woman laid the pill onto his tongue. The old woman sitting next to the man also opened her mouth, her head trembling, and stuck out her tongue.

"Eat to your health, granny." Nadezhda put a tablet onto her tongue.

One by one, all of the people sitting there began to open up their mouths and stick out their tongues. Nadezhda moved from person to person, keeping the open case balanced in her hand, taking tablets out of it, and laying them down onto tongues:

"Eat, my darlings, eat, my dears . . ."

Finally, it was Arisha's turn. She opened her mouth, stuck out her tongue, and saw the woman take a tablet out of the case. In the case, there were more or less a hundred of them; the woman broke into the next partition and took one out. Arisha guessed there were twenty-eight partitions in the case.

"Eat, deary." Nadezhda placed the tablet onto Arisha's proffered tongue, then moved toward the old man.

Arisha pulled her tongue with the tablet on it into her mouth. The tablet immediately began to melt in pleasant fashion. Her mouth felt fresh and chill. The tablet continued to melt, cooling the tongue and tickling the palate. Sucking on the tablet, Arisha inhaled gingerly and looked at the others taking their tablets. All of them were relaxed, not sitting as tensely as they had been at first. Some of them were smacking their lips with pleasure as they sucked at the pills. The woman with the scar put the penultimate pill into the bearded man's mouth, the last into her own, then threw the case into a corner with unexpected fury. The bearded man lifted his hands and gave her two thumbs up. Nadezhda awkwardly flopped down onto the floor next to the bearded man, embraced him, and joyfully clapped him on the shoulder.

The old man with the crutch sitting nearby moaned and shook his white head of hair. His face was blissful and seemed to have grown younger: His eyebrows rose, his eyes were half-closed, and his sucking lips stretched forth into a smile. Arisha suddenly felt a pleasant numbness spread through her entire body and realized that she couldn't take her eyes off of this old smiling face. The old man's face grew younger, his wrinkles ironed out, and his skin grew tighter and pinker.

'What a beautiful face!' Arisha thought enthusiastically. 'What beautiful eyes!'

The old man's eyes darkened. His face began to grow over with brown fur. It was divine. Arisha ceased breathing from sheer pleasure. The old man opened his mouth and snarled dully, exposing old, yellow fangs.

Arisha screwed up her eyes—so thoroughly had desire taken possession of her. Her heart was beating deafeningly. She opened her eyes. And sank down heavily onto her four paws. Before her lay a wide square bathed in moonlight. Ahead of her was a church with golden domes. Further away, there were a few more churches. Arisha sniffed the square. It smelled of alien, pungent, and alarming odors. Arisha took a few cautious steps, waddling clubfootedly and clawing at the stone. Then stopped. Lifted her snout and looked up. There was the familiar night sky with the stars and a large full moon. Battlements of white stone surrounded the sky. The sky's odor was familiar. The odor of the sky calmed and cheered Arisha. She let down her head. And saw an Oldun and two Younguns. They had come out onto the square from the church. Arisha roared at them welcomingly. The Younguns roared back and the Oldun pulled the frosty air into its snout, then blew it out noisily. Other Younguns and Olduns started to come out from the little square filled with fir trees covered in snow. Arisha moved toward them. Each step brought her great pleasure. She could feel all of her shaggy, many-pood body. It was calm and strong. Her woolen coat and a layer of lard beneath the fur reliably protected her from the extreme cold, which was making Arisha's little eyes water. She went out onto the square. There, Younguns and Olduns were beginning to gather. Arisha walked over to an Oldun and cautiously sniffed the air around his snout without touching it. The Oldun roared calmly. Arisha touched his frosty snout with her nose. The Oldun opened his maw and roared even more loudly, revealing his sharpened yellow teeth. A Youngun touched his nose to Arisha's behind. She quickly turned away and hit the Youngun slightly with her paw. The Youngun recoiled. A female Youngun cried out briefly, then easily and amicably grabbed Arisha by the shoulder. Snarling back, Arisha grabbed her by the paw. The others sniffed and snarled cheerfully. Two Younguns stood up on their hind legs and began to horse around. Snarling dully, a female Oldun grabbed one of the Younguns by the thigh. Two

Olduns sniffed quietly as they circled each other. Soon, all of them had gathered together on the square. Suddenly, everyone froze. Arisha also froze, realizing that something very important was about to happen. Everyone stuck their snouts up into the air and sniffed at the frosty air in anticipation. Suddenly, a chime rang out. And right afterward—resounding blows onto a piece of heavy metal hidden in the tall white tower that rose up next to the battlements of the wall. "Bom! Bom! Bom! Bom!" the blows rang out into the frosty night air. Everyone drank in the blows. Arisha also listened to them, entirely frozen. Each blow resounded in her shaggy ears and resonated in the thick bones of her strong, many-pood body. These blows *promised* something joyful, that for which they had all gathered here. Arisha saw the top of the tower from whence the reverberating blows were reverberating with her watery eyes. Above the tower, a golden two-headed bird gleamed in the moonlight. "Bom! Bom! Bom!" the tower rang. Finally, it let forth one final blow. Everyone froze. Six Olduns got up onto their hind legs and roared. The Olduns' roar signified one thing: "'Tis time!" The others roared back. And Arisha roared together with everyone else. "'Tis time! 'Tis time! 'Tis time!" rang out over the square. The roar made the square shake. And everyone tore forth from their places. Arisha tore forth with everyone else. She was running amongst *her own*, her paws pushing up off of the cold stone. Her heart had already sensed *whither* everyone was rushing. Having circumnavigated the church, everyone bounded toward the other building. Its heavy doors were closed. But could it really be that they would hold back the fierce desire of the *strong*? The shaggy stream tore the door from its hinges and poured up the marble stairs. Packed together with everyone else, Arisha burst forth into warm space. Her shaggy paws slid along the marble, her claws digging into carpet. The brown stream, pushing, puffing, and roaring, tore into a spacious enfilade. The antique parquetry creaked beneath their mighty paws. Overturned vases toppled down, marble statues staggered, and the pendants of chandeliers and candelabras tinkled. And a heart-rending cry of female foreboding sounded out in the darkness. 'Twas the Sovereigness! And Arisha's big heart responded to this cry with a sweet shudder of joy. The Sovereigness tore forward, pushing back the others. But how was she to compete with the strong and mighty? They pushed ahead, overtook, and knocked all those who screeched and howled down onto the carpet. The bones of the Sovereign, Sovereigness, and their children crunched between their teeth. Growling and shoving, Arisha stuck her snout between the strong and shaggy, reaching for those trembling in agony—for a hairless, sweetly smelling body. Her teeth dug in, pulled at, and broke apart weak bone. She tore something off and was immediately shoved away by another hungry one. Choking on the fountain of warm blood, she swallowed a trembling chunk. And, behind the brown mass of the strong and the shaggy, a small child sliding out of a window suddenly appeared in the darkness. A thought flashed through Arisha's small brain as quick as a frightened bird flew off: "Catch it!" And she rushed off against the flow of the brown stream, back toward the marble staircase and the doors. Rushed through enfilades, slid head over heels down the marble stairs, and jumped from the porch out into the frosty night. She froze, her ears and nose alert. And heard . . . nay . . . sensed the running of small, childish feet. She ran after it. Nimble feet urged forth by horror rushed across the deserted square. Arisha ran clumsily after it, breathing heavily. Suddenly, the small child disappeared. Arisha sniffed. She understood: It had hidden itself. A fitful trail led to the most enormous, most ancient Main Cannon upon the square. Arisha sensed something. She walked over swayingly. Got up onto her hind legs and looked into the cannon's black mouth. The darkness smelled sweetly of the Sovereign's young heir. Arisha stuck her snout in and clacked her teeth together. But couldn't reach it: The little thing was in deep.

Snarling with impatience, she pressed her back against the cannon and pushed. The Main Cannon was heavy. But Arisha's passion and rage ended up being stronger: the cannon wobbled and fell. The Heir rolled out of its mouth and rushed away. But it didn't even have time to take five steps before a clawed paw knocked it over, breaking its vertebrae. Arisha's fangs closed round its warm neck. A wheeze alone came forth from the Heir's mouth. Trembling with joy and impatience, Arisha began to chow down on the Heir. Its head cracked like an egg between her fangs, its bones cracked, and priceless blood spattered onto the stone. Choking and growling, Arisha swallowed its warm meat. Tears of pleasure and happiness poured thickly from her eyes. Arisha couldn't even see anymore, but, with her nose and tongue, she could *feel* the sweetness of young cartilage and the tenderness of the offal and the intoxicating warmth of the young heart...

Burping, Arisha stuck her nose into what was left of the Heir: torn pants in a pool of steaming blood. There was something in the pocket of the pants. Overwhelmingly intoxicated from how much and how quickly she'd eaten, she tore into the pants with her claws, blinked, and had a look. There turned out to be a fragment of something white in the pocket. It smelled new and sweet. Arisha took a closer look: this fragment was precisely like the white tower from which the blow had sounded forth. There was even a little two-headed bird on it. Arisha licked the tower. It turned out to be sweet... but this wasn't the sweetness of steaming blood... it was another sweetness... a new sweetness. Arisha took the tower into her mouth with her tongue. The tower cracked between her teeth. Arisha swallowed it and licked her lips. Took a step and immediately realized she'd overeaten. So much so that it was hard to walk. Drunk on meat. Stupefied. Then an Oldun waddled over to her swayingly. Sniffed. Licked the blood on the stone and drew its snout over toward Arisha. Its eyes were asking for meat. 'I'll burp up a little for the Oldun...'

she thought. But immediately changed her mind. 'No, that'd be a waste . . . '

Arisha opened her eyes. The old man's face was next to hers, but she could only see his profile. With his eyes closed, he was lying on his back on the concrete floor and sobbing. Arisha pushed herself up. Around her, people were lying down, sitting, and waking up. She stared dumbfoundedly at them. The old man coughed, moaned, and began to get up with great difficulty. The bearded man screamed, twitched, cursed, and began to breathe heavily. Nadezhda tossed and turned, muttering something as she did.

Arisha realized she was lying on her side and curled up in an uncomfortable position. She sat up. Her head was heavy, there was an unpleasant aftertaste in her mouth, and her mind felt a bit clouded. The people around her gradually got up and left. They were looking at Arisha in what seemed to be an unfriendly way, plus they weren't talking to each other. Arisha stood up and immediately grimaced: she'd been lying on her right leg *really* awkwardly. She limped over to the wall and leaned against it. The old man sat up, coughing. The girl who had brought him in was already sitting next to him and combing his long hair. Then she began to help the old man get up. Leaning onto the crutch and onto the girl, he did so, coughed again, then spat thickly onto the floor. Arisha pushed off of the wall and, favoring one leg, walked over to the exit. Her head felt heavy and empty, but her soul somehow felt calm and good. Leaving through the attic door, she went down the stairs toward the elevator. There, the people who'd come down from the attic before her were waiting and someone started to walk down the stairs. Arisha also kept silent; she didn't want to talk at all. The old woman with the trembling head was the person standing closest to the elevator, her forehead pressed against the door. The elevator came and the people went inside, filling it up completely. The elevator departed. Arisha was left alone. The old man came down from the attic leaning onto his crutch and the girl. As soon as he'd reached Arisha, the empty elevator arrived. The old man, the girl, and Arisha got onto the elevator and the girl pushed the button for the first floor. The elevator went down. The old man looked at Arisha silently and reproachfully. She moved her gaze off to the side. Right when the elevator stopped, Arisha vomited.

"You gobbled down the whole Heir." The old man smiled disapprovingly.

He pulled a handkerchief from his pocket and handed it to her. Shaking her head, Arisha took her own handkerchief out from her girdle and wiped her mouth off.

"Next time, don't be so greedy," the old man advised. "Share. Don't rush. That clear?"

Arisha nodded, breathing heavily.

"'Tisn't you alone who's been wronged."

The old man winked and waddled out of the elevator. The girl also left, holding him up from behind.

Having caught her breath, Arisha stepped over the vomit, in which she could just barely make out the pelmeni she'd eaten today in the Zagoryansk Working Cafeteria after her shift, then left the elevator.

It was getting a bit dark outside.

Arisha took out her long-distance talker and glanced at it: almost nine. Two guys with girls were sitting on the bench where the sharpener had been. One guy was playing "The Golden Mountains" on a *soft* balalaika, and the drunk girls were singing along with their unpleasant voices. Off in the distance, local hooligans were partying it up with *mollusks* underneath the poplars.

Arisha adjusted her kerchief and, with a calm stride, set off toward the underpass, where a red "U" had already been kindled in the darkening, dirty air.

A HOUSE OF TOLERANCE

THE QUINCE JAM OF the July sunset had already flown out and dripped down onto dustily stuffy ZaMoskvorechye, worn at and wearied by the day, when, having cleared itself a path with the infrasonic "Sovereign's Roar," a brand-new Merstallion the color of steamy blood belonging to Okhlop, one of the Sovereign's oprichniks, twisted and turned off of noisy Pyatnitskaya Street onto Vishnyakovsky Lane, then stopped, stopped, stopped outside of a pinkish-yellow mansion with white columns, milky windows, and red lights over the porch.

It was a calm and quiet evening on Vishnyakovsky Lane.

The big-bodied Okhlop didn't even manage to open the glass door on top of his Merstallion when a Tatar in white rushed down to him from the porch:

"Let me, let me *oh most humbly*, Mr. Oprichnik!"

They'd been waiting and waiting for the Sovereign's oprichnik on Vishnyakovsky Lane. The transparent roof of the Merstallion opened smoothly and the seat belt clicked as it unfastened. Grunting, Okhlop pulled his seven-pood body out of the low car.

"Let me, let me . . ." The Tatar takes the oprichnik under his brocaded elbow and helps him, wriggling like a white adder as he does.

Okhlop clambers out of his Merstallion unhurriedly. He is wearing the oprichniks' summer garb: a thin, brocaded silvery-scarlet jacket belted round with a wooden-holstered silver belt and a knife in a copper scabbard, tight bloomers made of scarlet silk, and short ankle boots made of Morocco leather. The oprichnik's curled forelock glistens with golden powder and a bell sways from his thick earlobe next to his rouged cheek. Okhlop's face is heavy, stern, and significant.

"Cover the head." Panting heavily, he points his chubby finger, ornamented by a platinum ring with a black sapphire on it, at a spotted Great Dane's head fastened to the Merstallion's bumper, which, judging by its stench and the weathered tip of its lilac tongue, has already been touched by some light decay, never mind the fact that those handy stablemen, the twins Matvei and Danila, had already cut it off of a frozen dog and fastened it to the car in Okhlop's estate by 5:17 this morning when the sun had only barely risen and hadn't yet managed to wake the twins' master, reaching with an insidious knitting-needle-like ray through the bedroom's open window and through the gap in the chintz curtains all the way to the swollen, half-open, mighty eye of the thunderously snoring Okhlop.

"I shall!" A black plastic bag rustles up into the gatekeeper's quick hands, then swallows the dog's sharp-eared head.

Catching his breath, Okhlop waits for the roof of the Merstallion to move back into place, turns sharply, the copper calkins of the heels of his ankle boots screeching sharply against the cobblestone, then, swaying stockily, frowning with low, thick eyebrows, mashing the dough of his heavy lips together, and shoving his belly forward, he climbs the porch steps.

"I prithee, I prithee . . ." The flexibly white Tatar outpaces him, overtakes him, and opens the door.

Okhlop goes in, banging his brocaded shoulders against the beautiful door jamb.

Everything is red in the antechamber—the walls and the ceiling and the carpet and the chairs and the girls' clothing behind the crimson security counter. The chandelier shines with raspberry pendants too.

"Helloo-o-o-o-o-o!!!" a girl sings, bowing her neatly combed head and smiling with crimson lips.

"Yo!" Okhlop breathes heavily, unfastening his silver belt with its weapon and hurling it onto the counter in front of the *maiden*.

"Good to see you in such hale health." The *maiden* promptly grabs the belt and puts it away.

"Where is she?" Okhlop gasps, pulling a handkerchief of the finest cambric from his sleeve and wiping at his triple chin with it.

"Our Commandress-in-Chief is getting everything ready!" The *maiden* winks playfully.

And Okhlop hasn't yet managed to answer with his usual "alrighty, then" when the drapes of heavy carmine damask stir and let pass into the antechamber a little, thin middle-aged woman in a blue hussar's uniform:

"Benefactor! Beloved!"

"Blue marten!" Okhlop's lips spread open, revealing his strong new teeth.

"How long-awaited your arrival is!" The Commandress-in-Chief kisses Okhlop's ring, straining her thin blue lips upward and standing on the toes of her hussar boots.

"Hello, hussar-maiden!" Okhlop kisses her little blue lips.

"Hello, darling!" The hussar-maiden's spurs ring out.

"I missed ye."

"It's us who've missed you!"

The hussar-maiden grabs Okhlop by the waist with her little hand and pulls him out of the antechamber:

"New ones have come! These are more like raspberries and cream than they are girlies!"

Okhlop waddles with a wobble:

"Ye already know I love my old favorites."

"Your old favorites are here along with the new ones!"

The hostess and her guest go into the salon. There, quiet music is playing, candles are burning, and twelve *maidens* in sarafans and kokoshniks are sitting modestly, their eyes cast downwards.

"Come in, dear guest, make yourself at home." Their madame snaps her spurs.

The *maidens* stand up, bowing to the guest at the waist.

"Yo, tender ones." Okhlop smiles.

"Health to ye, Ivan Vladimirovich!" the *maidens* sing back in unison.

"Our mares have grown tired of waiting for you, Ivan Vladimirovich, oh light of ours." The hussar-maiden strokes Okhlop's heavy hand. "The red maidens have dried up with grieving."

"I don't believe it!" Okhlop's stomach sways. "How can it be the nobles and zemsky bastards don't come knocking at yer door?"

"We kicked everyone out and refused them for you, good sir!"

"Ye respect the oprichniks, then?"

"How could we not respect the servants of the Sovereign? Mother Russia depends on all of you!"

"That's right! Show me yer merchandise!"

The Commandress-in-Chief walks round the circle of *maidens*:

"You already know Anfiska with the Cootchie, Tanechka the Headbutter, Lenochka the Warbler, Polinka the Raspberry, and Galinka the Tearer too, oh benefactor."

"I do."

"But, here, you don't know Anechka and Agashenka—they're new."

"I don't—show them to me."

The hussar-maiden brings over two young *new ones* and lifts up the red hems of their sarafans. And beneath their sarafans—young, stately, sweet bodies.

"Take a look, good sir, at how they are!"

Okhlop looks at their shapely little legs with his swollen eyes—their smooth knees, groins grown over with just a single little hair, neat little navels . . .

"Tender, affectionate, and skillful!" their mistress praises her goods.

"Nice," Okhlop mutters through clenched teeth.

"And here's Irochka the Cat-ochka, Natashenka the Fox-ochka, and another one—Irochka of the Juicy Hole-ochka—very new, from Saratov, bursting with health."

She brings over Irochka of Saratov and lifts up her sarafan. The young thing is white-bodied—plump, portly, white-eyed, and fat-cheeked. Her mistress turns her around:

"Marvel, my dear, at Irochka's little sit-upon. One might say 'tis a wheat bun and not a bottom!"

Irina's butt is broad and white. Mistress spreads *maiden*'s white cheeks apart:

"Look here, my dear, you see her lil' stuffed pastry?"

"I do."

"Have a taste of it and you'll never forget it!"

"We'll have a taste, then." Okhlop laughs, stroking the white bottom with his eyes.

The hussar-maiden sees, yes, she notices that the trunk of his member is already filling up with blood, stirring in his silk bloomers, rising like a horn.

"You've already become inflamed, our good sir!" She strokes and touches it tenderly through the silk with her small, nimble hand. "Beautiful girls, my soulful babes, oh how you've inflamed Mister Oprichnik!"

The girls laugh quietly, exchanging mischievous winks.

"Gimme Lenka and Tanka, plus this juicy one as an appetizer."

"Your desires are our law, oh benefactor."

"What'll y'drink, babes?" Okhlop embraces Lenka and Tanka.

"Champagne for me!" Lenka pinches his stomach.

"Lilac water with rum for me!" Tanka strokes the oprichnik's powerful behind.

"And what d'y'want?" Okhlop grabs Irochka by the chin.

"I dunno... haven't decided yet..."

"Why're ye so indecisive?"

The Commandress-in-Chief embraces Irochka around her chubby shoulders.

"She's very new, oh benefactor. Don't rebuke her."

"Right-o, we'll figure it out. Well, then, newbie, lead the way!"

Even though she's very new, Irochka of the Juicy Hole-ochka understands what it means to *lead*. She undoes the fly on the oprichnik's bloomers and releases his beast out into the wild. Okhlop has a mighty beast between his legs! Updated by ingenious craftsmen of Chinese medicine, it's been lengthened, hardened, outfitted with four cartilaginous inserts, a hyperwire spike, pellets in relief, a meat wave, and a mobile tattoo: a herd of wild horses sweeps across the oprichnik's member!

Irochka takes Okhlop by the member and *leads* him into the bedchamber. And the *maidens* start up their song:

> Come with us, sweet friend,
> Come with us, sweet friend,
> We shall begin to console you,
> Shall begin to please you.
>
> We shall fondle the white swan,
> Shall stroke the pure falcon,
> Clear eyes, tender hands,
> Hot, insatiable lips,
> Generous love is quick to act.

She leads the chubby oprichnik by his member. And Tanka and Lenka push him from behind. They walk down the hallway, following the party into the blue bedchamber. This is Okhlop's favorite of the four bedchambers: blue, lemon, emerald, and pink.

Barely have the doors of the blue bedchamber slid open when its entire population of *cheerfuls* sings out a toast to Okhlop:

"To your health, Ivan Vladimirovich, oh light of ours!"

Okhlop bursts into his favorite bedchamber and all the *electricals* and *cheerfuls* rush and stream over to him: the nudie pellets and the sliders and the squawkers and the chucklers and the combers and the rockers. They know, oh, do they ever know Okhlop the Sizable! Their smart brains are very familiar with the oprichnik's habits and his fixations too.

The *electricals* sing and squawk and giggle *desirously*. Out of his left pocket, Okhlop takes a handful of seeds, all glowing blue, as feed for the brand new and the crypto-new. Throws them to the *electricals*. They grab the *seeds*, swallow them, and become saturated.

"Thankee-e-e-e-e!!!" they squawk in unison.

Okhlop takes a sugared Ivan the Great Bell Tower that he'd broken off of a Sugar Kremlin out of his right pocket. Throws it to the *cheerfuls*. They catch it, running and dancing. And bring him various trays. And on the trays—champagne and lilac water with rum for the *maidens* and fermented lingonberry honey set out for their dear guest. Tanka and Lenka drink their champagne and their lilac water and Okhlop sips his honey out from its crystal chalice. And Irochka of the Juicy Hole-ochka holds the oprichnik's member in her hand, watching him and smiling.

"What're y'starin' at? Come on—drink with us!" Okhlop grabs her by her white neck and pours the hearty honey into her mouth.

Irochka swallows the lingonberry honey—chokes on it. Okhlop presses his meaty, carnivorous lips to white-bottomed

Irochka's scarlet mouth, forcibly feeding her even more honey. Irochka's body trembles, her breasts tremble, but she is unable to let go of Okhlop's member.

Tanka and Lenka chuckle, pinching Irochka's sit-upon. The *electricals* squawk and howl.

"Disrobe!" the oprichnik commands.

Suddenly, the *electricals* all go *quiet* and begin to dance slowly. Okhlop sits down in a chair, chalice in hand and member protruding.

Quiet music plays. The girls slowly undress to the music, writhing and winking. They dance naked, exposing themselves and approaching Okhlop. They wrap their arms around him and press their lips to him. Undress him:

"Lead!"

The girls grab the naked Okhlop by his arms and lead him over to the wide bed covered in blue silk.

"Fell!"

The girls knock the oprichnik over backward, stroke him with tender hands, stick their able tongues into the sweaty, secret places of his broad-meated body. Okhlop grunts with pleasure and purrs, his heavy member shuddering:

"Mortar!"

A copper mortar and pestle appear among the *cheerfuls*. The *electricals* put the sugared Ivan the Great Bell Tower into the mortar and hastily pound the sugar into powder. The *electricals* give the mortar filled with powdered sugar to the girls and bow. The girls sprinkle Okhlop's member over with powdered sugar. The little bell hanging from the oprichnik's ear rings out with the sound of the Ivan the Great Bell Tower. The girls bow to the sugared member. The oprichnik smiles:

"Onto the stake!"

Lenka and Tanka take turns sitting on the sugared member. And their sweet punishment begins. Lenka and Tanka ride on the member, screeching out as they do. And at the same time, Irochka tickles the oprichnik's gonads, gathering heart and courage. The *cheerfuls* also come to life: they crawl up, wrap round, and stroke in their own ways—cautious and afraid of interfering.

They're taking Okhlop *all the way*. The dough of his mug goes crimson and his lips fill up with blood:

"Tide out!!!"

Tanka jumps off of his horn and Lenka tumbles off of his chest. They grab his member with their hands, Irochka still clutching his gonads. The girls help the thick oprichnik seed to tear its way out from the trunk of his member. Okhlop roars like a bear, kicks up with the trunks of his legs, and thumps the babes on their bottoms. The member shoots out cloudy clots, the girls groan empathetically, and the *electricals* and *cheerfuls* are ecstatic.

"Repose . . . " Okhlop gasps.

Everyone freezes at once. Calming music sounds. Some time passes, then the oprichnik gives a new command:

"Infusion!"

Tanka pours a Tibetan infusion into his mouth, invigorating him, then brings over the chalice of honey. Okhlop washes down the powder, smacks his lips, and breathes freely with his hilly chest, coming to his senses as he does. The *maidens* just drink and drink. And the invisible singer doesn't even have time to finish a second song before the trunk 'tween Okhlop's legs has begun to stir.

Beginning to get drunk, the *maidens* clap and the *electricals* stir:

"Siphon!" Okhlop strictly demands.

The three girls cling to his trunk, tickle it, and polish it with their tongues. The oprichnik's member begins to rise again. Okhlop lays his eye on the white-bodied Irochka:

"Her!"

Irochka's friends prepare to sit her down on the sweet stake:

they put, oh yes, they introduce a relaxant suppository into her behind, then rub it over with pink oil so's to fulfill his order more easily. They hold Irochka by her white arms, measure her up, guide her, and press her delicately.

Irochka sits her *stuffed pastry* down onto Okhlop's member.

However, despite their medical precautions and oily preparations, a groan tears forth from between the girl's lips: The member is most wide in girth, most tuberous, and most troublesome for the young woman. Irochka groans, choking forth tears and biting her scarlet lips. Her accomplices hold her back—they press her sloped shoulders down, skewering her sit-upon even deeper on his member. A scream bursts forth from Irochka's lips.

"Take it!" Okhlop smirks.

"Take it! Take it!" The girls move Irochka's body up and down.

"Take i-i-i-it!" the *electricals* squeal.

"O-o-o-o-a-g-g-g-h!!!" Irochka cries out.

They shove her white bottom down, wedging the member mercilessly into it. Okhlop neighs like a foal, thrashing around on the blue sheet as if he were a seal or a sea lion. They jam Irochka down as she squeals. She's already trying to escape from the sticky stake, but her girlfriends, her comrades, don't let her, they hold her in place, then tug her down by her white breasts:

"Take it! Take it!"

And the Saratov whitefish *does* take it, does begin to adapt. She's not screaming anymore, but moaning. She moves up and down along his member. A moment later—and she's totally accustomed. And now, 'tisn't cries of pain tearing forth from her mouth, but of lust. Irochka gets so *into it* that she suddenly goes stiff with pleasure. She squeals, trembles like an epileptic, and squeezes her tits together:

"A-a-a-a-a-m-m-m-m-m-a-a-a-a-a!"

Okhlop can't restrain himself either and he explodes:

"O-o-o-a-a-a-a-r-r-r-h-h-y-a-a-a-a!"
Tanka and Lenka are sweetly surprised:
"Lo-o-o-ocket!"
The *electricals* tumble over backward:
"Swe-e-e-e-etness!"

Okhlop slaps the babes upon their behinds, pinches them, and growls. Irochka howls on the stake. The girls approve.

And thus do they pass the time . . .

At midnight, yes, even past midnight, Okhlop leaves the house of tolerance staggering and stumbling too. The girls accompany him in their sarafans and kokoshniks, holding him by the arms and singing:

"Don't leave us, oh pure falcon!"

The hussar-maiden strokes the member that's fallen asleep in the oprichnik's bloomers:

"Don't forget us!"

The flexible Tatar helps Okhlop sit down into his Merstallion:
"Happy trails!"

The Merstallion rumbles, winks its red eye, and drives off.

The girls wave to him with their kerchiefs:

"Health to ye, oh oprichnik of the Sovereign!"

KHLYUPINO

T̲HE COW MOOED AGAIN, shook its black-and-white head, and lashed Sasha with its dirty tail.

"Stay still fer a sec, ye devilish daughter!" Sasha cried out, kneeing the cow in its none-too-impressive belly. "A beast like ye oughta get torn apart by hooks . . ."

Sasha smeared its nipples with tronipple, deftly put a "daisy" onto them, then turned it on. The "daisy" purred, then the cow mooed and lashed out its tail.

"Stand still, ye beast, stand still or I'll . . . " Sasha grabbed the cow by its withers, kneeing its side.

The cow mooed unhappily.

"Stand still fer a sec, Daughty, Daughty, Daughter . . ." Sasha began to stroke the cow's warm withers. The cow mooed sobbingly and breathed heavily.

"It ain't painful, so what're ye given' me a hard time for?" Sasha stroked the cow.

The cow mooed sobbingly and breathed heavily, stepping into the sucking manure covered in straw. Three other cows that had already been milked by Sasha stood nearby, chewing hay.

"Okey dokey, then . . . " Sasha looked beneath the cow's belly, adjusting the transparent, dung-covered hose of the "daisy," through which milk was pulsing. Straightened herself up and wiped off the sweat dotting her forehead with the sleeve of her vatnik. "Okey dokey, then . . ."

The "daisy" squeaked out its "end of milking" signal, then turned itself off.

"Ain't bad at all." Sasha squatted down and started to remove the daisy from the udder. "My God, when's this sprang goan come to an end?"

Grabbing the "daisy," she set off along the uneven flooring toward the door, dragging the hose behind her. The cow mooed.

"Oh God . . ." Sasha remembered the hay.

She hung the "daisy" dripping with milk over a partition, walked over to the haystacks, planted hay onto her pitchfork, took it over to the cow, and laid it down. Resting the pitchfork against the wall, she took a scoop out from a container of coarse salt and shook it over the hay.

"Chow time . . ." She slapped the cow on its side, grabbed the "daisy," reeled in the hose, grabbed it, and left the stable, fastening the felt-upholstered door with a peg.

The backyard was wet and dirty. Sparse, fat flakes of wet snow were falling from the gray morning sky. Shoving his shaggy snout out of his kennel, Friendy surveyed her in dejected fashion. Winding up the dirty hose that stretched through the backyard from stable to cabin, Sasha walked over to the back porch, opened the door, dragged the hose into the poorly lit breezeway, and immediately shoved it into a barrel of water, hanging the "daisy" over the edge of the barrel. Took off her dirty boots, walked over to the door into the log cabin—to where the clean end of the hose stretched across the floor—in her woolen socks, opened it, and went in.

It was clean, warm, and bright inside of the log cabin because of a fluorescent light hanging over the table. Firewood was crackling in a big Russian stove. Two calves were lying in mangers next to the stove. Seeing Sasha, they let forth high-pitched moos. Quickly jumping up off of a stove bench, a gray cat rushed between Sasha's legs and began to rub herself there. Sasha kicked her gently:

"Get outta here . . . "

Took off her vatnik and hung it from a hook by the door. Stuck her feet into short, worn-out fur boots. Rinsed the filth from her hands in the washbasin, and wiped them with a dirty towel. Ladled water out of a bucket on a bench and drank greedily. Caught her breath:

"Oh, mama . . . "

Looked into the stove. Adjusted the burning logs with a long poker. Walked over to a separator in the corner, pressed a button, and looked at the indicators:

"Ain't bad at all."

Filled two one-liter bottles of milk from the faucet, put rubber nipples onto them, and gave them to the calves. The calves began to suck, their eyes of dark lilac bugging out.

"That's all. I'll send you to your mothers tomorrow," Sasha announced to them. "Ain't that cold any longer. And in here, ye piss and shit all over everything, ye lil' astronauts."

The calves sucked, smacked, and stretched out their little necks. The kitty walked over again and began to rub against her leg. Waiting for the calves to be done sucking, Sasha was thinking about sour cream:

'Should get six packs no problem, I'll finish the briquette . . . there should be six . . . or five . . . nah, six . . . six would be good, so's to just send it today . . . otherwise I'm goan have to wait all the way till Monday . . . and there might not even be a car . . . there'll be six or there won't be . . . maybe there won't be enough . . . '

When there was just a little milk left in the bottles, Sasha took them away from the calves, removed the rubber nipples, and poured them into the kitty's bowl:

"Here, ye little nuisance."

Meowing, the cat darted over to the bowl and began to quickly, quickly lap at the milk.

"Okey dokey, then . . ." Sasha rinsed out the bottles in the washbasin and put them on the shelf.

Poured a glass of buckwheat into a little cast iron pot, added water, threw in a pinch of salt, put in a spoonful of melted butter, covered the pot with a smoke-stained cast-iron lid, grabbed the pot with a little oven fork, and shoved it into the stove. In a large pot, peeled and chopped potatoes, a carrot, and two onions were resting in water, left over from yesterday evening. Sasha went out into the breezeway, took a can of Chinese pork stew from a cupboard, brought it into the cabin, opened it with a can opener, and dumped it into the large pot. Added a bay leaf and salt, grabbed the pot with a big oven fork, and immediately slid it into the stove. Adjusted the logs, on the point of burning out, with the poker:

"Okey dokey, then . . ."

Turned on the separator. It began to purr.

Sasha opened up a new packet, took out six little cups made of argentine plastic and six lids with *living* pictures on them: A red cow winks cheerfully with its big, black eye, and shakes its head, around which scarlet letters flare up in the shape of a necklace: KHLUPINO SOUR CREAM, 15%.

Having placed the cups into the underframe, she waited for the separator to stop knocking and squeaking and the green light to blink.

"Let's go!" Sasha put the first little cup beneath the nozzle and pressed the red button.

It filled up with sour cream. Sasha lined up the next cup. Sour cream slid from the nozzle like a white worm.

"Come on, sweetheart, come on, darlin'. . ." Sasha filled up the cups.

Having filled up a fifth cup and put down a sixth, she began to pray:

"Fer the love of Christ . . . oh Lord . . . let this be Thy will . . ."

Snarling, the separator filled up the sixth cup.

"Oh God!" Laughing joyfully, Sasha put a faceted cup beneath the nozzle.

The separator squeezed out a half cup of sour cream, then turned itself off.

"Oh, well done! Oh, my little smarty!"

She kissed the separator's semicircular metal top and turned on the "reset." Turbid whey murmured its way through the hose stretching toward the door. Sasha took her *pistol*, sealed the six cups with argentine-blue foil, put lids over them, grabbed them, and, pressing the bundle to her bosom, carried them into the cupboard:

"Okey dokey, then . . ."

In the cupboard, there was a plastic board lying on top of a barrel of sauerkraut and on the board was a box with precisely the same winking cow on its side. Sasha opened the box. Cups of sour cream were tightly packed into it. There were exactly six spots to fill. Sasha put them into the box, closed it, sealed it with a broad strip of packing tape, popped in the code, and put down the date: 3/19/2028.

"That's it!" Sasha returned to the cabin, took her long-distance talker off of the table, turned it on, and dialed.

The talker squeaked and flashed forth a tiny, indistinct hologram: A guy with a sleepy face raised his head from his pillow:

"What is it?"

"Yer sleepin'?" Sasha asked.

"Sash . . ." The guy smiled, yawned, and stretched. "Yesterday I . . . was hangin' round with the Anikins."

"Yer livin' well. When ye goin' to the city?"

"I must needs go today . . ."

"Really?"
"Mhmm."
"Can ye come grab a box from me?"
"A box? Alrighty . . ."
"When'll ye be by?"
"Well . . . what time is it? Oy, nine, motherfuck . . ."
"Nine."
"I gotta go by ten. I'll come by now, Sash."
"See you."

Sasha extinguished the hologram and turned off the talker. Looked into the stove, piled up the coals with the poker, then raked them over to the pots. A single firebrand burnt stubbornly and undyingly among the orange coals.

"Well then, get over here, y'little snake . . ." Sasha raked the firebrand out of the stove and into the ashpan, closed the mouth of the stove with a tin flap, reached up, and opened the damper of the chimney pipe.

Having taken off her half-length felt boots, she put on her proper boots, grabbed the still smoldering and burning firebrand with wrought-iron tongs, went out into the breezeway, walked through it, turned right, went out onto the porch, and immediately threw the firebrand into the front garden, into the dirty, sunken snow:

"Get outta here . . ."

The firebrand hissed.

Sasha gazed out from the porch and onto the sparse huts of the village. Nobody was visible. The Kopylovs, Sotnik, Fly, and Petukh all had smoke coming from their chimneys. Hens and a pig were circling around Gudilikha's rickety hut. A murder of crows circled round over the nearby forest.

Sasha got down from the porch and walked over the planks past the front garden and the storehouse. Walked by the storehouse and into the outhouse. It was gloomy in here and smelled of thawed shit. Raising her skirt, Sasha lowered her leggings, then pulled down her woolen underpants. A stream of urine splashed down, then gurgled. Sasha pulled a copy of the newspaper *Rus'* that had been cut into quarters off of a nail in the wall, brought it up to her face, and read a fragment of a headline: ATION WITH ENORMOUS RESULTS. Beneath the headline was a picture of the Minister of the Bowels of the Earth's face with its neatly trimmed beard. This newspaper was printed in the provinces and none of the pictures were *living*, as they would be in an equivalent newspaper printed in the capital.

Having finished urinating, Sasha wiped her groin with a piece of paper with the minister's face on it, tossed it down, stood up, pulled up her panties and leggings, then left the outhouse. A magpie flew unevenly over her head. Sasha grabbed a pile of firewood from the storehouse and carried it to the cabin, carefully stepping on the boards sinking into the mud. Got up onto the porch, pushed the door open with her right hip, walked through the breezeway, immediately dumped the firewood down next to the stove, chose three thinner logs, and put them on top of the stove to dry. Shook off her blouse, changed into her short felt boots, and looked at the calves. Having drunk their fill of milk, they were lying in straw and chewing it with their funny little mouths. Sasha took the glass with the remnants of the freshly churned sour cream, a big spoon, then sat down on the bench by the window. And, looking through the window overgrown with geraniums, she ate the sour cream.

During this time, nothing was happening through the window.

Sasha put the empty glass down on the edge of the table, licked the spoon, and put it into the glass. The kitty began to rub up against her legs.

"Ye've only just eaten yer fill!" Sasha kicked her away.

Friendy began to bark in the backyard. A motorcycle's rumbling became audible and Sasha watched Vanya approach through the geraniums.

She stood up from the bench and went out onto the porch. Having stopped, as always, by the fence of the front garden, Vanya turned off the motor and slid off of the three-wheeled motorcycle's voluminous silvery body emblazoned with the words CHICKEN WORLD.

"Ye got here quick!" Sasha grinned, shivering at a sudden burst of wet wind and hugging herself by the elbows.

"To get somewhere quick, I just throw my belt on in a lick." Vanya smiled at her with his little tobacco-stained teeth.

He opened the motorcycle's storage compartment, then waddled over to Sasha, his feet chunking through the muck.

"And I thought ye were goin' on Monday."

"I ain't goin' on Monday, they can't make me." He came up onto the porch, stood next to Sasha, and looked her in the eyes, the smile not leaving his face.

"I got real lucky, then." Looking away, Sasha opened the door and let him into the breezeway.

"Ye got lucky, that's fer sure."

Vanya went into the breezeway, opened the cupboard in business-like fashion, picked up the sealed box, and took it over to his motorcycle. Sasha followed after him:

"I thought I wouldn't get a whole box, but I did, glory be to ye, oh Lord."

"Calves suckin' ye outta house and home?"

"Yeah, outta milk . . . it is sprang after all."

"It's sprang, stands ta reason."

Vanya put the box into the motorcycle and closed the mud-spattered door. Wiped his hands on his vatnik and looked Sasha in the eye:

"Got a cup fer me?"

"A cuppa tea?" Sasha smiled.

"Ma still ain't stoked the stove, our generator died, and we're outta diesel."

"I got a cup."

Sasha walked over to the porch and looked around.

Vanya set off after her. Following Sasha into the cabin, he took off his cap, crossed himself before the icons, hung his cap from a hook, and smoothed down his sparse, disheveled hair. While Sasha was pouring water into the kettle, he sat down at the table, put his swarthy hands with their big, prominent nails half-clenched into fists in front of him, and looked around:

"A week ago, I delivered two canisters, but this morning—drip, drip, ain't a drop."

"Yer livin' above yer means." Sasha put a mug down in front of him, put a teabag into it, then sat down across from him.

"Ma just watches yon bubble about the orphan all day."

"*Alevtina?*"

"Mhmm."

Ivan was watching Sasha. She sighed and looked out the window:

"I glance at the news alone—and that ain't even every day."

"I don't glance at 'em at all."

"As it should be."

Sasha glanced out the window again. The wall-clock's pendulum indicated 9:30.

"Ye ain't goan be late?" Sasha glanced at the clock.

"Nah!" Vanya waved his fist. "They'll wait. I ain't their mule."

The water came to a boil. Sasha stood up, brought the kettle over, and poured the water into the mug.

"Ye ain't goan have some too?" Ivan took a bundle of paper out of his pocket and began to unwrap it.

"I already did."

"I brought ye a lil' present."

Vanya unwrapped the paper. In it was the Kutafya Tower of a Sugar Kremlin.

"Woah there." Sasha put the kettle down onto the table and took the tower. "Where'd ye get that?"

"My brother-in-law brought it."

"It's real pretty."

"They know how to make 'em," Vanya looked at Sasha. "Gimme a knife."

Sasha pulled a narrow drawer out of the table, took out a large kitchen knife with a worn wooden handle, and handed it to Ivan. Ivan took the tower back from her, laid it out in his left palm, drew back the knife, then broke the tower in half. Handed half to Sasha and sprinkled sugared crumbs into his mouth:

"Sit down, have a drink."

Sasha poured herself some boiled water, put a teabag into it, and sat down, stirring her tea with a spoon. Vanya dipped his half of the tower in his tea, sucked at it, and took a bite. Took a drink of tea. Sasha dipped her half into the tea, sucked at it, then washed it down. Looked out the window. Vanya was gnawing at the hard sugar and looking at Sasha:

"My brother-in-law in Medyn heard a new yarn about the Sovereign's daughter-in-law," he said, sipping his tea loudly.

"About Nastyona?"

"Mhmm. So, at the Kremlin, there's a beautiful woman who's got three poods of shit lurking in her gut, she bends over to bow, a half-pood breaks off, then she continues on her way like a peacock . . ."

" . . . and two more accumulate."

"Ye already heard it?" Vanya laughed.

"Ye-ap."

"Like a peacock, huh?" Vanya laughed, winking at her.

"Why shouldn't she walk round like a peacock? She ain't hardly milkin' cows."

"No, she ain't, that's fer sure. They milk 'em fer her."

"They milk the cows and do everythin' else."

"That's fer sure."

They fell silent and sipped at their tea. A long-distance talker on the table suddenly rang out. A tiny, indistinct hologram rose up: an old woman's face wrapped round in a kerchief.

"Tha' . . . who . . . who the heck's that?" the old woman asked, squinting.

"Yo Mama!" Sasha answered mockingly, then sipped at her tea. "Who're ye tryin' to call?"

"Nastya."

"I ain't no Nastya." Sasha grinned.

"Nastya at the Kremlin!" Vanya added.

She and Sasha laughed. The old woman vanished.

"Why ain't ye get 'Rainbow' fer yerself?" Vanya asked.

"Why the heck would I do that?"

"I mean . . . everything's bigger. And ye see clearer."

"It's fine how it is."

Sasha looked out the window, sucking at the sugar and drinking her tea. Vanya kept glancing at Sasha. Two dogs began to bark in the village. Friendy growled, then barked. Having barked their fill, the dogs fell silent. Friendy whined and squealed. Then he too fell silent. A plane flew by.

They drank their tea and finished their towers in silence.

"Well then," Vanya wiped at his knee. "I gotta go."

"Yer off?" Sasha stood up.

"I'm off," he grinned. "Thankee fer the tea."

"My pleasure."

Vanya stood up, walked over to the door, took his cap off of its hook, put it on, and pushed it back to the nape of his neck. Opened the door, stepped into the breezeway. Sasha followed him out. In the gloom of the breezeway, Vanya suddenly turned and hugged Sasha awkwardly. Sasha stood there without moving.

"Ye think I'm a bed-hopper?" he asked.

"I don't think nothin'," Sasha sighed.

Vanya tried to kiss her, but she moved her lips away from him.

"I offend ye?" Vanya asked, taking hold of her cheek.

"I ain't get offended."

"What is it, then?"

"Nothin'."

They stood there for a moment. Vanya held Sasha by the cheek. Friendy growled in the backyard.

"Sash."

"Wha'?"

"Can I come back later today?"

"If ye want to."

Vanya tried to kiss her again. Sasha pulled away again.

"What is it with . . . that . . . " He stroked her cheek. "What's with ye?"

"Nothin'."

"Ye got somethin' goin' with Fyodor?"

"Nothin' goin'."

"He calls?"

"Sometimes."

Vanya sighed.

"Get goin'. Or ye'll be late," Sasha said.

He stroked her cheek.

"So, I'll see ye later?"

"If ye want to."

He smiled in the gloom, pulled away, and adjusted his cap: "OK, then."

He turned and went from the breezeway out to the porch. The door closed behind him. Sasha remained standing in the hallway. Walked over to the door of the cupboard and touched the latch bolt. She could hear Vanya walk over to his motorcycle, cough, then start it up. Friendy barked. Sasha turned the latch bolt upwards. The motorcycle drove away. Friendy stopped barking. Sasha turned the latch bolt to the left.

A calf in the log cabin mooed out in its thin, little voice.

DISFAVOR

T HE SIGHTLESS GRAY HAZE of the autumnal dawn abutted the edge of the Yaroslavsky Tract. The liquid clock on the dashboard *dripped out* 8:16. And, immediately, a kopeck-sized circle of sun shone forth onto the clock, indicating that somewhere off to the east, to the right of a bustling road, beyond the autumnal PodMoscovian fog, beyond the ashy mildew of cloud pierced by holey, flickering pines, behind the sad shoals of flocks of birds flying away and the rainy spill, the real, living Russian sun was rising.

And a new day begins—October 23, 2028.

"Twould be better for it not to begin . . ." Komyaga thought, taking out a cigarette, then immediately reproaching himself aloud for his cowardice:

"Enough of that. Don't die 'fore your death, oprichnik."

Pops always loved saying this in perilous moments. 'Twas his saying. And it helped. Is he saying so now too, in yon perilous moment? Or remaining silent? The perilous moment lasts and lasts, oozing salty drops that accumulate and gather at such perilous times. This hour dripped forth, overflowed, then, after that hour, an entire perilous day rolled and surged forth as if 'twere a wave in the ocean. It knocked him from his feet unremittingly and dragged him out, filling his mouth with sea. Is it possible to speak whilst covered over in salty wave?

"Shall they LET me speak, now *that* is the question . . ."

Komyaga brought the hand holding the cigarette to the dashboard and a cold flame flashed out of it, lighting the tip. He took a drag of soothing smoke, then blew it out over his mustache. And turned the malleable wheel to the right, maneuvering off of the tract. Roundabouts overcome by morning traffic flowed past, high-rise buildings flickered by, then he came to forest and zemsky settlements, sparsely populated, dogs barking from behind slanted fences, tattered kittens atop violated gates, and voiceless roosters in burs and burdocks. And now—a turn to the left, a birch forest, abandoned dwellings, ashes, three rusty Chinese tractors, a *new* little village belonging to the votchina, a real hearty one, then another, then young pines, then old ones, then a plowed field, another field and another and another, a sinuous squiggle around a pond filled with ducks and a single goose, a watchtower, undergrowth with traces of recent felling, a green fence, solid and *stately*, with an inextinguishable guard beam shooting up over it and strong five-meter-high gates.

Komyaga braked.

The green security eye squinted out over the gates and the oprichnik in the Sovereign's red Merstallion replied with three flashy blue sparks. The gates shuddered and slid off to the side. The Merstallion drove forward, along a straight road strewn with fallen leaves, through a centuries-old forest, thick, untouched, and shrouded in a light fog. A verst later, a grove of oak trees opened up, a linden alley flashed by, the orangerie flickered forth, a fountain surrounded by statues of white marble and juniper cones, balls, and pyramids rose up, an eternally green lawn with many craters from shell blasts and an old oak split apart by a ruthless direct hit spread out, and, like a pinkish-white horseshoe, the manor belonging to the formerly most excellent gentleman in *favor*, the okolnichy Kirill Ivanovich Kubasov, now in *disfavor* for three months and eight days, swam up, approaching in all of its magnificent splendor.

Komyaga rolled over to the front porch, cut his four-hundred-horsepower engine, and the Merstallion's transparent roof opened up. Whilst the oprichnik was getting out of his trusty automobile, a butler scampered down the porch steps:

"Welcome, Andrei Danilovich . . . welcome, good sir!"

The butler was getting on in years, but agile, stately with golden-olive livery, and handsome with gray sideburns and sleek snout.

"Yo, Potap," Komyaga answered gloomily, tossing down his cigarette.

"Thou hast not deigned to visit us for a long time—oh, such a long time!" The butler shook his big head. "Allow me to park your car in the garage."

"I shan't be here long," Komyaga adjusted his black caftan.

"I must needs shield the dog's head from the crows. They'll peck it to bits in a moment!"

"Well, you do that . . . " Komyaga squinted up at the windows of the manor, stroked his exquisite beard, and began to climb up the steps of the wide porch.

"Filka!" the butler grunted into the long-distance talker hanging from his lapel in a commanding tone as he rushed after Komyaga. "Deal with Mr. Oprichnik's vehicle!"

And he himself rushes to clean the dust from Komyaga's back with a cambric handkerchief:

"'Tis true the crows are scattered hither and thither these days, good sir—a sight to behold! Black clouds of 'em! They circle round and sully, circle round and sully . . . "

"Crows? From whence?" Komyaga asked with a nervous morning yawn.

"From the set-aside fields, where else, my good sir Andrei

Danilovich? At present, everything's been set aside all the way to Bolshevo, just like it is here. The zemskys didn't deign to sow winter cereals, as they await a new law governing sharecropping anon. Which means: waiting for the Sovereign to either allow everyone to go off onto their own freedman's land without hindrance or, contrarily, to work for the nobility. So Chinamen and the votchina alone sow their fields. That's how it is these days in PodMoscovie!"

"A new law governing sharecropping..." Komyaga thought gloomily, looking at the bulletproof glass doors swimming smoothly open in front of him with eyes tired from a sleepless night. "That old *vexation* again. Are we all to trouble ourselves with it once more?"

The doors swung open. And, immediately behind them, an enormous entrance hall lit up with its spiral columns, a chandelier shaped like an Egyptian palm, a carved ceiling, a mosaic stone floor, *living* lions of white marble, and two tall sentries in the same golden-olive livery as Potap.

"Where's your master?" Komyaga threw his caftan and black-velvet shapka with its sable hem into Potap's hands.

Left in a red brocaded jacket belted round with the oprichniks' regulation belt, a knife in a copper sheath, and a pistol in a wooden holster, he rubbed his palm over his head, smoothing down his hair without touching the forelock covered in golden powder.

The marble lions roared. Komyaga winked at them severely and yawned grimly:

"Well, where's Kirill?"

"He's deigned to go swimming in the pool, m'lord." Potap gave the oprichnik's clothing to a hunchbacked valet, then scurried across the marble ahead of Komyaga. "At present, for more than a month, our hearty master has once more taken to chill water, may God give him health!"

"The big, meaty boy's been swimming..." Komyaga thought

enviously, arching his brow gloomily. "The universe is falling to pieces, the earth trembles, and *his excellency has taken to chill water, m'lord.*"

Komyaga went after the butler through enfilades of rooms, his iron-shod boots rattling the inlaid parquetry. They passed through one hall, then another, then went downstairs—and there it was, the bathing hall: spacious, painted, with sea waves, stones, and marble figures. Three naked people were swimming in the pool, struggling with the waves: the okolnichy Kubasov and two of his concubines—the sisters Mmm and Yummy.

"Andrei!" With booming voice, the okolnichy took note of who'd entered.

"Kirill!" Komyaga raised his right hand, put it to his brocaded chest, then lowered his head.

"Andrei!" Kubasov splashed water at the oprichnik, but it didn't reach him.

"Kirill," Komyaga smiled wearily.

"Jump in!" the fat okolnichy rode a wave.

"The water is most cold." Komyaga looked at the thermometer.

"Fifteen degrees! Jump in and it'll freshen you up!" Kubasov splashed him again, this time managing to hit him.

"No, my dear." Komyaga wiped the drops of water from the brocade.

"Ach, thou'rt so fussy." Kubasov laughed. "Let's dive, girlies!"

All three of them dove beneath the water. The miniature Mmm and Yummy hugged the okolnichy's fat legs beneath the water, pressed themselves to him, and pushed, pushed, pushed his excellency's body forward, like a naval mine, as he kicked his legs desperately. While they swam through all fifty arshins of the pool, Komyaga managed to sit down in a wicker chair, take out his cigarette case, and light up.

"O-a-h-h!" Kubasov emerged, breathing greedily, and rode the waves.

Mmm and Yummy held onto him.

"Oy, how deathly . . . oy, I can't . . . " Kubasov breathed.

"I didn't know you were a deep-sea diver." Komyaga smiled wearily.

"Oy, how deathly . . . Oy, how good . . . " Kubasov blew his nose noisily into the water and Mmm and Yummy wiped his face.

"Enough. To shore!" he ordered.

His concubines shoved him over to the steps. He began to drag his ten-pood body out of the water, Mmm and Yummy pushing at his monstrous buttocks.

"To shore, to shore . . . " the okolnichy muttered.

Vanka, the pool attendant, leapt over to help, grabbing him by his powerful hand and handing him a red robe made of viviparous terrycloth.

"Get outta here!" Kubasov stamped his wet foot and Vanka disappeared.

Jumping out of the waves, Mmm and Yummy dressed the okolnichy in his robe.

"Fo-a-a . . . paradise . . . " Kubasov said in his bass voice, approaching Komyaga.

Komyaga stood up.

"Well, hello, oprichnik." Kubasov smiled with his swollen, flushed, wet face.

"Hello, okolnichy." Komyaga smiled back, preparing to embrace Kubasov and moving the hand with the cigarette off to the side.

Kubasov hesitated with a smile. Then, suddenly, with a short wind-up, he delivered a strong slap to Komyaga's face. The loud blow swam through the bathing hall, echoing off of the tiled walls. And, as if summoned by this sound, the dark figures of the okolnichy's bodyguards rose up in the bright space of the bathing hall.

Komyaga moved back, the cigarette slipping from between

his fingers. Stunned, he held onto his cheek with his left hand, as if he were checking if it had fallen off.

Kubasov walked right up to him, his belly making contact with the oprichnik. His face had instantaneously become menacingly impenetrable and his lips were sternly contracted.

"Wherefore have you come?!" he asked deafeningly.

"Kirill . . . " Komyaga muttered.

"Wherefore have you come?!" Kubasov grabbed Komyaga by the shoulders and gave him a shake.

The golden bell hanging from the oprichnik's ear rang out thinly. But even this familiar ringing couldn't help Komyaga out of his daze.

"Kirill . . . Kirill . . . " He screwed up his thick brows perplexedly. "Kirill . . . Kirill . . . "

"Who are you?! Who?" Kubasov gave him a shake.

"I'm . . . Komyaga."

"Who are you, motherlover?! Answer me!"

"Komyaga."

"Who?! Who?!!" the okolnichy cried out, shaking him.

"Your friend!!" Komyaga suddenly cried out in such a way that the okolnichy stopped.

Komyaga threw out his arms. The oprichnik's face had gone pale, but his left cheek was flooded with red.

"I'm your friend! Andrei!"

Kubasov stared at Komyaga with his furious little eyes.

"Wherefore have you come?" he asked in a whisper.

"Pops's been arrested."

Kubasov watched him attentively. His swollen face was focused and his little eyes narrowed. He licked at his wet lips. Then grabbed Komyaga violently by the arm, turning around and dragging the oprichnik behind him:

"Let's go!"

Komyaga followed him, stumbling and muttering as he did:

"Not arrested in the strictest sense, but merely detained by the Sovereign for a day in order to justify himself. For the Sovereign has elected Potyka to lead the oprichniks. And, as such, has given the oprichniks over to its young wing. And thanks be to God."

"Let's go, let's go . . . " Kubasov dragged him along.

They left the bathing hall and Kubasov dragged Komyaga over to the elevator:

"Let's go, let's go!"

"Our Sovereign knows best, of course, it stands to reason." Komyaga looked back at the guards with machine guns.

Kubasov stepped into the mirrored elevator after it opened, pulled Komyaga in, and pressed the button for floor three. The elevator went up. Komyaga looked at his own reflection:

"Potyka used to abide in the left wing, but, only just now, they—"

"A sweaty affair!" Kubasov laughed loudly, jabbing his finger at his own reflection. "And where there's sweat, so shall there be blood. And tears! Right?"

Komyaga looked gloomily at Kubasov in the mirror.

The elevator stopped. Kubasov got out hastily, pulling Komyaga by the hand:

"Over here . . . to the eternal lair . . . "

Outside the elevator were standing four men in black with machine guns. Further away opened up the okolnichy's spacious office with three bulletproof windows mirrored on the outside, into each of which was built a cannon. Two shooters were sitting by the cannons to the right and left. A massive leather armchair was next to the cannon in the middle.

"Here, here!" Kubasov dragged Komyaga away over to a desk.

A large mirror lay on the desk, on which were laid out dozens of neatly cut lines of cocaine ready to be snorted. There was also a sweaty carafe of vodka.

"Well, there . . . " Komyaga thought gloomily, "as always . . . "

And began to speak.

"So, Kirill, what I wanted to ask was—"

"Come on, come on!" Kirill pushed him toward the desk and, having picked up a golden tube, leaned over to the mirror himself and promptly pulled a line into each nostril.

A guard immediately appeared and filled a shot glass with vodka. Sniffing briefly, Kubasov emptied the shot glass back into his mouth, exhaled, then immediately snorted a third line, tossed the tube down onto the mirror, and imperiously pointed at Komyaga with his fat finger. With a reluctant sigh, Komyaga took the tube, unhurriedly snorted up a single line, then another, then sat up. The guard brought him a glass of vodka. Komyaga drank and sighed relievedly. But Kubasov tapped his fat finger against the mirror demandingly:

"Wheel horse on the right! Wheel horse on the right!"

Komyaga was compelled to bend over and snort up a third line. Chuckling joyfully and noisily, Kubasov stroked Komyaga's back and shook his finger threateningly:

"And all because the gas is gone. The cross-eyed bastards've sucked it all up!"

Komyaga straightened up, took out a handkerchief, and wiped at his nose. Kubasov grabbed him by his brocaded jacket:

"The country needs to be put in order, hm? That's what this is about, huh? You get it, huh? Don't you? Hm?"

"Of course I understand, Kirill Ivanych, how could I not?" Komyaga's eyebrows arched. "Our Sovereign's contrived a great business for us. And thanks be to God."

"Our Sovereign is a sewer rat!" Kubasov pronounced with a grin, pressing his swollen face toward Komyaga. "He should be quartered on Lobnoye Mesto, hm? Maybe even *sixthed*, huh? Or *ninetieth'ed*, hm? Then thrown to the hounds so's the hounds can really savor him, hm? For all that which is good, for all that which is comely. For all that which is distant, for all that which is wide."

Komyaga was silent.

"There." Kubasov pointed toward the cannons by the windows. "My three graces. I love them."

"Kirill Ivanych," Komyaga pronounced calmly. "I know that the Sovereign called you last night."

"He did!" The okolnichy nodded cheerfully, baring his teeth. "He asked me to usurp the throne."

"Kirill, I'm being serious . . ."

"And he was too! He said he'd come with Monomakh's Cap. To crown me. The Patriarch would come too. And you know what—I agreed. Although, Komyaga, I'll tell you the truth: heavy, oh so heavy is Monomakh's Motherfuckin' Cap! But I agreed! What else am I to do?! They'll be here by lunchtime! I'm getting ready. Look out there, Komyaga . . ."

Kubasov walked over to the middle window, sat down in the armchair, removed the safety on the cannon, and fired a short burst out onto the lawn. Three silent charges flared up, then down on the lawn.

"Welcome, you little rats!" Kubasov laughed.

"Kirill Ivanych, listen—"

"No, you listen to me!" Kubasov suddenly punched him in the side. "There's no heat on you! Why'd you think to come to me? You think I'll tell you who to give yourself up to, hm?"

"Hold on just a moment—"

"Or do you want love from me? Love heals, y'know."

"Kirill . . ."

"Love, Komyaga! Love! That should be clear, hm?"

"Kirill . . ."

"Love shall save the world, Komyaga, love and love alone!"

"Listen, Kirill!" Komyaga raised his voice. "Tomorrow, we're going to live in a different country. Tomorrow shall already be too late! The Sovereign's preparing to sweep out the ranks! And the bristles in his broom are most numerous. You shan't be able to seclude yourself here for all time! Time is of the essence! What did the Sovereign say to you?"

Kubasov brought his finger up to his big, narrow-lipped mouth: "Shh . . . Just a moment."

He tiptoed over to the desk, pulled out a drawer, took out a big, black Mauser, cocked it, aimed quickly at Komyaga's forehead, and fired. Komyaga's brain splashed heavily out of the back of his head and onto the floor. Komyaga staggered backward and tumbled over. The guards and the shooters by the cannons didn't budge.

Kubasov looked at Komyaga lying on the carpet. Picked up the spent cartridge case from the mirror, twirled it around in his chubby fingers, and sniffed at it. Put it back down onto the mirror. His eyes came to rest on the Sugar Kremlin atop a short marble column in the corner. He fired at the Kremlin. Bits of sugar flew forth from it.

"There . . . " Kubasov sighed, then laid the Mauser down onto the desk. "In drinking, I shall not get drunk, in eating, shall not eat my fill, and, in sleeping, shall not fall asleep. Amen."

He walked slowly over to the window. Approached it and squinted through it.

A murder of crows made a circle above the lawn before landing in the fresh black craters.

"Set not eternal limits," Kubasov pronounced, then laughed both quietly and joyfully.

TRANSLATOR'S NOTE for
The Sugar Kremlin

O N MY FIRST NIGHT in Russia, Vladimir took me to dinner at Café Pushkin. He was most excited for me to see that the menus were written in pre-revolutionary orthography, a kitschy touch, if also one of complete historical authenticity, that represented (represents) a broader yearning for the antediluvian ubiquitous among Russian elites. At first, the chubby and bespectacled waiter—with his visibly sweaty palms, he much resembled a *chinovnik*'s assistant in a miserable modern adaptation of Gogol—brought me the English menu. Vladimir politely insisted that he bring me the proper *Russian* menu instead, then, as we determined what we'd order, Vladimir quizzed me about the old spellings on the menu, me joking about how *War and Peace* had ostensibly hemorrhaged hundreds of pages after reformers had removed the hard sign from after every hard consonant, where it'd had its place in the old orthographical system. Vladimir and I were very near to the heart of Moscow, where money came from all of the country's provinces to "get washed," but the powerful people around us longed for nothing so much as the kitsch of an imperial Russian past, which, at Café Pushkin, had been recreated in meticulous fashion by Andrei Dellos, a one-time restorer of antique furniture whose great-grandfather had been a caterer for the Tsar's court.

A few weeks later, my friend Ben Hooyman (who had, like me, grown up in Wisconsin) and I traveled to the outskirts of the city to see a monastery that had been transformed into a museum, eating big, dry hunks of gingerbread being sold at a kiosk out front as we walked. The monastery had been burnished to an uncanny state of unreality—it was unthinkable that the past had ever taken place here. But, gazing out over the outskirts of Moscow from a big hill, at the ocean of tenements at our feet, I remember telling Ben how I found it vaguely frightening to be in Russia. "It feels like dancing with a bear. . . and the bear's kinda pissed at you . . ." I said, thinking of how state power made itself felt in various contexts where it didn't in the so-called west: at the border, for example, the border agent looking at your passport like the foreknowledge of one's own imprisonment. "You think so?" Ben said. "I don't know if I feel that." "The ambient menace in the air? A premonition of a violent act that may never be committed?" "Yeah . . . I don't know, man . . ." Ben said, bemused by the wordiness of my philosophizing. We wandered back to the metro and returned to the center of the city—making our way toward Red Square, Moscow's central "erogenous zone," as Vladimir would often put it, a sexual metaphor suggesting that Moscow had rather perverse taste in the bedroom, blood, whips, and chains appearing as the sex act's central players began to ascend toward orgasm. I don't think Ben and I ate at Café Pushkin that night—also not having yet found our way to the more glamorous side of Moscow nightlife, endless plastic surgery, perfect silicone bosoms, G-wagons, Birkin bags, bad cocaine, private drivers, clubs you couldn't get into without paying a small fortune for bottle service—but wherever it was we did go, we doubtlessly smirked whenever we set eyes on the Gogolian archetype of sinister men who bore some resemblance to Yuri Nikulin: *chinovniki* with blood on their hands as they paged through kitschy menus embroidered with antiquated orthography.

That is what *The Sugar Kremlin* is about: the old orthography of the Café Pushkin menu, the dancing bear I could sense snarling at me at the border, and the nondescript men with their paunches, their tonsures of thinning hair, the nondescript men who commit awful acts of violence by way of paperwork, then slink off to luxurious eateries where nubile women lay rolls of frozen *salo* into their mouths, lasciviously smearing brutally spicy mustard onto their toad-like lips before licking them clean . . .

Upon reading the initial draft of this brief note, Vladimir warned me that it sounded like "a young journalist reminiscing about his first trip to wild, wild Russia . . ." *Where was the book*? As such, some further explanation: my purpose in writing this brief note is to suggest that, as Vladimir states in his interview with Josh, *The Sugar Kremlin* represents a system of mirrors facing each other on opposed platforms (as if in a train station) and that, by way of these mirrors, the "real phenomena" of Russia are transmuted into a meta-reality that is more real than reality itself. The worst error critics and readers make when engaging with Vladimir's work is to assume that his "visions" are the product of his imagination alone (the delirium of a mind rather than a kaleidoscopic eye processing real things out in the world). That which I bore witness to as a young translator in Moscow were the traces of certain tendencies Vladimir develops into an entire metaphysical system in *The Sugar Kremlin*. I still believe that, were I to have followed the thread of faux-archaism I had teased out, I could easily have found myself walking across a Red Square made entirely of cocaine with the Sovereigness, riding along with Komyaga on his fatal final drive at the novel's end, drinking a cup of irradiated tea complete with the turret of a Sugar Kremlin, raging against the Sovereign with Petrushka, in line with the devious soon-to-be lovers, just as disappointed as they are to discover the rigorous quota system in place at queue's end, watching Amonya's high jinks with Marfusha on Malaya Bronnaya, at the Happy Moscovia public house with the motley company Vladimir depicts there, or on the wrong side of the torturous poker wielded against a dissident scribe (myself) . . . I was perceptive enough to realize that the unfamiliar Russian world I had been thrust into contained many signifiers of the metaphysical system Vladimir develops in his work. And perhaps there's a certain irony in the fact that, during all of the time I spent in Russia, the images cast by Vladimir's system of mirrors set up on the platforms of, say, Belorussky Station were more real to me than the banal, humdrum world that surrounded me. The menace I felt as my friend Ben and I gazed out over the Moscow suburbs was an electricity perceptible in the air, one I could only feel thanks to what Vladimir had taught me in and through his books. My sincerest hope, then, is that this book might help Anglophone readers to sense similar vibrations in their own national psychospheres . . .

Eternal thanks to my дичь-consultant Yelena Veisman for her keen eye, to my Wisconsin buddy Ben Hooyman who's never found a rabbit hole too deep to get to the bottom of, to Andrei of The Untranslated for *keeping me honest*, and to Jack Hargreaves, whose hard work has made it so that the Chinese is now legible and accurate in its transliterations and glossed translations. Thank you also to the Columbia Slavic Department for allowing me to teach this book to a big lecture of undergrads in the required department-wide Slavic Cultures survey course. I think the students liked it—think they got it—but I also removed the anal-sex-brothel-fantasia chapter before distributing the PDF. Some things are better left untasted until grad school.

VLADIMIR SOROKIN was born in a small town outside of Moscow in 1955. He trained as an engineer at the Moscow Institute of Oil and Gas, but turned to art and writing, becoming a major presence in the Moscow underground of the 1980s. In 1992, Sorokin's *Collected Stories* was nominated for the Russian Booker Prize; in 1999, the publication of the controversial novel *Blue Lard*, which included a sex scene between clones of Stalin and Khrushchev, led to public demonstrations against the book and to demands that Sorokin be prosecuted as a pornographer. His award-winning works have been translated throughout the world, most recently by Dalkey Archive Press and NYRB Classics.

MAX LAWTON is a translator, novelist, and musician. He has translated many books by Vladimir Sorokin, including *Blue Lard* (NYRB Classics), *Their Four Hearts*, and *Dispatches from the District Committee* (both from Dalkey Archive Press).

JOSHUA COHEN was born in 1980 in Atlantic City. Called "a major American writer" by the *New York Times*, and "an extraordinary prose stylist, surely one of the most prodigious at work in American fiction today" by the *New Yorker*, Cohen has published novels (*The Netanyahus*, *Moving Kings*, *Book of Numbers*, *Witz*), a collection of stories (*Four New Messages*), and a collection of essays (*Attention*). He was named one of *Granta*'s Best Young American Novelists, and his awards include the Matanel Prize, the National Jewish Book Award, and the Pulitzer Prize for Fiction.